HIGH

WATER

HIGH WATER

Patty Flores Reinhart

High Water by Patty Flores Reinhart

This is a work of fiction. Names, characters, places and incidents are the products of the author's imagination or are used fictitiously. Any resemblance to actual events, locales, or persons, living or dead, is entirely coincidental.

Front cover artwork by Valeriya Simantovskaya/Shutterstock.com.
Back cover cat mask artwork by robin.ph/Shutterstock.com.
Author photo by Jana Marcus.

ISBN: 9798230030300

a PennedSource Production

In memory of Grandma and Luciano

*For my wonderful girlfriends. Thank you for
always being there for me.
For Bob, who helped me return to Venice after
almost 30 years, and for Aaron
. . . always for Aaron.*

Do not be dismayed by the brokenness of the world.
All things break. And all things can be mended.
Not with time, as they say, but with intention.
So, go. Love intentionally, extravagantly, unconditionally.
The broken world waits in darkness for the light that is you.

L. R. Knost

PROLOGUE

"Okay, thank you," said the casting director who didn't even bother to look up at me as she continued perusing through my resume. "Now, I'd like you to do it again, but this time—can you do it with an accent?"

Seriously? Crap.

"I'm sorry," I responded, feigning ignorance. "Is this character supposed to have an accent? I didn't read anywhere in the character description that she speaks with an accent."

"Well, she is Hispanic, sooo yeah," said the casting director. "Can you do an accent?"

Although I was born in El Salvador and Spanish was my first language, I moved to the United States with my family when I was three years old. At that young age, I learned English quickly and, unlike my parents, I've never spoken it with any trace of an accent. Asking me to, "Say the lines with an accent," especially when the role does not specifically call for that, is like asking black actors to, "Do it a little more *urban*." It is an insulting euphemism that perpetuates narrow-minded stereotypes.

My hesitation caused the casting director, seated at the table in front of me inside the cold, impersonal, windowless audition room, to finally look up at me expectantly.

I swallowed hard. "Um, yeah. Sure."

I proceeded to give my best impersonation of a stereotypical newly arrived immigrant with an extremely limited proficiency of the English language.

When I left the audition, I passed through the waiting area—a room full of young women who looked similar to me, all of us vying for the same tiny role in a TV crime procedural consisting of one short scene with only five lines.

This is bullshit. You guys can have it!

* * * * *

I parked my car two blocks away from a little black-box theatre on Pico Boulevard, southwest of the UCLA campus in Los Angeles, California. I ran all the way to the theatre and spotted my friend and roommate, Mayra, just outside the entrance, waiting for me. Mayra and I met during our freshman year at UCLA in a theatre history class. We became instant friends and had been roommates since our sophomore year.

"I'm so sorry!" I yelled out as I got closer. "My audition ran late, and I got stuck in traffic."

"No worries," she said. "The show doesn't start for ten minutes. How did your audition go?"

"Annoying," I said. "They wanted me to read the character with an accent."

"Ugggh," Mayra groaned. "Sorry, mija."

Mayra and I were both Theatre Arts majors at UCLA. We were at the theatre that night to watch a production of *West Side Story* that she had auditioned for, but didn't get the part, which made no sense to me because she was an international student from Puerto Rico, has a beautiful lyrical soprano voice, and would have been perfect for the role of Maria.

"I still think you should have auditioned for this show," Mayra told me after finding our seats. "Don't you want to play the part of Anita again? You were so good!" she said referring to a production of *West Side Story* I was in three summers ago.

"Thanks," I responded. "Yeah, I thought about it, but I want to expand my horizons, you know? There's gotta be other roles I can play. I don't want to be seen as a one-trick pony."

"I don't know, chica. It always feels like slim pickings for us artists of color. At least in *West Side Story* it makes sense to have an accent," Mayra said, in her own thick Spanish accent. Until she began attending UCLA, she had lived her entire life in Puerto Rico. Although Mayra enjoyed performing, her real passion was in costume design and she figured that she had a better chance of making a living as a costume designer, which she could pursue either in New York or by staying in Los Angeles. She still hadn't decided.

For as long as I could remember, I had dreamed of moving to New York City right after graduation, but as that time drew near, I started having serious doubts. Are there even any roles for someone like me on Broadway?

The lights dimmed. The whistling and finger snapping began.

When the character, Tony, appeared for the first time and sang the song, "Something's Coming," I was confused. Then the main ingenue, Maria, had her first scene, and I was further baffled.

"What?!" I mouthed to Mayra, who answered me by rolling her eyes and shaking her head in disbelief.

At intermission, the house lights came up and Mayra and I sat in bewildered silence.

"What the hell was *that?*" I finally said. "Why in the world did they cast a black Tony and a white Maria? It completely messes up the message and plot of the story. It's illogical."

"Well," said Mayra, "I heard through the grapevine that the director and the actress who plays Maria are good friends, and he cast that actor as Tony because he's tall, good-looking, and has a really great voice."

"Okaaay," I said, still not comprehending this rationale. "So, the director was willing to thoroughly disregard the key message of this well-known musical just because he didn't want to bother holding more auditions so he could find actors who appropriately fit the roles? And what about you? Jeeez, you would have been the ideal Maria, but instead he chose to play favorites just so he could completely miscast his friend?"

"Um-hm," Mayra uttered through pursed lips.

"That really pisses me off."

"Seen enough?" asked Mayra.

"Yeah," I said, "Let's get out of here." We left before the second act began.

"Meet you back at the apartment," said Mayra and we got into our separate cars.

All the way home, I ruminated over what I had just witnessed.

West Side Story is unmistakably a play about racism and racial tensions, specifically between white and Puerto Rican gangs in an urban setting. Tony, a white boy, and Maria, a Puerto Rican girl, fall in love against that backdrop of bigotry and hatred. The Jets must be played by Caucasian actors and the Sharks must be played by Latinx actors for the story to make sense.

When I got back to our apartment, Mayra said, "Thanks for coming with me tonight. Sorry it was such a waste of time."

"It's okay," I said. "I'm sorry you didn't get that role. But maybe it's just as well. Clearly that director doesn't know what he's doing."

"It's so stupid," she said. "I don't understand! Why is it so difficult for this industry to figure out what 'diverse casting' really means?

"You're preaching to the choir, mija," I answered.

"Well, I've got some homework to finish, then I'm going to bed," Mayra said, crestfallen. "Goodnight."

"'Night," I said and headed for my room.

A director friend of mine, Brad, wanted me to audition for his next play at a small community theatre in West Hollywood and had given me the script to read. He told me he thought I'd be great for one of the lead roles. I was both flattered and excited about the possible opportunity as I crawled into bed and began reading the play.

By the time I finished reading it, all I could think was, *Is this guy high?!*

* * * * *

The following morning, Brad and I met for coffee at the Starbucks in Westwood. I arrived first and after ordering my latte I found a table next to the window.

When Brad showed up, he waved to me as he got in line to place his order. After getting his drink, he strolled over to me with a big, goofy grin, blue eyes twinkling.

"Hey, Frankie. So, what'd you think?" he asked taking a seat.

"Dude," I said, pushing the script over to him across the table. "I am not at all right for this role."

"What are you talking about? You'd be perfect," he insisted.

"Um, hello? This role is specifically written for a black woman. Aaand, look at me! That ain't me."

"I think you're wrong. You could totally pass for a light-skinned black woman."

I could not believe what I was hearing.

I took a deep breath. "Look, this play is unquestioningly about the ongoing discrimination and racial inequity experienced by young black men at the hands of police in this country, so you can't just throw in any actors for these roles. Besides, for us actors of color, there are so few roles that are even written for us, I would not dare insinuate myself into a situation where I clearly don't belong. It would not only be wrong, but also embarrassing for me to even show up! People of color are not interchangeable!"

"Well okay, first of all," he said, "I still think you could totally play this role. And secondly, aren't you the one who's always complaining about the lack of inclusivity and diversity?"

"Oh, my God, Brad!" I exclaimed, trying to keep my voice down, but I could feel my blood begin to boil. "Tokenism is not the same thing as diversity. There is nothing 'progressive' in the willy-nilly casting of people of color if it completely distorts the story so that it doesn't follow any logic. What true inclusive and diverse casting should mean is that if a play, TV show, or movie does not specifically call for characters to be played by actors of a particular ethnicity in order for the story to feel plausible, then why not cast actors of any ethnicity and color? Like *Hamilton*, for example. Or the TV show, *The Good Place!*"

He sighed heavily in exasperation. "Look, I don't understand what all the bruhaha is about. I think it's absurd to make such an issue about a person's race. I don't even see color. I treat everyone the same. My first priority as a director is always to cast the *best* actor for the role. It doesn't matter what color they are. The best actor deserves the role."

This was making me crazy. I knew that losing my cool was not going to help me get my point across, so I needed to tread lightly.

"Brad, please believe me when I tell you that I know you mean well when you say that. But what most writers and directors in theatre, TV, and the film industry fail to recognize is that to declare that you are 'colorblind' means that if you don't see color, then it is a convenient way for you to absolve yourself from seeing racism and inequality, either . . . or from taking any responsibility for your part in maintaining the status quo."

"That is really offensive, Frankie," he said, raising his voice. "I am not a racist!"

I could feel the eyes of everyone inside the Starbucks turn our way and I had to fight the uncontrollable urge to break out singing, "Everybody's a little bit racist," quoting the lyrics of one of the songs in the hilarious and irreverent musical, *Avenue Q*.

"I am not calling you a racist, Brad," I said. "I'm just trying to explain that the misuse of the term 'colorblind casting' has contributed to a lot of questionable miscasting. Last night I saw a production of *West Side Story* that did just that. Colorblind casting is not the ideal that we should be striving for in order to achieve true diversity, but rather, colorful casting when it makes sense!"

I really thought that when *Hamilton* burst upon our collective national consciousness with its colorful cast, that would put an end to this debate. But obviously, that *West Side Story* production and this conversation proved the confusion still exists.

What I also didn't admit to Brad at that moment was my fear that if I couldn't attain professional status by becoming a member of Actors' Equity soon so that I could audition for a production of *Hamilton,* in any role, by the time the rights to *Hamilton* were released to non-professional theatre companies, I would probably be too old to perform in it. Musical theatre already favored younger actors, and even more so for women. Sadly, the only other well-known musical written for Latinx actors, *In the Heights,* is also mainly comprised of younger characters, leaving me and other Latinx actors competing for an already limited number of roles, which we will all age out of rather quickly.

The longer we argued, the more apparent it became that Brad and I were at a standstill.

"I'm really sorry, Brad, I just can't audition for this show."

I never heard from him again.

* * * * *

I once read an op-ed piece that broke down the racial make-up of the people who control various institutions, and the numbers were quite revealing. Everything from who decides what TV shows get developed and aired, what books are published, what music gets produced, which news stories get covered, and who directed the 100 top-grossing films of all time, worldwide across the board, the percentages overwhelmingly indicated 85-95% white people. How will we ever achieve an end to racism and the lack of representation of people of color in the arts or anywhere else in society if we continue along this existing paradigm?

So, is it any surprise that I would be questioning my chances in pursuing a musical theatre career on Broadway, which in the past decade has become a bastion of expensive, over-produced, Disney juggernauts, as well as other overblown, fluffy, empty-calorie entertainment spectacles that jack up ticket prices, making it economically difficult for the exact population that is underrepresented on those stages from being able to even afford to see them? But why am I surprised that Broadway is just another institution run by people who, for the most part, do not look anything like me, where the almighty dollar rules over all major decision-making, above true artistic innovation and inclusivity?

I loved studying theatre, but I often wondered if selecting that major was a mistake. Throughout my years at UCLA, every time a non-theatre student asked me what my major was, and I replied, "Theatre Arts," without fail, I often received the same response: "What are you gonna do with that?" Good question.

* * * * *

I returned to the apartment after my failed meeting with Brad and found Mayra seated at the kitchen table, in front of her laptop, tears streaming down her face.

"¡Ai, chica!" I said. "What's wrong?"

"¡Mira!" she said, pointing to her computer screen. "Look what that asshole has done!"

I stood behind her, watching the news video footage of the children and babies who had been separated from their parents and were being warehoused at various immigration detention centers along the U.S. southern borders.

"Oh, my God," was all I could utter, barely audible.

"What is going on in this country?" Mayra cried.

We continued watching in horror. I felt sick to my stomach. "I can't look at this anymore," I finally said, and Mayra closed her laptop.

"Why are people allowing this to happen?" she whispered.

I had no answer.

I sometimes lie awake at night worrying about all those children as a result of the madman disguised as our President enforcing his racist, inhumane policies. How will the distress those children are experiencing right now affect their emotional well-being and future?

I felt fortunate to have migrated into the U.S. during a window of time when the country still embodied the ideals represented by the Statue of Liberty, welcoming the tired, the poor, the huddled masses yearning to breathe free. But perhaps that was only the ideal and never the reality. Certainly, during this horror show that is the current Presidential administration, my adopted country often feels unrecognizable.

I entered this country legally, and with my Green Card I was awarded the privilege of permanent residency. When I finally became a United States citizen and obtained my first U.S. passport I was filled with tremendous pride. The great irony is that today, with that bigoted tyrant in our White House, I have never felt more vulnerable and fearful of being uprooted from my life and deported back to a country I no longer have any memory of or a connection to. I cannot begin to imagine how scary it must feel to be an undocumented immigrant at this time. I don't get why it's so hard for political leaders to understand and appreciate the utter desperation it takes to summon the courage to leave your entire world behind for the prospect of a better life. Many of those undocumented immigrants who make the treacherous journey into the U.S. are aware that life may not be automatically easier for them. They often toil at jobs that require extreme physical labor at very low wages, the likes of which most Americans will never experience, but those hard-working immigrants are motivated and thrive on the hope that someday it will be better for their children and all the generations to follow.

I called my grandma for some much-needed wisdom and words of advice.

Grandma and I are not actually related by blood. She is the mother of my stepdad, but my only remaining relative after my parents were killed in a car accident when I was sixteen years old and she became my legal guardian. Despite the fact that she and I are not even the same race—she and my stepdad being white— my grandma immediately loved me without reservation from the moment we first met. Grandma was the first adult in my life who exemplified truly unconditional love. I experienced an instantaneous bond with her, and she made me feel fully accepted and valued without having to prove my worthiness.

"Identify people's fear," my grandma explained over the phone, "and isolate a common enemy on whom all the blame can be placed for everything that is causing the fear. That is the perfect combination for the making of a tyrannical leader. It's precisely what Hitler did to galvanize his followers, resulting in World War II and the annihilation of six million Jewish people. And unfortunately, that's what is now happening not only here, but throughout many countries around the world where tribalism is gaining popularity as a result of autocrats stoking those fires of fear."

"I know, Grandma. That's why it's so scary."

"Try not to let it get you down, Frankie. I know it's difficult, but eventually we'll have another Presidential election and I still feel optimistic that our Democracy will prevail. We can get through this."

I also shared with her my recent frustrations in the world of acting and my awkward meeting with Brad. "I feel emotionally drained and exhausted," I said. "I am so sick and tired of explaining and having to teach people what it feels like to live in my skin!"

"I know, sweetie. I'm sure it's really disappointing when the people you assume will be your biggest allies turn their back on you when you call out their biases."

"Yes! You totally get it. It feels like abandonment. To make matters worse, it often seems like people view my complaints about diversity as just 'sour grapes' over my inability to get the part."

"I'm sorry, Frankie," Grandma replied. "I think it boils down to a lack of imagination, an absence of curiosity, and just plain laziness on their part."

"I don't know what to do, Grandma," I moaned. "I probably should have picked a different major. Why didn't I select journalism? Then again, is a writing career any more stable than a career as a performing artist? Maybe I should have been a linguistics major instead and pursued a career in the travel or tourism industry, become an interpreter or something."

"Well, hon, you certainly do have a gift for languages. You are a true Renaissance woman and talented in so many areas."

True to form, Grandma was giving me much more credit than I felt I deserved. Over the past year I had been taking Italian as an elective and absolutely fell in love with that language! I had studied French in high school, but despite being a native Spanish speaker, and both Spanish and French being Romance languages, French did not come easily for me. It makes my mouth hurt. My tongue and jaw feel stiff and achy after straining to capture the correct pronunciation. Italian, on the other hand, so similar to Spanish, felt more natural.

"That's what these college years are all about," Grandma continued. "It's okay if you still haven't decided what you want to do. Sometimes you need just a little more real-life experience to help you sort that out. The most important thing is that you worked really hard to be the first person in your family to graduate from college! You should be very proud of yourself and, whatever you decide, you know you'll always have my full support."

* * * * *

One week later I made the decision to apply through the UCLA language program for the opportunity to live and work in Italy for the entire summer after graduation in order to immerse myself in the language and culture, with the goal of becoming fluent.

My application accepted, I studied Italian with even more zeal and used the remainder of the school year to conduct research and prepare for my trip. I put New York City and Broadway on indefinite hold, graduated with honors, and packed my suitcase with the hope that this trip would help me figure out what to do with my life.

Chapter 1 - FRANKIE

Venice, Italy
Tuesday, June 18, 2019

It's midnight, and I'm walking through a ghost town.

The streets are devoid of the throngs of tourists I had envisioned. All the businesses are closed behind rolling metal shutters, and except for a few water taxis cruising the canals for people such as myself who have just arrived at this late hour, it is eerily quiet. There is no one around to ask for directions. Despite the emptiness of the streets, I'm not afraid. For some reason it doesn't feel unsafe to be walking alone at this hour. I imagine during the day this is one of the busiest areas, so close to the bus stop and train station, but the fact that all the restaurants and stores are closed does surprise me. I had the impression, because of the famous annual Carnevale di Venezia, that Venice was a "party town."

I really want to take one of those water taxis. I could have taken one directly from the airport, but the man working at the information desk warned me that they are terribly expensive, especially at this late hour, and suggested that taking the bus was a better option. But right now, I'm questioning my choice. It would be a lot easier to get around this city in a water taxi than trying to navigate on foot from where the bus dropped me off, but I have no idea how much they cost, and I am hesitant to spend the cash I have on me. I have enough money to last for a while, but until I receive my first paycheck from the hotel where I'll be working, I need to be frugal. Besides, my Italian is rudimentary at best. I may not be able to speak nor understand well enough to communicate exactly where I need to go and not get ripped off in the transaction.

The problem is I'm surprisingly disoriented, since I didn't enter the city coming out of the train station, the way I had always imagined after seeing that famous view in old movies, such as *Summertime*, starring Katharine Hepburn. No, instead I arrived, anticlimactically, on a bus from the airport that dropped me off at Piazzale Roma in the industrial Santa Croce district. Instead of crossing over the Ponte della Costituzione, the bridge that would take me north toward the Cannaregio district where I will be staying for the next three months, apparently I made a wrong turn. The blue dot on my phone's GPS shows that I am now heading in the completely opposite direction toward Dorsoduro.

I am totally discombobulated in this city of labyrinths. Oh, well—I'm on an island, or rather, a series of islands connected by bridges. How lost could I get?

My plan had been to fly directly from Los Angeles to London, then on to Milan. Unfortunately, immediately after my plane arrived in London, the Italian air traffic controllers decided to go on strike for six hours, leaving me stranded at the Heathrow airport. *Who only strikes for six hours?!*

After waiting in Heathrow for almost seven hours, I was finally able to get the next available flight directly to Venice, getting me here at this late, desolate hour. The destination, of course, was always Venice, but I had hopes of spending a couple of days in Milan first. Afterward, I would have taken the romanticized train ride into Venice, arriving at the Stazione di Venezia Santa Lucia and step out onto the fondamenta, or canal walkway, to see the iconic green domed church, la Chiesa di San Simeon Piccolo, welcome me from across the Grand Canal, just like in the movies. Instead, I arrived at the Aeroporto di Venezia-Marco Polo at 10:30 p.m. where I bolted to catch the last bus of the evening leaving for Venice.

Had I arrived during daylight hours I could have taken an affordable vaporetto. Unfortunately, the waterbuses have stopped running for the night. That would have saved me this long trek through the city, destroying the wheels on my rolling suitcase as I pull it over the cobblestones and uneven surfaces of these ancient stone walkways and bridges.

Aside from improving my Italian, my hope is that this stay in Venice will provide me with some great material for writing. How could it not? Already, simply getting here has been an adventure and I still haven't even arrived at my final destination.

So, here I am, finally walking in the correct direction—I hope—and see on my left the steps to the train station. I stop and look to my right across the Grand Canal, and there it is—the Byzantine metal dome of the famous church, glinting green under the light of the full moon. I pull my suitcase up the steps and stand on the landing, directly in front of the station entrance and look out at the city I already love and take in the view I have been imagining ever since I saw the movie, *A Little Romance*, while at a friend's sleepover during the 8th grade. I marvel at the panorama for several moments, then continue making my way to the Cannaregio district, the northernmost of the sestieri.

Paying close attention to the blue dot on my phone, I head northeast toward Calle Carmelitani. I cross over Ponte della

Guglie and continue straight ahead. I turn right, cross over two more bridges, turn left, cross over the Ponte Vendramin, and step onto the Fondamenta de Ca' Vendramin. I have arrived!

"Buona sera! You must be Frankie?" I am greeted by the middle-aged man behind the reception desk of the Hotel Vendramin, with whom I spoke over the phone when I was stranded at Heathrow. "I am Paolo."

"Buona sera," I reply, complete exhaustion overtaking me. I just realized I have been traveling for 24 hours straight. "Si, sono Frankie."

"Ah, is your given name Francesca?" he continues in English.

"Actually, it is Francisca," I explain. "It's a Spanish name. I don't really like it, so I go by Frankie. But I like Francesca better."

Smiling politely, he says, "I will show you to your room." He leads me up a flight of worn, white, marble stairs. As I set foot on the landing on the second floor that opens up to an inviting portego, the reception hall feels oddly familiar to me. I follow Paolo toward the left corner of the portego, down a short hallway, where he unlocks a door and leads me into the most beautiful bedroom I have ever seen. An inexplicable sense of déjà vu washes over me

"Here is your key," Paolo says handing it to me. "Since you are an employee, your room will not be cleaned every day, but only once a week. You will have access to our laundry facility for washing your clothes. Your breakfast is also included every day. In the morning, Luciana will be working the front desk. She will set you up with your first training session. You will be assisting Maria in the kitchen, the dining room, and every morning preparing the breakfast for the other hotel guests. If you have any questions or need anything, do not hesitate to ask."

I appreciate him explaining all of this in English because I am thoroughly sapped and I'm not sure I would have been able to follow any of it if he had been speaking Italian.

"Grazie. This is amazing!" I say, indicating the stunning high-ceilinged room.

"Benvenuta a Venezia! Buona notte."

"Buona notte," I say, closing the door.

I cannot believe my eyes! This must be how the daughters of the Venetian aristocracy lived during the Italian Renaissance. The walls of the room are swathed in a peach-and-cream-colored brocade wallpaper, with a matching duvet cover on the bed. The lamps and wall sconces are made of elaborate Murano glass, exactly like the ones I saw in the lobby downstairs and in the portego. There is a small bathroom with a pedestal sink, shower stall, a toilet, and the ubiquitous European bidet.

I walk over to the large window spanning almost the entire height of the wall, open the French doors, and push back the heavy green wooden shutters. I step outside to a balcony overlooking a narrow canal and the Ponte Vendramin, the bridge over which I crossed earlier. As I continue admiring my lovely view under the moonlight, the bells of the church across the canal begin chiming, joined by a few others somewhere in the distance. When their pealing subsides, it is completely silent.

No cars. Of course! That's why it's so incredibly quiet. I've never experienced a city that felt so still at night.

Yawning, I re-enter my room, leaving the window and shutters slightly ajar to allow fresh air to flow through, and get ready for bed. I'll unpack tomorrow. Right now, I just want to sleep. I quickly send a group text to my grandma, to Mayra, who is spending her summer interning at Universal Studios Hollywood in the costume department, and to a couple of other friends, letting them know I have finally arrived, safe and sound. Using my European adaptor, I plug my phone into an outlet next to the small, ornate writing desk by the window.

I slip into the bed and pull the fluffy duvet up to my chin. As I close my eyes, I hear the soothing and hypnotic sound of water from the canal lap against the fondamenta below.

Chapter 2 — FRANCESCA

Murano, Italia
Lunedì 12 settembre 1550

It is an unusually chilly morning for this time of year as Alfredo and I make our way across the laguna from Venezia to the island of Murano. Despite the heavy woolen blanket wrapped around my body, the damp fog seems to penetrate all the way down to my bones. Poor Alfredo. I feel sorry for the oarsman who must row our sandolo, exposed to the frigid air. Perhaps the exertion is keeping him warm. Surely, his strong, muscular arms are a testament to all the physical labor he is accustomed to. I feel myself blush. A girl of sixteen years should not be thinking about a man's body in this manner. Fortunately, even if he could see the color rise in my cheeks through the fog, he is too busy navigating and watching for other sandoli to avoid collision.

We are fortunate today because there are not many other boats on the laguna, and Alfredo has made this trip often and has enough experience that I am certain he could find his way with eyes closed. Alfredo was born and raised on Murano, after all. I have full confidence in him.

To our right is the island of San Michele appearing eerily out of the fog. We are halfway to Murano. As we pass by the small island, the sun begins burning through the mist, but the temperature is not yet warmer. I shiver as I pull the blanket tighter around me.

"Non è molto più lontano, signorina Francesca," Alfredo assures me. "It is not much farther. We are almost there."

"Si," I answer, through chattering teeth.

By the time we reach Murano and the rio dei Vetrai, the closest entrance by boat to the main glass factory district, the fog has completely lifted to reveal a bright, sunny day.

"Che bellissima!" Alfredo sighs as he takes us through the canal toward our destination—the Fornace Briati glass factory on the Fondamenta da Mula—and I am uncertain if he is referring to the promise of a beautiful day or the beauty of his homeland.

My errand today is to check on the status of a special order for the grand party at the Palazzo Vendramin in two months.

*   *   *   *   *

I came to live at the palazzo with my mother's younger sister, Zia Veronica, after both my parents died during the terrible storm of 1543. I was nine years old at the time and my mother had insisted on obtaining my first holy communion gown from the renowned lace makers on the island of Burano. After their excursion to the island, my mother and father were on their way back to Venezia when their boat capsized, and they both drowned, along with their oarsman.

My mother suffered a difficult pregnancy and birth with me, which left her unable to bear more children. Therefore, I am an only child. My father came from a noble family and as the eldest son, he was the only offspring encouraged to marry. This is how the families of the aristocracy in Venezia maintain their wealth, because if every son married and had sons of their own, the family's fortune would soon dissipate within a few generations. Subsequent sons remain single, while continuing to live comfortably in the ancestral home. Thanks to Venetian law, male heirs are allowed equal share of their parents' inheritance, which affords them enough money to last the rest of their lives. My father's younger brother, Maffio, however, is a man of greed and vice. He squandered most of his inheritance on gambling and extravagant purchases, causing him to acquire a great amount of debt by the time of my parents' death. In order to pay off those debts, he sold my family home, and then left Venezia in self-imposed exile to avoid any further legal entanglements and altercations with the long string of enemies he accumulated due to his feckless behavior. Having no concern for me, he left me without a place to live. That is when my Zia Veronica came to my rescue and brought me into her home, the Palazzo Vendramin, property of her wealthy benefactor, Domenico Vendramin. I doubt that my uncle has any knowledge of what became of me and I assume he does not care. The feeling is mutual.

My mother and her sister were also born into a noble family, but in a society that mandates exorbitant dowries, it is similarly customary for only the eldest daughter to marry. Thus, my Zia Veronica, being the youngest daughter, faced the uncertain future shared by the many daughters of Venezia. She could be sequestered away in a convent, which also required a dowry. She could become the aging spinster aunt, forever and completely financially dependent on the head of the household, without any more freedom than she would have within a convent. Or she could choose the life of a *cortigiana onesta*: an honest courtesan. Zia Veronica chose the latter.

Unlike the *cortigiana di lume*, the common street prostitutes who live and work near the Ponte Rialto, the *cortigiana onesta* is considered an intellectual woman of culture, a stark contrast to the typical wealthy Venetian women of nobility, who are seldom allowed an education. Many of them cannot even read and rely on their husbands for *everything* because according to Venetian law, a married woman is the subject and property of her husband. Those noblewomen are also seldom seen in public and rarely venture beyond their domestic boundaries. While my Zia Veronica wears lavish gowns in vibrant colors and moves, unencumbered, among influential circles of artists, poets, and politicians, the women of the Venetian upper class are only permitted limited access to the civic world by the Church during parish feasts. My zia's beauty, intellect, and charm have made her successful, and she enjoys a sumptuous life of parties where she entertains wealthy merchants and members of the Venetian elite. Thus, my frequent trips to Murano where Zia Veronica commissions and obtains all the fine glassware used when she hosts her elegant gatherings.

Three years ago, at the age of thirteen, when my zia decided I was old enough to assist her in this endeavor, she began sending me to the glass island for her elaborate purchases.

"Francesca, I cannot possibly serve my guests with the same goblets I used at the *salone letterario* last month for the *festa di Carnevale* next month," she would say. And off I would go to the sequestered island.

However, it is not the single reason I make the long and often uncomfortable journey to Murano. I come to see Giovanni.

Giovanni is the nephew of Lorenzo Briati, one of the greatest glassmakers in all of Murano. Giovanni was born in Padova and orphaned at the age of four when his parents, younger brother, and infant sister all succumbed to a typhus epidemic. Although Giovanni was also ill, he miraculously recovered and his father's older brother, Lorenzo, sent for Giovanni and raised him as his own.

I met Giovanni on my first trip to the renowned isle of glass when Zia Veronica asked me to bring back a wine carafe she ordered as a gift for her benefactor. I walked into the small front room of the Fornace Briati, which is used as a showroom for a few pieces created by Maestro Lorenzo as examples, and a youth of sixteen years of age greeted me. When he first turned to look at me, I felt as if I could not breathe, for he stared at me with the most exquisite eyes I had ever seen. They were neither green nor blue, but an exceptional combination of both colors, with small flecks of gold. They remind me of the laguna at twilight. I cannot wait to see them again.

* * * * *

Alfredo has pulled up to the side of the Fondamenta da Mula. He secures the sandolo to the colorful mooring post in front of the Fornace Briati with a rope and steps onto the fondamenta. I grab my satchel, and he reaches his hand to help me climb out.

"I will return an hour before sunset to take you back to Venezia," he tells me.

"Si. Va bene," I say. "Grazie."

Alfredo's mother, sister, brother, his brother's wife and their two young boys still live on Murano and run a successful fruit orchard. Alfredo enjoys visiting them during these glass-finding expeditions. Zia Veronica knows perfectly well it does not take me all day to check on the progress of her orders, but she generously indulges me and Alfredo by providing us with these little excursions outside of Venezia for a few hours.

"Ci vediamo," he says as he climbs back into the sandolo and pushes away from the mooring post. I wave goodbye watching Alfredo continue rowing up the canal. Just as I am about to enter the Fornace Briati, I realize that I left the blanket inside the sandolo. Still chilled, my body covered in gooseflesh, I go inside the building quickly to warm up.

"Buongiorno?" I call out. The small front room is empty. "Hello? Is anyone here?"

"Buongiorno!" Giovanni says, as he enters from the courtyard, which adjoins the small showroom, the glass factory, and the family's living quarters. And there are those eyes! No matter how many times I have seen them, they never cease to take my breath away. "Francesca! Have you forgotten your cloak on such a chilly morning? You must be freezing. Come! I will take you to the furnace area so you can warm up and you can see how your zia Veronica's special order is coming along."

"Yes, please. Thank you," I say, and follow him out through the courtyard.

"After such a hot summer, the cold fog this morning was strange, no?" Giovanni says as we enter the factory where we are greeted with a blast of warmth emanating from several furnaces used by the glassmakers. "Now that it has burned off, the day will warm up quickly."

The heat from these furnaces is intolerable during the summer months, which is why all the glass factories were closed for the past three months and have only recently reopened.

"Sit here, Francesca," Giovanni indicates a stool by the entrance. "I cannot wait to show you. This is something very special. I will be right back," he says, and walks deeper into the factory. Moments later, he returns with his Uncle Lorenzo.

"Ah, Francesca!" cries Lorenzo, upon seeing me. "Buongiorno, bellissima!"

"Buongiorno, Maestro Lorenzo. I have come to check on the status of the chandelier my zia has commissioned."

"Si. Guarda! Look! I have invented something very new and different." I can see Giovanni behind his uncle, beaming with pride and he walks over to stand next to my stool so we can both observe what is about to be demonstrated. "As you know," continues Maestro Lorenzo, "chandeliers are not normally part of our collection, but when signora d'Aragona told me she wanted something unique for her next gathering, I decided to surprise her with this."

We watch as Maestro Lorenzo lifts his pontello, takes a molten glob of liquefied glass out of the furnace with the end of the iron rod, alternately heating it and shaping with a borsella. He uses this tong-like tool and other instruments to manipulate the pliable substance and creates what appears to be a garland or leaf.

"Oh!" I gasp. "Che meraviglia!"

But then he does something astonishing. After heating the garland one more time in the furnace, he places it over another pontello and coaxes the soft, molten glass so it drapes over the rod. When he removes the glass from around the metal rod the piece looks as though it is a fallen leaf in mid-flight. It is like magic.

"Mio Dio!" I exclaim. "How in the world did you do that?"

"Uh-uh," he scolds, good naturedly. "It is bad enough I let you see this much. I cannot give away all my secrets. Venezia's Council of Ten would put me in prison if they knew."

"Maestro Lorenzo, you must not do anything that will jeopardize your safety!"

Lorenzo chuckles. "Do not worry, Francesca. I trust you not to give me away. Besides, this is all I will show you. It is only a small portion of the chandelier I am creating for your zia Veronica. The first of its kind!"

"She will be so pleased, Maestro Lorenzo. It will be the envy of all Venezia!"

"I will have it completed by next week and Giovanni will hand deliver and install it himself."

I look up at Giovanni in surprise. The glassmakers of Murano are normally not allowed to leave the island in order to preserve their secrets and are threatened with imprisonment or death if they or anyone in their family try to escape.

"I have been granted special permission by the Glassmakers Guild to leave the island," Giovanni explains. "Since I am not technically a glassmaker, myself, but simply an employee who assists with the commissions and sales, they are allowing me some leniency from the strict guidelines."

"My nephew continues to break my heart by refusing me the satisfaction of becoming my apprentice," says Lorenzo. "He has artistic talent running throughout his veins. He would be a fine glassmaker. But no! Instead, he wishes to leave us all behind to attend l'Università di Padova to study what? Gruesome bodies?"

"Zio," Giovanni groans. "You know it is my wish to study medicine. The university's discoveries in anatomy will someday help us find cures for the vast epidemics that too often sweep through our cities, taking the lives of countless people such as my parents and siblings."

Maestro Lorenzo sets his tools down on his workbench and places a gentle hand on Giovanni's shoulder. "Si, Giovanni, I know. I am sorry, my boy. I am merely teasing. You will make an excellent dottore, or whatever else you set your mind on. I will miss you when you are gone, that is all."

Giovanni nods and for a moment, there is an awkward silence.

"Are you hungry, Francesca?" he asks abruptly. "Cook has prepared a picnic lunch for us. We can go to the Campo Santo Stefano. It is warming up nicely, and we can eat under the shade of a tree."

"Si," I reply. "It sounds lovely."

"D'accordo, ragazzi," says Maestro Lorenzo. "I will complete one more small piece and close up for the noon meal. Enjoy yourselves. Divertitevi!"

I wait in the courtyard while Giovanni gathers our picnic from the kitchen. He comes out with a large basket, a blanket, and his drawing utensils.

"After we eat, I will sketch you while you read to me from your latest work," he says, and we exit through the showroom onto the fondamenta, turn right, walk a few steps, and cross over the bridge to the Campo Santo Stefano.

There is a small grass area right next to the canal where Giovanni spreads out our blanket. As he begins unpacking the basket, the smell of sardines and olives makes my mouth water.

He sets out a bowl of pine nuts and raisins, a plate of hard cheese, and freshly baked bread. Lastly, he pulls out a small plate of biscotti and Vin Santo wine, my favorite.

"My, what a feast!"

"Buon appetito," he says, and we both dive in as if we haven't eaten in days.

After our meal, feeling satiated and drowsy, we lie on our backs and stare up at the cerulean sky. Only on the island of Murano are we afforded such freedoms, where the codes of conduct are not as strict as they are in Venezia, which is why we can enjoy our picnic devoid of a chaperone.

"When will you be leaving for Padova?" I finally have the courage to ask. "And how will it be possible for you to leave Murano for such an extended period of time? Will it not present a threat to your family?"

Giovanni sits up quickly and looks at me. "Francesca, that is one of the reasons I did not want to take on the title of apprentice. Since I was born outside of Murano and not officially a glassmaker, zio Lorenzo believes that he can convince the authorities that he has taught me none of his secrets and I will be granted permission to leave. My zio would prefer that I wait one more year so my cousin, Giuseppe, will be old enough to continue his father's trade after I leave. It is the least I can do after all he has done for me. He has been a father to me."

"Will you be sure to let me know when the time comes, so I can say goodbye?" I can feel the sting of tears, which threaten to spill from my eyes as I sit up to meet his gaze fully.

"Francesca, I would never leave without letting you know first. Do you not know me better than that?"

The lump in my throat prevents me from speaking and I drop my head.

He takes my hand in his and says, "Francesca, look at me." He lifts my chin with his other hand. "Come with me to Padova."

My eyes widen in surprise, yet he continues in earnest. "You are of age now. We can marry! Did you know the university has begun admitting women into their classes? Think of it. You could be among the first women to earn a degree! What better place than Padova for a talented writer such as yourself?"

My head is spinning. His enthusiasm is irresistible, but this is far too much information, too fast.

"Giovanni! Such dreams! How could we possibly do this?"

"Why not? We are both of age and your zia is well able to afford your dowry. However, you have my heart with or without a dowry," he says, placing my hand on his chest. "Surely your zia does not expect you to follow in her footsteps. I am not passing judgment on her occupation, but you have options, Francesca. You have choices. You have *me*."

While I have avoided picturing myself following in my zia's footsteps, I have also been unable to imagine what other kind of life I might have.

"I am an orphan—"

"As am I," he interrupts.

"Yes, but although my zia has been a mother to me, just as your zio has been a father to you, she is not obligated to provide me with a dowry."

"There is no harm in asking her," he says quietly. "And as a poet herself, I would imagine she, of all people, would be thrilled to see you further your education and writing career. Think about it. Imagine the life we could have!"

A life outside these islands on this laguna? A life away from Venezia—the only home I have ever known? A life as Giovanni's wife?

Si! I nod and lace my fingers through his.

"Please promise me you will think about it, yes?" he pleads. "And when you feel the time is right, talk to your zia about our nuptials."

"Yes," I finally assure him. "I promise. Now, can we please go back to our picnic and not be so serious? Alfredo will be coming by to take me back to Venezia before we know it. And I still have not seen your most recent drawings."

"And you must read me your latest work. Also, I have a surprise for you."

"Another surprise?" I laugh.

Giovanni pulls out one more item from the picnic basket, wrapped in rough linen. He gently removes the cloth and reveals a small vase. It is made of the most striking millefiori glass.

"I made this for you," he says, handing it to me, then whispers, "But you must keep it a secret. If anyone asks you who made it, please tell them that it is the work of my zio."

"Giovanni!" I whisper in return. "You made this? Your zio is right. You do have a talent for glassmaking."

"This is merely a trinket. I do not possess the skill to do what he does. My artwork would be better suited for anatomical renderings. I have heard Andreas Vesalius, the chair of Surgery and Anatomy at the university, is working on a book of anatomical discoveries. If I get there in time, I could conceivably assist him."

"Grazie, Giovanni," I say, holding the vase to my bosom. "I will treasure it. And yes, I will keep your secret."

"Now it is your turn," he says. "Read to me and I will draw your portrait."

After carefully wrapping the vase in the cloth, I place it in my satchel and extract several pages of parchment.

"My zia has asked me to write a commedia to be performed at the upcoming salone next month. She has invited me to attend the entire evening of festivities. It will be my first time presenting my work in public."

"And you will be the belle of the ball, naturalmente!"

I smile at him and commence reading.

While Giovanni quietly sketches, the birds sing sweetly in the trees, a mellow breeze offers a respite from the midday heat, and for the next remaining hours before Alfredo returns on the sandolo, we forget about rules, dowries, expectations, uncertain futures, and possible goodbyes.

Chapter 3 — GIO

Venice, Italy
Wednesday, June 19, 2019

The sky changes from indigo to purple and pink as the sun rises on another day in La Serenissima, the most serene of all cities, my Venezia. I stretch and yawn, while sitting on top of the wall of the rear courtyard, overlooking two canals—the rio della Tetta and the rio di San Giovanni Laterno. Both canals intersect directly behind the bookstore where I live and work.

The heavens continue to lighten, and soon the sandoli pass by on their way toward the Canal Grande and the Campo della Pescaria. In ancient times, these small boats used to be navigated by an oarsman, but today, they all have small motors. Every morning, these boats cruise by, usually carrying two to four men in each, all heading out to the open marketplace to purchase the catch of the day, which will be served at the various restaurants and hotels. By midmorning, the mouthwatering culinary aromas of the wonderful delicacies prepared with all of that fresh seafood will permeate the air. The thought of it makes me hungry.

"Gio!" Luigi is calling me. "Giovanni! Dove sei? Where are you? It is time for breakfast."

Perfect timing! Climbing down off the wall, I head inside. We always enjoy our colazione inside the bookstore as opposed to the kitchen upstairs. It gives us a chance to discuss the news of the day and prepare to open the store.

"Ah! Ciao bello! There you are. Buongiorno!"

Ciao, I yawn sleepily, and he pats my head, affectionately.

"You are a good boy, Gio," Luigi says as he serves me my breakfast. "Mangia. Buon appetito."

Stretching and yawning again, I begin eating.

"A-hah!" Luigi exclaims. "So, you stayed out late again last night, my friend, eh? One of these nights I will follow you and see where you go off to."

Oh, mio Dio! I think. *Please don't.*

Luigi lets out a chuckle as he pats my back. "No, Gio. Do not look alarmed. I am joking. Have fun while you are young. We all have plenty of time to be old, but youth is fleeting and is over too quickly."

I glance up at Luigi. He appears to be in a melancholy mood this morning.

Sensing my thoughts, he says, "Si, Gio. I am worried today. The business has been quite slow, and it is becoming harder and harder to make a decent profit."

Well, I think to myself as I continue eating, *maybe if you would spiffy the place up a bit so the customers might actually find what they were searching for without having to dig through piles and piles of books, which are stored in no apparent logical order, it might make a difference.* But I do not speak this out loud because I have made this complaint many times before to no avail. He doesn't seem to listen. Or perhaps, he doesn't understand.

"The problem is," he continues, "people come here because of the novelty of the place. The fact that our unique little bookstore floods every year during the acqua alta season makes it a big tourist attraction during the dry months. But the rest of the year, when there are not as many visitors and the high waters prevent even the locals from being able to move around the city, there is very little business."

Not to mention the fact that the dry season seems shorter each year, I think. *And the acqua alta has become more frequent.* But the simple fact that we have too many books no one can reach is the main problem, as far as I'm concerned. Luigi needs to hire extra help to assist in organizing it all. They could sort through the piles to inventory what should stay and what we could get rid of. The two of us can only do so much. He spends most of the day manning the cash register and chatting warmly with everyone who comes in. I do my best to help the customers find what they are looking for. My flexibility and dexterity allows me the ability to climb over the hard-to-reach piles. I also keep an eye out for shoplifters. The chaotic mountains of books make it far too easy for people to sneak them into a backpack or purse—another reason it is difficult to make a profit. But Luigi refuses to check the bags of the customers before they exit. He is far too good-natured and trusting. If it were up to me, things would be different. All I can do is give them the evil eye as they depart if they appear suspicious.

"Si, Gio, I know," he says, somehow reading my thoughts. "This place is a disaster, and we need to do something about it."

Infine! I sigh. Finally.

"I need to look into hiring someone to help us," he continues. "I would not be able to pay them very much, but like you, they could live here. You would not mind some companionship, would you? There is plenty of room in our apartment upstairs, and in exchange for room and board, I could also pay them a small wage to help us organize these volcanoes of books. Besides, Sofia and I are feeling the emptiness of our nest ever since Cristina went away to Padova for university. A little company could be nice."

Sofia is Luigi's wife. She does not care for the bookstore because she says it makes her feel claustrophobic. I cannot say I blame her. She is often busy with her own job as the Marketing Director for the Teatro La Fenice, Venezia's famous opera house. Their daughter, Cristina, has completed her third year at l'Università di Padova, where she is studying to become an attorney. I envy her. If I had the means, I too would be attending l'Università di Padova.

Cristina loves living in Padova and has discovered a freedom there which she did not feel within the confines of this island city. Although it is a short train ride to Venezia from Padova, she does not visit very often, especially during the crowded summer months. "Too many tourists!" she complains. Sofia and Luigi miss her terribly. I think it is one of the reasons Luigi enjoys having me around. He is often lonely.

Instead, Sofia and Luigi visit Cristina in Padova, where they all stay at the home of Luigi's brother, Roberto, with his wife and their children during most holidays. When they go to Padova, Luigi closes the bookstore and I stay behind as a house-sitter. Although Luigi has casually mentioned bringing me along to join their family holidays, I prefer remaining where I am. I am afraid that being so close to the university I cannot attend would make me terribly sad.

I thank Luigi for the breakfast as I wipe my face. After my late night, I would love a short catnap before we open the store, but I do not think there will be time this morning. If business is slow today, I might sneak a quick shuteye on the big, soft chair next to the back door, which leads directly to the canal. During business hours, we keep that door to the water entrance propped open with the chair. People love to have their picture taken seated there because Luigi has painted the words, "Fire Exit" on the door. It is his little joke. Often, the customers ask to take pictures with Luigi and me as well. If our customers purchased as many books as the number of photos they take, Luigi would be a wealthy man.

"You are a handsome boy, Gio," Luigi tells me. "The ladies cannot get enough of you. You keep them coming back. You are my lucky charm."

He gives me too much credit. People simply enjoy the bookstore. It is quirky and charming, matching Luigi's personality. He is a good man.

"Well," Luigi says, "it is time to begin our day. Do not worry, Gio, the summer months are here, and the tourists will be good to us. Andiamo!"

I follow him out through the front courtyard, where I inspect the postcard racks while he unlocks the heavy wooden doors that open to the Calle Lunga Santa Maria Formosa. Luigi hangs the "Aperto" sign on a nail in one of the doors. Our bookstore, the Belli Libri dell'Acqua Alta, is open for business.

Chapter 4 — FRANKIE

Venice, Italy
Wednesday, June 19, 2019

I am doing homework at the kitchen table. How do you spell school? Is it s-h-c or s-c-h? This is one of those tricky English words with too many letters and some are "silent" like my teacher says. I look at Mami. She is banging pots and pans. It is very loud. I don't know where Papi is. They had another big fight. "Mami?" I say. "How do you spell school?" "Eh?" she says and sounds mad. "You don't know how to spell school? What's the matter with you? You don't pay attention in class? ¡Sinverguenza! What are you doing? Talking and playing around with your friends instead of paying attention? Go! You go to school and learn how to spell!" It is cold and rainy as I walk down the street to my school. I stand in front of the building and see the sign. It is spelled s-c-h. I knew it! I just wasn't sure. I cry, sitting on the steps in front of my school in the rain. I will stay here for a long time until it gets dark. Then Mami will be worried and feel bad that she yelled at me for not knowing how to spell school and Papi will feel bad and not drink too much beer so he will stop fighting with Mami . . . Papi is scolding me. I am in trouble again. I am always in trouble. I want to ask him how come grown-ups can do bad things and they don't get in trouble, but I just stay quiet . . . "Francisca!" Mami shouts. "I told you to wash the dishes!" "I did," I say. "What is this?" she yells, pointing to a piece of food I did not scrub off of a plate. "Sorry, Mami," I say. "I ask you to help me and all you do is make more work for me! Why can't you do what I tell you?" She bangs a pot on the counter. "Why? Whyyy? Whyyy?"

Awakening with a start, my heart pounding, for a moment I experience the unsettling sensation of not knowing where I am. The squawk of seagulls is accompanied by the clanging of church bells. Ah, yes. I recognize the brocade wallpaper and sigh with relief as I stretch and rub the remaining sleep from my eyes.

I get up and pad over to the window. The smooth terrazzo floor feels cool on my bare feet. I behold my first view of Venice in the morning light from my balcony. To the left, there are several boats traveling along a wider canal, which intersects the one I am standing above. That must be the rio di Noale, which leads directly to the Grand Canal. In the short span of time I have been standing here, I have seen three water taxis and four sandolos, making me appreciate the fact that the Hotel Vendramin is situated on this quiet residential canal and not on a busier one.

Across the canal is a small campo. The square is abuzz with activity, a significant difference from my arrival just a few hours ago when my footsteps echoed along the empty streets. There is a restaurant in the campo and all the outdoor tables are filled with people enjoying their breakfast. Breakfast. I'm famished! But before I go downstairs to eat and meet my fellow employees, I need to check in with my loved ones.

Walking back into the room, I retrieve my phone from the desk. There are several responses to last night's group text. I read through them and reply with a short message reminding everybody that I will send a weekly email with news and photos, but I prefer not to correspond via text while I'm here because I want to be "in the moment" and not feel tempted to constantly stare at my phone. Also, I will be turning off my phone each night. Again—to avoid temptation.

"Seriously, Frankie?!" was Mayra's retort when I informed her of this decision before I embarked on my trip.

"Yes, I am dead serious," I shot back. "I don't want to experience my trip with the agenda of taking pictures and going through my day planning what I'm going to post. I feel the need to reevaluate our Instagram culture and social media obsession. There's gotta be a better way of determining the success of our days other than the number of 'likes' we receive and how many followers we have."

"¡Coño!" Mayra said in exasperation. "But I'm going to miss you, Frankie. An email once a week is not enough. Why do you have to completely cut yourself off? Can't you at least send me a text every now and then?"

She had a point, and I agreed to send her an occasional text and photos to let her know I was thinking of her. But I also shared with her my experience while on vacation last summer with my grandma, when we were watching several tourists enjoying an afternoon on some paddle boats and I observed a young woman in one of them. She fluffed up her hair, adjusted her flirty off-the-shoulder peasant blouse, held her phone out, and took a selfie. I could picture her post in my head: #livingmybestlife.

"That's so sad," said Grandma right at that moment, bursting the thought bubble in my head. "Here's a beautiful girl, all dressed up, taking a picture of herself because she's all alone, but she'll probably post on Facebook, Twitter, or whatever, that she's having the best time ever, and 'Oh, isn't my life perfect and fabulous?' I sometimes feel sorry for your generation, Frankie. You all have become slaves to your phones and living your lives online! Back in my day, we didn't rush to answer every time our phones rang. If it were important, the person would either leave a message or call back later. Our day wasn't constantly interrupted with pings, dings, buzzes, or other ridiculous nonsense. It's no wonder you kids are so stressed out. Your brains don't get a chance to rest with all of that 24/7 noise."

I have seen and experienced firsthand the amount of distress Grandma was talking about brought on by the concept of Fear of Missing Out. FOMO has plagued my friends and me all through middle school, high school, and college. And while the proponents of social media allege that it has brought us closer together and helps us build community, the high rates of depression and anxiety among adolescents and young adults seems to prove otherwise because we essentially feel more isolated despite the amount of time we spend observing other people's lives through our phones.

When I ran into an ex-boyfriend on campus a couple of years ago, he asked me why I had unfriended him on Facebook. "I thought we could at least stay friends," he said. "Just because we're no longer together, it doesn't mean I'm not still interested in how or what you're doing."

"I can't," I admitted. "It just makes me too sad to see you having fun and enjoying life without me. It hurts too much."

Sure, I could refrain from going online and looking at all those posts but come on! Do any of us really possess that kind of willpower?

I remained quiet as I continued watching the young woman in the paddleboat and sadly agreed with everything Grandma said. Whether it's Instagram, Snapchat, TikTok, Twitter, Facebook, or any other platform—people present themselves at their most polished and least vulnerable, and more often than not, all it does is leave everyone feeling sad by comparison.

"Comparison is the thief of joy," Grandma said, surprisingly reading my thoughts. "I'm sorry, Frankie. I know I go on and on about it, but I just think this whole social media thing has gone too far. You do realize, don't you, that nobody's life online is an accurate depiction of what's really going on. At best, it's *only* the 'Best of' and at worst, it's completely curated to the point where it doesn't represent anything genuine at all! Not to mention the major part social media played in all the shenanigans that wreaked havoc on the 2016 Presidential election, for heaven's sake! What a nightmare. Now we're having to endure that pathological lying, racist, anti-Semitic, white supremacist, misogynistic, infantile, inarticulate, imbecilic, out-of-control, sociopathic, narcissistic *disgrace* taking up residence in *our* White House. Just look how awful *his* presence is on social media. Not only has he normalized hate speech, but he has also turned bold-face lying into a daily common occurrence to the point where we have become almost numb to it. And who the hell does that wife of his think she is, telling us her focus is on the issue of cyberbullying. Give me a break! Arrrgh! Don't let me get started!"

Her tirade made me laugh so hard. Grandma never shies away from speaking her mind, and she doesn't suffer fools lightly. It's one of the many reasons I adore her. She shook her head in disgust and joined my laughter.

"You know," Grandma continued, "even though I complain about our obsessions with these phones, I admit they do come in handy. I tell you what—back in the 1960s, when we were all marching for Civil Rights, we could have used this technology to organize and reach out to even more people. And the ability to take videos would have gone a long way in capturing the police brutality many of those protestors experienced."

"But Grandma, videos of police brutality have been appearing all over the news for years and nothing seems to change. What is it going to take to finally bring an end to all this deeply ingrained racism?"

"You're right," she said, solemnly. "I wish I had an answer for that. All we can do is stay vigilant . . . and VOTE! Anyway, no technology is either all good or all bad. Like everything in life, it depends on how you use it."

It was with that experience in mind that I decided, before this trip to Italy, I would come off *all* social media and deleted all of my accounts and apps. Mayra, along with several other friends thought my decision was nuts because they couldn't imagine being out of touch and missing out on whatever everyone else is doing at any given moment.

Grandma, of course, thought it was a great idea.

* * * * *

After a quick shower, I try to find something to wear that isn't too wrinkled. I'm starving and I need to get to the dining room before they stop serving breakfast. Walking through the lovely portego on my way to the lobby, that odd feeling of recognition floods over me again. Before embarking on this trip I did a lot of research about this hotel. It must just be that I recognize this room from the photos I received via email during my application process and that's why it feels familiar.

Inhaling a strong whiff of coffee, I race down the stairs and step into the lobby. The young woman behind the reception desk, who looks to be around my age, greets me with a dazzling smile. "Buongiorno!"

"Buongiorno," I reply. "I'm Frankie."

"Ah, si! Paolo told me to expect you. I am Luciana. Please take a seat in our dining area and Maria will be with you shortly. After you eat, she will explain your job."

"Grazie," I say, once again grateful she speaks English, and walk into the charming dining area. Of course, my main purpose for being here is to practice and improve my Italian, but it's a relief to get off to a gradual start.

Most of the palazzi in Venice have undergone massive renovations, and the Hotel Vendramin is no exception. This first floor, with the lobby, dining area, and main entrance at one time must have been the basement and storage area in the private home of one family. It is at the same level as the canal, which would have made it easy for supplies to be unloaded off boats by the servants. What is currently the main entrance of the hotel is probably where the noble family members would have boarded their private gondola.

Walking around the delightful room, I take careful notice of all the authentic details, which make me feel as if I've been transported back in time. All the furnishings appear to be genuine antiques and every well-crafted lighting fixture is made of Murano glass. At the far end of the dining area is a magnificent floor-to-ceiling, elaborately carved, wooden cabinet where all the pastries, fresh bread, and fruit are arranged for the enjoyment of the hotel guests. Above the counter with the food is a shelf of knickknacks and something catches my eye. Stepping closer to get a better look, it is a small, multicolored vase, housing a single blush-colored long-stem rose.

"Millefiori," a voice behind me says and I jump, startled.

"Oh, mi scusi," says a woman. "I did not mean to scare you. I am Maria." She speaks all of this in Italian. And so, begins my first lesson.

"Oh, buongiorno," I respond, flustered, my Italian sounding stilted to my own ears. "Io sono Frankie."

"Benvenuta, Frankie," Maria says, extending her hand. She looks to be in her late 30s and has a warm, maternal air about her. I like her immediately.

I shake her hand. "This vase is unlike anything I have ever seen before. What did you call it?"

"Millefiori," she says. "It means, a thousand flowers. It is a special type of glassmaking from Murano. Come! Please sit down and I will bring you coffee. You drink coffee, yes?"

"Sì! Un caffè latte per favore."

"Va bene," she says. "Make yourself comfortable. Help yourself to bread and pastries. I will make your coffee and after you finish eating, I will show you the kitchen and tell you about your duties."

"Grazie," I say and select a table closest to the cabinet, where I can continue admiring the little vase. I may need to bring something similar back to Grandma.

I don't care how good Starbucks is, nothing can beat an authentic caffè latte in Italy. The bread, fresh butter and cream are also unsurpassed. Or it could simply be all food tastes better when traveling somewhere exotic. Nope. I think food is just better in Italy. Period.

I eat slowly and deliberately, allowing myself to enjoy every bite without guilt or fear. I've battled with an eating disorder for most of my adolescence and maintaining a healthy relationship with food is an ongoing process.

After my breakfast, Maria gives me a tour of the kitchen. Since the hotel only serves a continental breakfast of coffee, tea, juices, bread, yogurt, pastries, and fresh fruit, the kitchen is used for the sole purpose of storage and preparation. We will not be doing any cooking. Each morning a boat arrives with fresh supplies and it will be part of my job to unload the goods and help Maria set out all the food. She shows me how to use the elaborate copper espresso machine, which is a work of art and seems far too pretty for practical use. How quintessentially Italian! The Italian aesthetic of beauty seems to make everything ordinary a masterpiece.

The breakfast service is from 7:30 to 10:30 a.m. daily and the only drawback is that I must report for work at 6:30 a.m.—I am not a morning person. After the breakfast service is over, Maria and I will clean and prepare the dining area for the following morning. She tells me we will likely be finished no later than noon and I will have the remainder of the day to do whatever I wish. Plus, I will have each Monday off. Not bad.

"Paolo explained to me that you are here a few days early due to travel problems," Maria says.

"Yes. Originally, I was not supposed to arrive until tomorrow and then begin work the following day."

"Well," Maria continues, "it is up to you if you want to begin tomorrow or the day after. It is okay if you want to wait. This way you can do some sightseeing."

"Oh, yes! That would be wonderful. There is so much I want to see."

"Va bene,'" she says. "Luciana at the front desk can answer any questions you may have and help you with reservations, tickets, and directions."

"Great! Thank you, Maria."

"Prego. Ciao. Ci vediamo."

"Ciao!"

The entire conversation with Maria in Italian has worn me out, but I'm proud of myself for getting through it. Nevertheless, the excitement of exploring the city infuses me with a surge of energy and I quickly run upstairs, back to my room to retrieve my purse, water bottle, and phone. First on my list: Piazza San Marco!

* * * * *

After purchasing a Rolling Venice card for youth ages 14-29 directly from Luciana at the reception desk, I am now able to enjoy unlimited rides on the water buses. Most visitors must obtain their vaporetto tickets from Actv kiosks at specific locations throughout the city. While the self-service machines are translated in several languages, they can be confusing, and I'm relieved I don't have to deal with any of that. She also gave me a map, in which she circled several popular landmarks and suggested I obtain my first vaporetto at the Ca' d'Oro stop. I thank Luciana profusely for all her invaluable help and head out for my first adventure in Venice.

I could easily enter Ca' d'Oro on my phone's navigation, but instead I choose to follow the line Luciana drew in red pen on the map and allow myself to feel like a true explorer! Grandma, who believes that GPS has eliminated the serendipity and whimsy of getting lost, would be tickled by my adventurous spirit.

"It's so easy to miss out on wonderful discoveries when your attention is occupied with staring at the blue dot on your phone. Some of the best twists of fate can occur when you find yourself lost," she once told me.

After crossing over the Ponte Vendramin, I turn left on Strada Nova and keep walking until I cross another bridge. I continue on Strada Nova until it dead ends at a canal and turn left. The next bridge I cross turns into Calle San Felice, which curiously becomes Calle del Pistor for no apparent reason. At Ramo Ca' d'Oro I make a right and that street suddenly changes into Calle Ca' d'Oro, which finally leads me to the vaporetto stop. I am rewarded for my labyrinthine excursion with my first daytime view of the Grand Canal! I am bowled over by the majesty of it and feel as though I might cry from joy. It is breathtakingly beautiful.

There are numerous watercrafts on the canal, and it resembles a liquid freeway, minus lane markings. Along with the many vaporetti, there are small motorboats, water taxis, and gondolas. The water taxis are lovely, highly polished wooden boats trimmed in chrome, similar to the ones I saw showcased one summer at the Concours d'Elegance on the west shore of California's Lake Tahoe. There, those boats are owned and maintained by wealthy boat collectors and aficionados. But here, they are common utility vehicles. Further evidence that everything in Italy, no matter how ordinary, is gorgeous. The highly shellacked wood of the water taxis makes them appear like golden jewels, glinting under the sun. They are all extraordinarily pretty. But the gondolas! Those are *magnificent.* So dramatic in the contrast of their red and gold plush seating inside a shining black hull, immediately making me feel as if I've stepped through a portal back to the Italian Renaissance.

I'm also getting my first look at some of the famous palazzi that line the Grand Canal. Most of them date from the 13th to the 18th century and housed noble Venetian families who spared no expense to show off their wealth through the ostentatious opulence of their ornate facades.

I board the next vaporetto that arrives and have the good fortune to find a seat at the front, where I have an unobstructed view of Venice from the water as we motor down the reverse S-shaped canal, south, toward the Fermata San Marco. This is fantastic! It's all the sightseeing I need to do. I could happily ride the vaporetto up and down the Grand Canal all day long.

The foundation on which this unique city sits is man-made and was built by using long timber piles, which were driven into the mud at the bottom of the lagoon. The wood absorbed all the silt and sediment carried by the lagoon, and over time it petrified and kept the wood intact for hundreds of years. It is an absolute engineering marvel of the world!

The vaporetto arrives at my destination, Fermata San Marco, directly in front of the Giardini Reali. A sign in English for the tourists proclaims it the Royal Gardens, and is one of the extremely rare green spaces in the city. I disembark, along with the majority of the passengers. Not surprisingly, we all seem to be headed in the same direction. We file past several souvenir stalls along the Riva degli Schiavoni, which leads straight to the famous columns of Saint Mark and Saint Theodore, Venice's patron saints, at the Piazzetta. This little square is an extension of the Piazza San Marco and directly in front of the Doge's Palace. Other than the Piazzale Roma, where the bus dropped me off last night, all other open spaces in the city are called campi, or fields. Quite the misnomer, since there is nothing field-like about those public squares, comprised mainly of brick and stone.

Together, the Piazzetta and the Piazza San Marco, the principal square of Venice, served as the social, political, and religious center of Venice throughout its illustrious history. Today, it is one of the most iconic and frequently visited tourist sites in the world. Also making it one of the most crowded, which is undoubtedly the case today. However, I have been expecting this. It is summer, after all, and the height of tourist season throughout Europe. I will not allow the crowds to dampen my enthusiasm as I resolutely take my place at the end of the long line of people waiting their turn to enter the famous Basilica San Marco. It's barely noon. I have all day.

Fortunately, the queue moves surprisingly fast, and soon I am stepping through the ancient arched entrance into the golden mosaic belly of this masterpiece of Byzantine and Gothic architecture, where we are required to remain in some semblance of a single file as we proceed across the main floor, toward the altar.

Making my way around the pews, I notice a distinct horizontal smudge on all the interior marble columns as well as on the walls. This must be a water line mark left from a previous flooding of the entire Basilica during an aqua alta event.

I had read that throughout history, Venice and its inhabitants have endured the occasional flooding of their exceptional city during winter storms, which they refer to as the acqua alta, or high water. The watermark on the columns and walls is about four feet high. I am guessing the ground floor of the Basilica is around four or five feet above the Piazza level outside. Therefore, the water must have gotten up to a height of ten feet for the Basilica to flood. Wow. That's a lot of water! How can the Basilica withstand that type of flooding year after year?

Arriving at the front of the main altar, I notice a young security officer keeping a close watch on everyone. I smile at him in greeting as I pass by, but he is no-nonsense, and maintains his serious demeanor as he continues his surveillance. My curiosity is killing me so I risk a possible stern reprimand by asking him a question.

"Excuse me?" I say, indicating the watermark on the nearest column. "How many times does the Basilica flood each year during the acqua alta?

"Mai," he replies. Never.

Wait. What? I always assumed that flooding inside the Basilica and Piazza San Marco was a naturally occurring yearly event, given its precarious location and all the images I've seen on the news.

"The watermark you see was created by the flood of 1966," he continues. "To date, it remains the worst flood in the history of Venezia. The water rose high enough to fill the crypt below us up to the ceiling. Since that time, there have been two other big floods in 1979 and 1986, but neither as bad as the one in 1966. In 2018 we experienced the fourth worst flood ever in recorded history. Many native Venetians continue to leave as the acqua alta becomes worse and more frequent with each passing year. If this continues, Venezia will become a city solely comprised of hotels, restaurants, and souvenir shops. No one will be able to live here any longer."

I recall a conversation with my grandma last year. "Frankie, I am filled with equal parts guilt and anger at what my generation has done. Or rather, failed to do," Grandma told me. "I am so sorry for the absolute mess we are leaving you kids with. It wasn't just my generation, though. The ones before mine and after are also to blame. We neglected to get a handle on this thing before it spun out of control. Now, our poor planet is practically on life support and your generation is left with the daunting task of performing triage. And once again, that moronic climate denier in the White House is only making matters worse by refusing to acknowledge the *science*!"

The city of Venice is over 1200 years old. The acqua alta phenomenon of unusually high tides that cover parts of Venice for a few hours, then slowly retreat, has always been a part of its history. Yet, according to what the security guard is telling me, the four worst floods in the entire recorded history of the city took place within the last 50 years. So, while it is widely known that the city of Venice has been sinking over the centuries, understandably due to its tenuous foundation, it is becoming fairly obvious that the steadily rising sea levels, as a result of global warming, have further jeopardized the future of this extraordinary city. This breaks my heart.

I thank the security guard for his information and continue the rest of my tour of the Basilica.

Two hours later, as I exit the Basilica, I take in the swarms of tourists throughout the Piazza San Marco. There appear to be tour groups of every nationality and I hear a myriad of languages as I walk the parameter of the piazza through the arcades, where I locate a gelateria and indulge in my first gelato. Stracciatella! It is basically the Italian version of chocolate chip ice cream, but so much better. The rich, creamy delight is the precise definition of decadence. Delizioso!

While finishing my ice cream, I observe that the line of people waiting to ascend the Campanile is rather short. The bell tower is one of the most recognizable symbols of the city and the tallest structure in all of Venice. I seize the opportunity to experience the 360-degree view the observation deck at the top has to offer of this unique and historic marvel.

Emerging from the elevator to the observation deck, I immediately feel my eyes well up. Oh, Venice! In all my travels, never have I been in a city that fills me with such wonder that my emotions cannot keep pace with what my vision takes in. From the top of this 323-foot structure, which was originally built as a watch tower and lighthouse, I can see the renowned picture-postcard church, Santa Maria della Salute, across the Grand Canal, and I have a bird's eye view of Piazza San Marco, the Doge's Palace, and Basilica. The rest of the city is a jumble of red terracotta-tiled roofs covering buildings of brick, marble, and stone, which in the light of the late afternoon sun, become even more imbued with an intense color palette of umber, russet, amber, sienna, and ochre. I see innumerable church bell towers, and beyond that the lagoon, Adriatic Sea, and the Dolomites mountain range.

I am overwhelmed by this city. It is a living, breathing, open-air museum. One whose powerful yet delicate beauty and its future sits precariously atop humanity's decision as to whether or not it deserves our protection.

Chapter 5 — FRANCESCA

Venezia, Italia
Martedì 19 settembre 1550

"Be careful!" An angry shout comes from outside the open window in the dining room of the Palazzo Vendramin. "Maestro Lorenzo did not painstakingly create this work of genius so you could destroy it in one moment of negligence."

Zia Veronica and I are finishing our colazione, and she looks at me with wide eyes as she rises quickly from the table to look out the window.

"Giovanni?" she calls from the balcony. "Cosa sta succendo?"

"Ah, Buongiorno, signora d'Aragona," I hear Giovanni say from down below on the canal. "Mi dispiace. I am sorry for the disturbance, but your servants do not seem to understand the care with which they must handle this delicate shipment. It involves much unique glasswork—unlike anything anyone has ever seen."

"Ragazzi!" Zia Veronica shouts down to her servants. "Please listen to Giovanni's instructions. This is an extremely important piece."

"Grazie, signora!" Giovanni answers.

Zia Veronica returns inside. "Your bel ragazzo has quite the temper, Francesca," she teases.

"Or one could call it passion," I respond coyly.

With eyebrows raised, she gives me a knowing look. "I am well aware you have strong feelings for him, Francesca, but always remember that marriage is a contract, above all else. Marrying for love is a luxury seldom experienced outside fairy stories, your parents being the exception. My dear sister and your father had the good fortune of falling in love within an arranged marriage."

"It surprises me to hear you say that zia, given the romantic nature of your poetry."

"Yes," she concedes. "However, let us not forget that the only reason I am even allowed to write as I wish is because I could not marry. While being a courtesan allows me certain freedoms, a woman's options are always limited. Your mother and I were fortunate that our parents allowed us to be educated by our older brother's tutor. As I am sure you are aware, that opportunity was highly unusual. Sadly, when our brother fell ill and died at the age of nineteen, your mother became the eldest child, and thus, allowed to marry. If our brother had lived, however, she would have joined a convent, no doubt. I do not believe the life of a courtesan would have suited her."

I, of course, am well acquainted with this family history, but it is not until this moment that the complete impact of those events hit me. Had it not been for my uncle's death, I would not exist.

"Maritar o monacar," I recite the old Venetian saying.

"Essatamente," my zia says. "Marry or enter a convent. Women have few alternatives, Francesca. Which is why I encourage you to not get caught up in fantasy."

I have not yet told my zia about Giovanni's plans to study in Padova and his invitation to have me join him. It is as if she has read my mind.

"And while I do not wish to place any pressure on you at your sixteen years of age, you must soon decide which direction you wish to take," she continues. "Or, you could choose to learn the skills of the cortigiana onesta, but you must do so while you are in your prime in order to secure a proper benefactor. Also, bear in mind that you have become accustomed to our way of life here. You are educated and have had the rare opportunity of experiencing a world not available to most women. But make no mistake—your exposure to literature, art, and culture would disappear once you are married to *anyone*. Even if you married a nobleman, you would inevitably be excluded from participating in public life and would be relegated to observing the goings-on from the 'safe distance' of your palazzo window. Whereas, the courtesan, similar to the male courtier, can remain actively involved in public affairs. I am afraid that taking you in as my charge after the death of your parents has been both a blessing and a curse to you, Francesca. I am deeply sorry."

The genuine sorrow with which she says this startles me.

"Zia, please do not apologize. I owe you my life! I understand everything you are saying. While I cannot imagine a life in a convent, I must admit that, like my mother, I am not sure I possess all the qualities required to become a successful courtesan such as yourself. At least if I married for love, would that not make up for the loss of certain privileges?"

Before my zia has a chance to respond, Domisilla, the maid, enters the dining room to inform her that Giovanni is awaiting instructions in the portego.

"We must continue this discussion another time, Francesca," says my zia. "For now, let us go see this *masterpiece.*"

During the next hour, after my zia shows Giovanni where she would like the chandelier hung, he meticulously installs it in the center of the coffered ceiling in the portego, where my zia greets and welcomes her guests before adjourning to the dining room for the elaborate dinners she hosts, followed by entertainment in the salone. When the task is completed, Giovanni calls us back into the room and the three of us stand back to admire Maestro Lorenzo's artistry.

"It is extraordinary!" Zia Veronica exclaims with delight. "Your zio has surely outdone himself!"

While most chandeliers are made of either wood, iron, bronze or a combination of materials, this one is made of bronze and embellished with a dozen glass garlands, such as the one I witnessed Maestro Lorenzo create during my last trip to Murano. Zia Veronica asks one of her servants to light the candles on the chandelier, and we all gasp in awe as the added glass ornamentation enhances the brilliance of the candlelight.

"He is a virtuoso," Giovanni proudly proclaims.

"It is amazing!" I say. "Oh, zia, your guests will surely be impressed."

"Si!" she agrees. "This next gathering will be the most memorable one yet. Giovanni, it must be exciting to be under the tutelage of the world's greatest glassmaker. No doubt, you will learn to become a master yourself"

Giovanni glances at me quickly and with my eyes, I try to communicate that I have not informed my zia of our discussion the other day.

Without missing a beat, he replies, "Mio zio is blessed with remarkable talents. And my young cousin, Giuseppe, is already showing great promise."

"Giovanni," my zia says thoughtfully as she slowly paces around the room, admiring her latest acquisition. "Would Maestro Lorenzo be able to produce candelabras to match this fine chandelier?"

"I do not see why not," he replies.

"Wonderful! Please relay my request to have him create two more pieces, which will adorn my dining table."

"Of course, signora. However, I am not sure he will be able to have them completed in time for your next gathering."

"Non importa," she says. "If they are completed in time, fantastico! If not, they will be used and appreciated during all future festivities."

"Very well. Nevertheless, I will convey the urgency, and I am sure my zio will do his best to complete them in time. And I will hand deliver them myself," he says, sneaking me a sly smile.

"Bravissimo!" Zia Veronica exclaims.

"Signora," Domisilla re-enters the room. "Alfredo and Marco have prepared your gondola and are waiting."

"Grazie," Zia Veronica tells her, and turning back to Giovanni says, "Allora, I must now leave you, for I have an important appointment with the mask maker at Ca' d'Arte. Francesca, will you please go to my chamber and retrieve my cloak and pouch? I wish to give Giovanni his payment."

"Yes, zia," I say and quickly return with the items she requested.

Handing Giovanni one ducato, she says, "And here is something extra as a deposit for the next pieces. This may give your uncle added incentive?" She winks and gives him two lire coins.

"Grazie. You are most generous. We are always at your service, signora d'Aragona."

"Va bene. We will see you again soon, Giovanni. Arrivederci!"

"Arrivederci!" Giovanni and I cry out in unison as we watch Zia Veronica descend the stairs to her awaiting gondola.

Giovanni regards me with those exquisite eyes, and before he has a chance to utter a word, I say, "Si, Giovanni, I *know*. I have not yet shared our plans with my zia. She has been extremely preoccupied with preparations for her upcoming salone."

"I understand," he says. "It has barely been one week since we last spoke. But I do hope you will have this conversation with her soon so we will have enough time to wed before I need to depart for l'università."

"She worries a great deal about my prospects. I do not wish to further concern her at this busy time with all the uncertainty of the future we discussed."

He nods in comprehension. "And after all she has done for you, you do not wish to appear disloyal."

"Si!" I say. "Exactly!"

"It is precisely how I feel about my zio Lorenzo. But there can be no doubt that they both want what is best for us, even if that means following a very different path than what they had originally imagined."

I abruptly pivot away from him in frustration.

"It is far easier for a man than a woman!" I say bitterly. "Men have always had more choices and liberties."

"Yes, Francesca. You are right," he says gently. "But together we can be stronger than separately. Do you not believe this to be true?"

"Si," I turn around slowly to look at him. "But I am afraid," I admit. "I have never left these islands, Giovanni. And what if the university does not accept me? What then? Will we ever return to Venezia? Will we ever be able to see our loved ones again? I applaud your ambition to become a dottore, Giovanni, and I think you will be greatly successful, but a life in Padova feels uncertain for me, personally, and so far away. If I knew we would spend the rest of our lives on Murano, with the mere distance of the laguna between me and the only home I have ever known, I would feel less uncertain and scared."

"Of course. It is reasonable. But I pledge to you, right here, right now, Francesca Cartelli, I will never allow any harm to come your way as long as I have breath in my body."

"Oh, Giovanni!" I embrace him fiercely, and I know with every fiber of my being that his promise is the purest truth in all the world.

We separate, and with his fingers, he tenderly caresses my cheek.

"And now," he says, his reluctance obvious, "I must be off. The sooner I return to Murano, the faster my uncle will begin work on your zia's next sensation."

I laugh lightly, knowing that while her extravagances may seem frivolous, my zia has a huge heart, and she generously provides a livelihood for many people including, but not limited to, the glassmakers of Murano and the mask makers here in Venezia.

"We will see each other soon, bellissima." He takes my hands in his and places a gentle kiss on them. "Alla prossima."

"Si, until next time, caro mio."

I watch him walk down the stairs and wave as he glances back at me one more time before disappearing from my sight. I run to the window in the dining room and peer down from the balcony as he is about to climb into his sandolo. Giovanni gazes up from the fondamenta to the balcony and blows me a kiss. He steps into the sandolo, unties it from the mooring post, picks up the oar, and pushes away from the fondamenta. I continue watching him from the balcony as the sandolo moves out toward the rio di Noale and turns left—north, toward Murano.

Chapter 6 — FRANKIE

Venice, Italy
Monday, July 29, 2019

Sipping water, I stare at the little blue pill in my palm. A small motor boat on the rio della Sensa captures my attention as it slowly passes by my table under the shade of an oversized umbrella on the Fondamenta de la Sensa. Each day when I'm faced with taking my medication, I wonder how much longer I will need to do so.

I signal to my waiter when he comes back outside from the restaurant.

"Would you like anything else, signorina?" the waiter asks.

"No, grazie," I respond. "The check please."

"Molto bene," he says as he removes my empty plate, stained black from my odd but delicious meal of Spaghetti alla Veneziana. A local dish made with cuttlefish cooked in its own ink, it tasted better than it looked and when I closed my eyes, the flavor was really no different from any other tasty plate of spaghetti. But when the waiter first set it down before me, I could have sworn someone spilled motor oil all over my lunch! It is the specialty of the house, here at the Osteria Ai 40 Ladroni. Of course, I had to try it. Paolo, back at the Hotel Vendramin, highly recommended this restaurant and I will report to him that I was not disappointed.

I look down at the little blue pill again.

* * * * *

"Frankie, if a person suffers from diabetes, heart disease, or high blood pressure, they will need to take medicine in order to keep them healthy, right?" my grandma once said, referring to my blue pills, the Zoloft I've been taking for the past six years. "So why is this any different?"

"I don't know," I replied. "I just feel like I should be able to overcome this somehow. Like my depression is a phase and I just need to figure out how to deal with it."

"If you had a broken leg it would be unthinkable to deny you medical attention, and no one would dare tell you to 'just get over it.' Frankie, you've been through a lot."

"We both have, Grandma."

"Yes," she agreed in a hushed voice, and after a big sigh continued, "While losing my child is the worst thing I could ever imagine happening and my worst nightmare come true, I am a grown-ass woman. You were just a kid and far too young to have to deal with so much trauma. It's perfectly understandable that you would be struggling. And it's okay to accept help while you try to find your footing. And it's also perfectly fine if it's something you need to continue taking for the rest of your life."

"I feel like I've been such a burden to you, Grandma."

"Frankie," she said, unexpectedly taking on a stern tone. "I don't ever want to hear you say that again. Do you hear me?"

I nodded mutely. Tears appeared in her eyes, which immediately caused me to completely lose it. She enfolded me in a tight embrace as we both wept.

"Taking care of you has saved me. Don't you understand?" she continued as she held me. "Without you, I would have found it impossible to have a reason to get up every morning." Looking directly into my eyes she said, "Sweetheart, our struggles don't make us burdens. Our struggles are what connect us and make us human. It is a sign of strength, not weakness, to ask for help and accept it. You are way too hard on yourself and expect too much. Please go easy on yourself, Frankie."

I'm way too hard on myself. *Gee, I wonder where I learned that?*

I know my parents loved me, but I often felt they placed unrealistically high expectations on me. Perhaps this is a common theme among children of immigrants. When you leave behind everything you have ever known to begin a new life in another country, the stakes are extraordinarily high and a lot of pressure winds up falling on the shoulders of the children to ensure that all the sacrifices made were worth it.

* * * * *

"Dónde están las casitas?" I asked my mami as I looked out of the small airplane window. Where are the houses?

Even though my mami had explained to me that we would be *flying,* my little three-year-old mind could not comprehend why I didn't see any of the houses I would normally look at while riding in a bus or car. Thus, began our journey from El Salvador to the country which would become our new home—the U.S. of A.

In 1996, shortly after my birth, mom enrolled in English classes, which she would attend in the evenings while my father stayed home with me. Mom had dreams of someday going to the United States of America because she believed a future in El Salvador held little opportunities for escaping poverty. Even after the civil war ended in 1992, life there remained difficult and increasingly dangerous.

My mom's English teacher had connections with an agency in the United States that hired domestic workers and nannies, while providing them with work visas and Green Cards. Mom saw this as her big chance to attain a better life for us, and she seized it. This required that she leave my father and me in El Salvador for one year as she worked for a family in the U.S. as their housekeeper and cook while going through the process of obtaining visas and Green Cards for the two of us, so we could join her.

Mom left El Salvador when I was two years old and when she returned to take us with her back to the U.S., I did not remember her. I was only three years old, but I have memories of being at the airport with my father and some family friends, waiting to welcome her back home after being away for a full year. As soon as my mom saw me, she ran to embrace me, but I remember pulling away from her and saying, "You're not my mami." I also remember her crying, right there in the middle of the bustling airport.

My father often showed me photos of my mom throughout that entire year she was away, but the woman crying and trying to hug me, who kept insisting that she was my mami, felt like a complete stranger to me.

I have no idea how much time passed before I finally warmed up to her. Several months later, by the time we were on that airplane on our way to the States, I finally felt comfortable with her and understood that she was indeed my mami. But I often wonder whether that lost year of bonding played a significant role in why she and I had such a turbulent relationship at times. By all accounts, experts claim that the first five years in a child's life are extremely important and what happens during those first few years can have a significant impact on a child.

The three of us settled in Los Angeles, California, but shortly after we arrived in L.A., my father's alcoholism became unavoidably apparent. Unlike my mom, he never wanted to leave El Salvador. Unfortunately, he never fully adapted to our new home and became increasingly miserable. He often took out his resentment on my mother during horrifically violent drunken rages.

My father's anger was further exacerbated by the many times he was unfairly stopped by police on his way home from working the graveyard shift at the factory where he was employed. The situation became worse after 9/11, when men of color, who have always been disproportionally targeted, became even more at risk. A brown man driving around during the wee hours of the morning in L.A. created enough cause for suspicion to warrant all manner of unfair treatment from the police.

Each time my father experienced one of those humiliating stop-and-frisk procedures, he sunk deeper into despair. The irony was the fact that the one time it would have been beneficial to pull him over, there were no police officers around to help prevent the tragedy about to unfold. Just four years after arriving in the United States, my father crashed his car into a telephone pole and died instantly. The one saving grace was that no other cars or passengers were involved.

After his death, the wealthy family my mom worked for offered to have us both live in their house, while my mom continued to work as their domestic help, thus, saving my mom having to pay rent on an apartment as a single parent. This made it possible for her to save money and not have to worry about being able to afford childcare for me while she worked. Throughout my elementary school years, we lived in a lavish mansion in the ritzy residential enclave known as Bel-Air, a hop, skip, and a jump away from the campus of the University of California, Los Angeles.

My mom eventually left domestic employment after taking several secretarial courses and obtained administrative office work. We moved into a small apartment in Burbank, a suburb of Los Angeles in the San Fernando Valley. Although we never had a lot of money, we weren't dirt poor either. My mom always made sure we had enough food and clothes and even managed to take us on some nice vacations. Eventually, we both became proud U.S. citizens. She was the embodiment of the American Dream, and I am her legacy.

When my mom met my stepdad, I was entering middle school and right smack in the thick of adolescent angst. My stepdad was a good man, but after several years of just mom and me, his sudden presence in our lives was hard for me. It also happened to be at that point when my mom and I were having the most problems. We fought regularly and the combination of my teenage insecurities and what felt like her constant criticism, made me become increasingly withdrawn, despondent, and angry. As with most females, I was socialized and indoctrinated in a cultural belief that I must be a "good girl" in order to be acceptable, and God forbid I should ever display any anger.

Instead, I turned my rage inward where it manifested as depression and eating disorders. But my stepdad brought with him the greatest asset—my grandma!

My mom and stepdad had been married for three short years when their car was hit by a drunk driver. Unlike my father's collision all those years earlier, this drunk driver walked away unscathed, but managed to kill the two people in the car he hit head on at 90 miles per hour.

I never had the chance to meet my stepdad's father, who had died two years before my mom and stepdad met. He had been a successful businessman and founded the moving company jointly owned and run by my grandma and stepdad. The business was hugely profitable, and we lived a comfortable life. Since my stepdad was an only child, and he and my mom never had children together, I will be the sole heir to this fortune when, God forbid, my grandma passes away.

I would gladly give it all up in a heartbeat if I could have my parents back.

After my parents' accident, the remaining two years of high school became unbearable. Fortunately, Grandma understood that we were going to need help and enrolled us both in grief counseling. With the help of a great therapist and eventually some meds, I managed to get through the remainder of high school and accepted into one of the finest universities in California. My grief and the guilt I felt over my complicated relationship with my mom continued to haunt me throughout my college years, but Grandma's love and encouragement supported me like a life raft.

I also continued seeing the same wonderful therapist. She helped me tremendously when she suggested that I had what is called complex PTSD. She explained that unlike regular post-traumatic stress disorder, which is generally related to a single event, complex PTSD arises from experiencing a series of events, such as ongoing abuse, or one prolonged event such as living in a war zone. My therapist stated that with the trauma I experienced from all the loss, separation, alcoholism, and exposure to domestic abuse, it was a miracle that I turned out as high functioning and well-adjusted as I am.

Understanding that my depression and anxiety have legitimate origins and are not a reflection of "weak character" gives me hope, because when you grow up with parents who are not inclined to acknowledge it or who negatively judge other people's mental health struggles, it's very easy to minimize, trivialize, and downplay what's going on in your head. My therapist also explained that it is quite common for certain cultures to avoid any discussion or acknowledgement of mental illness because it is a subject that remains taboo, along with addiction and domestic violence.

"All three of your parents would be so proud of you, Frankie," Grandma said as she embraced me in one of her bear hugs at my graduation ceremony last month. "I know your mom could be really hard on you at times, but I also know she loved you very much. It's crazy that being a parent is the hardest and most important job in the world, and yet, every single day millions of babies are born and sent home with parents who have no idea what they're doing. It's terrifying! That any of us manage to make it out alive is a miracle. What I'm trying to say, Frankie, is that your mother and father did the best they could with whatever skills they had. It's not an excuse for the pain you experienced, but if I've learned anything in my old age it's that if we assume everyone, from the time they wake up each morning until the time they go to bed, is doing the absolute best they can, it makes life a little bit easier. The same philosophy will also help you forgive yourself, Frankie. You also did the best you could with your mom, and you needn't beat yourself up for being a typical teenager. It was your job to assert your independence, push the boundaries, and question authority. That's called *growing up.* Everyone has to go through the process of realizing their own deep knowing, and that requires clearing up all the static from the old noise and finding the answers within yourself."

"Oh, Grandma!" I cried, bowled over by her wisdom and compassion. "What would I ever do without you?"

She hugged me for a long time and said, "Listen, I want you to stay in Europe as long as possible."

"Grandma," I laughed. "It doesn't work that way. I can't stay indefinitely. My seasonal work permit is only good through September. After you join me in the fall, and we travel for a few more weeks, I'll have to come home, back to 'real life' and become an adult."

"Well," she continued, stubbornly, "I just think while you're young and free, you should travel, travel, travel! I wish I had the chance to do that when I was your age."

"We'll have such a blast exploring the rest of Italy together!" I said.

Now that I am an adult and finished with school, she had recently sold the moving company and finally retired. For the first time since my parents died, she is free to go out and enjoy herself without any time constraints or the constant stress and obligation of running a business on her own as well as the responsibility of raising me.

* * * * *

Placing the little blue pill in my mouth and washing it down with the remaining water in my glass, I recall what my therapist always says: The ability to take action requires hope.

I text a photo of my black spaghetti to Mayra and retrieve a notebook and pen from my purse to write down the details of my unusual lunch. Then I stare at a blank page for several moments. Other than basic journal entries I haven't been able to write anything of substance since I arrived in Venice despite all of the interesting things I have seen and done. Writer's block was the last thing I expected to experience in such a fascinating location. I frustratingly shove the notebook back in my purse.

"Grazie, signorina," the waiter says as he hands me the check for my lunch.

I hand him some Euros and before he leaves, I open my trusty map and ask him what the best way is to get over to the Belli Libri dell'Acqua Alta bookstore. The waiter suggests that instead of walking, it might be faster and easier to take the vaporetto from San Marcuola Casino to the Rialto stop. I thank him once more, don my fabulous hat that makes me feel like I'm starring in an Italian film, and walk south toward the Grand Canal.

While conducting online research for this trip, I had come across an image entitled, "The world's most beautiful bookstore" and found several more pictures of the quirkiest shop I have ever seen. The proprietor of the store appeared in photographs wearing galoshes and gaiters, standing in water up to his knees. I adore bookstores, and decided I would have to pay this one a visit. When I asked my coworkers back at the hotel about it, they all agreed it was a must-see.

"Ah, yes," Paolo had said. "Luigi and his bookstore are very popular with the tourists."

Maria told me that her older sister and Luigi's wife, Sofia, have been longtime friends since childhood. "And Luciana, at the front desk, was also a schoolmate of their daughter, Cristina," she added.

"Wow," I said. "Everyone seems to know each other in this city."

"Si," Maria agreed. "Venezia is a city that often feels like a small village. You cannot go very far before you fall into the water, so we all bump into each other frequently."

I chuckle to myself as I recall Maria's comment and board the crowded vaporetto heading south on the Grand Canal. It never ceases to amaze me that no matter how many times I float along this extraordinary waterway, I feel as though my eyes are playing tricks on me. How is this place possible? It is simply too dazzling, too stunning and enchanting to be real.

I disembark at Rialto and head northeast. As I cross over the rio della Fava, I stop on the bridge to take a picture of a splendid gondola passing underneath. The young gondolier briefly pauses from his rowing to look up at me and says, "Bellissima!"

I smile and wave. "Grazie mille!" I could get used to these Italians.

When I arrive at the intersection where Calle del Mondo Novo turns into Calle Lunga Santa Maria Formosa, I check my map again. Yup, I'm in the right place. I continue on Calle Lunga

Santa Maria Formosa and just before reaching the next canal, to my left is the entrance of the Belli Libri dell'Acqua Alta.

Walking into a courtyard, I step inside to another world.

Greeting me is a handwritten sign hanging from the end of a long table that reads:

WELCOME
to the most beautiful
Bookshop in the World

Piled on top of the table is a disorganized heap of posters, magazines, and several small bins containing bookmarks. To my right is an easel displaying a large, vintage map of Venice. Next to it is a stack of novels haphazardly housed inside a rusting, red wheelbarrow. Past the wheelbarrow is a lone tree, providing some much-needed shade and also one of the few spots of green that compliment all the hard surfaces, which make up most of this city. The tree is surrounded by several tall, rotating display racks of postcards. As I walk forward toward the main entrance, I pass several milk crates, crammed with calendars.

Upon entering the store, I am stunned by the sheer volume on display.

"Buongiorno! Benvenuta!" The enthusiastic welcome comes from the jovial proprietor, Luigi, whom I recognize from the photos I've seen online.

"Good afternoon," I say as I amble through, amazed.

The room feels overstuffed with wall-to-wall books, magazines, maps, and who knows what else, along with a number of customers. It's a bit of sensory overload. Dubbed the Beautiful

Books of High Water because it does indeed flood during the acqua alta each year, and everything is arranged so chaotically it appears as if all the books have been swept in by the daily tides. What strikes me most are the incredibly creative bookshelves. Apparently, in order to keep all of this merchandise from becoming damaged and sodden during the acqua alta, mountains of books are stored and displayed in waterproof bins, canoes, kayaks, and bathtubs. However, the undeniable attention-grabbing centerpiece within this eccentric library is the full-size gondola, complete with a mannequin gondolier, dressed up for Carnevale!

The bizarre nature of the shop continues to fascinate me as I wander past the gondola toward the back of the room where the imaginatively peculiar atmosphere is reflected in what is labelled as a fire escape—a door leading directly to a canal, propped open by a chair, inviting passersby to stop, relax, and enjoy a good read. Right outside this exit is yet another gondola, this one in the water tied up to a mooring post next to the door, providing another cozy reading nook.

I continue my tour and discover that the place is much larger than I anticipated. There is an entire second room, just as filled to capacity as the first one. As I look more carefully at the titles, there appear to be both new and used books, all mixed together. I also realize that there is some form of sorting system to all the books, albeit unruly. In the first room there are several texts devoted to Venice alone, along with more books on travel, as well as books on art, cinema, sports, food, and music. The second room is packed with comic books, bestsellers, poetry, and an entire section allocated to one of Venice's most famous citizens, Casanova.

I notice another exit leading out to a side courtyard. Walking outside, I let out a yelp of surprise. Oh, my God! This is unbelievable! Old encyclopedia tomes, the kind no one ever buys or uses anymore have been turned into a colorful staircase, leading up to a lookout spot in the corner, where the high courtyard walls meet above the adjacent canals. On the two walls someone has painted an arrow with the words, "GO UP, FOLLOW THE BOOK STEPS, CLIMB, WONDERFUL VIEW." More encyclopedias fully cover the remaining walls of the courtyard, making me feel as if I've stepped into a bibliophile's version of Wonderland.

This place makes me so happy! I take a ton of pictures and spend the good part of an hour perusing through the mounds of books. I could come here every day for an entire year and never go through it all. The amount of inventory is overwhelming. How does the shop owner keep track of it all?

After rummaging through several crates of calendars, I choose one with gorgeous watercolor renderings of Venice scenes. Grandma will love this.

"Ah, yes," says Luigi as he places the calendar in a small shopping bag. "This is a good one. Very nice pictures."

"This one, too," I say, spontaneously grabbing a postcard I'll also mail to Grandma. "I love your store," I say when he hands me my change. "I will certainly be returning."

"Are you visiting Venezia for a while?" he asks.

"I will be here the entire summer. I am living and working at the Hotel Vendramin."

"The Hotel Vendramin! Wonderful. I know it well."

"Yes," I say. "Paolo, Maria, and Luciana all send their regards. My name is Frankie."

"Piacere. Io sonno Luigi," he says, extending his hand to me, and gives me a complimentary bookmark with a picture of him reading a book, while sitting on top of a stack of volumes, floating in the water. "It is a pleasure to meet you, Frankie. And yes, please come back. Feel free to stay as long as you like. There are many nice reading areas."

"Yes, I noticed," I say. "I will definitely take you up on the offer."

I turn the bookmark over to the other side and see that it is a replica of the many yellow directional street signs posted on the buildings throughout the city. This one reads, "Per S. Marco" with a black arrow.

"Grazie!" I say as I wave the bookmark.

"Arrivederci, Frankie. Hope to see you again soon."

Oh, you will, I think as I stroll out to the Calle Lunga Santa Maria Formosa. What a treasure find! It is a hidden gem inside a city, which is already a grand jewel atop the Adriatic Sea.

Chapter 7 — GIO

Venice, Italy
Monday, July 29, 2019

It is her! She is here—the signorina I have been waiting for my entire life.

I spotted her as she entered the bookstore and I quickly hid behind a tall stack of magazines, precariously perched on top of a kayak leaning on its side, and observed her as she quietly strolled through our beautiful chaos. She is lovelier than a Botticelli portrait of Venus. Ah, Venus, the luminous goddess after whom Venezia derives her name. This signorina is your rival!

I felt too shy to dare approach her, and instead admired her from a distance as I clandestinely remained hidden from view and delighted in watching her. Fortunately, like many of our first-time customers, she was too absorbed in our vast collection to notice me.

As she paid for her items, I eavesdropped from behind one of the bathtubs and heard her tell Luigi that she will be here in Venezia for the entire summer and would be returning to our little store. Oh, happy day! I will have the opportunity to see her again. But my heart already aches from missing her as I watch her leave our store and exit through the front courtyard out to the street.

I must follow her.

I glance back at Luigi who is sharing a laugh with an older couple from Germany. He will not miss me. I won't be gone long.

Running out through the courtyard to the main entrance, I carefully peek to the right, in the direction I saw la signorina walk. There she is several meters ahead. I follow at a safe distance, while keeping her in my sights, which becomes difficult among the crowds the closer we get to Piazza San Marco, where she appears to be headed. But her flowing white dress and blue hat make her easy to spot.

After several minutes, we both emerge onto the Riva degli Schiavoni, east of the Doge's Palace. I follow her as she turns right toward the Piazzetta. She pauses at the Ponte della Paglia, one of the best spots to view the historic Ponte dei Sospiri. Taking advantage of the large number of people waiting their turn to pose in front of the famous structure to obtain their Instagram selfies, I am able to get fairly close to her.

She stands on the ponte resting her hands on the stone balustrade, admiring the Bridge of Sighs. After snapping a couple of pictures with her phone she places it back in her purse. No selfies for her—especially not with one of those obnoxious selfie sticks. Of course not. She is far too classy for such nonsense! She remains on the bridge a while longer before continuing to walk in the direction of the Piazza.

As I follow her, I am all but trampled by the people on the ponte who rush toward the balustrade to snap a photo of the young couple in a gondola, sharing a kiss as they pass under the Bridge of Sighs. What madness! By sunset, this canal will have a parade of gondolas with other such lovers. No doubt, this particular twosome took advantage of the relatively cheaper cost of a gondola ride *before* the sunset hour to partake in this bizarre ritual. Sunset is the most expensive time for a gondola, but this specific trek under the Ponte dei Sospiri will be at a premium.

I do not understand this phenomenon. The famous enclosed, limestone structure with its small, barred windows did not obtain its name from some romantic legend. No, on the contrary—the bridge connects the Doge's Palace to the jail where prisoners, who were found guilty as criminals and traitors, after receiving their sentence in the Doge's Palace, would sigh as they crossed over to the prison because they were seeing their beloved city for the last time before spending the remainder of their lives incarcerated. Sharing a passionate kiss or a marriage proposal under the Bridge of Sighs is equivalent to having a romantic interlude directly in front of the Tower of London, on Robben Island, or Alcatraz. Poor, silly, misguided tourists!

I run to catch up with la signorina. She walks past the Campanile, turns left, and makes her way over to the Caffè Florian, where she sits at one of the outdoor bistro tables in the cool shade of the arcades, away from the intense slanting afternoon sun. A cameriere in a crisp white dinner jacket and carefully ironed black trousers takes her order. After he departs, she sits quietly, watching several small children as they race around the Piazza, sending pigeons into frenzied flight. She smiles. I cannot help but notice how far more observant she seems compared to the average tourist. She does not obsessively stare at her phone while waiting for the cameriere to return with her order, but instead takes out a small journal and begins writing in it. Naturalmente! She is a *writer.* But of course! She is obviously an intellectual.

The waiter brings her a spritz, and she thanks him, bestowing him with a beautiful smile. I am surprised by the unexpected pang of jealousy deep within my solar plexus. Ridiculous. La signorina is merely being polite. She continues her writing while taking casual sips of her spritz. After placing the journal back inside her purse, she takes out the postcard she bought at our bookstore. Yet another example of her unique nature. Who bothers sending postcards anymore? This can only mean that she cherishes nostalgia and is a romantic at heart. Just like me.

When she completes her writing, she places the postcard and pen in her purse and takes another sip of her spritz. She closes her eyes for a moment and her hands move delicately, rhythmically, in time to the small orchestra, set up in front of the Caffè and immediately outside the arcades, playing a sweet, haunting rendition of *Time to Say Goodbye*. Che bellezza!

The Campanile tolls. I have been gone longer than I intended. I should return to the bookstore. I reluctantly and cautiously step out from behind the column where I have been conducting my surveillance for one last glimpse at La Signorina Bellissima. I want to remember every detail of her loveliness until we meet again. I know I will be anxiously awaiting her return to our bookstore in the days and weeks to come.

I silently bid her farewell and cross to the north side of the Piazza toward the Clock Tower. Walking through the arched entrance to the Merceria, one of the most popular shopping streets, I make my way amid the throngs of tourists, back to the bookstore with my heart full of felicità e amore.

Chapter 8 — FRANCESCA

Venezia, Italia
Sabato 21 ottobre 1550

I gently rap on the door of my zia's bedchamber.

"Avanti," I hear Zia Veronica's voice from within and I open the door. Domisilla is assisting my zia perform her daily toilette. Seated at her dressing table, Zia Veronica is wearing an elegant gown of luxurious emerald velvet, celadon taffeta, accented with delicate white lace and ribbon, which shows off her complexion and copper tresses. Domisilla completes the finishing touches on my zia's hair.

"You asked to see me, zia?"

"Si. Have a seat, Francesca. Domisilla is almost done." I quietly settle myself in a chair next to the window. As I observe Zia Veronica with her maidservant, I remember the many times I sat watching my own mother dress and prepare herself for receiving guests. I feel a pang of longing and miss those quiet, special moments with her. My mother also possessed the same rich, auburn hair as Zia Veronica, but my own dark mahogany mane I inherited from my dear father. Now, I have only fleeting images of their physicality. If not for the one portrait of my parents, painted shortly after their wedding day, which is hanging up on the wall of my bedchamber, I would not be able to recall their faces at all. That portrait is one of the few treasured items my zia managed to salvage from my home before my father's greedy younger brother, Maffio, took possession and sold it all to appease his creditors. Fortunately, I still retain strong memories of my mother's gentle, loving nature and my father's strength and humor. My father delighted in making me laugh, and in his presence I felt both protected and playful. As a child I took that joyful invulnerability for granted. Now, with an uncertain future staring me in the face, I realize just how unique my loving, stable family was.

Domisilla places the hair-brush on top of the dressing table beside a small box and retrieves a strand of pearls nestled in the ivory-colored satin lining of the box. This necklace belonged to my grandmother, who left it to Zia Veronica upon her death, many years before I was born. My grandmother also left the matching pair of earrings and bracelet to my mother, which I now have in my possession. Domisilla places the pearls around zia's long, graceful neck and fastens the clasp.

"I am finished, signora," says Domisilla. "Do you require anything further?"

"No, grazie, Domisilla. That is all. When Signor Vecellio arrives, please let him know I will be with him shortly."

"Si, signora," Domisilla says with a slight curtsy and exits, closing the heavy door behind her.

"You look beautiful, zia. That color suits you. Are you entertaining someone special today?"

"Grazie, Francesca." Zia Veronica stands and walks over to her full-length looking glass, a most generous gift from her wealthy benefactor. This work of art ornately framed with gold leaf is a rare commodity, worth a small fortune, and provided Maestro Lorenzo the equivalent of an entire year's wages for this one commission alone because of its hazardous properties. The glassmakers of Murano are regularly exposed to dangerous chemicals in producing their art, but Venetian mirrors, which require the use of mercury, known as The Silver Devil, pose a special threat and has brought many glassmakers to their deaths.

"Yes, it is lovely," Zia Veronica says smoothing down the stiff folds in her gown, admiring the dress as she turns to look at it from every angle. "The dress maker delivered it this morning and, fortunately, it is a perfect fit. Signor Tiziano Vecellio will be arriving shortly to begin work on my portrait."

"How exciting! I am sure Signor Vecellio will do a wonderful job of capturing your likeness. Is this commission a gift from Signor Vendramin?"

"Why, yes," she replies and turns to look directly at me. "And speaking of my dear patron Domenico, that is precisely the topic I wish to discuss with you."

A painful constriction spreads through the middle of my chest as my breath catches. I have a dark foreboding of what this conversation might entail. With care so as not to wrinkle her gown, Zia Veronica lowers herself onto the settee directly facing my chair. Taking a deep breath, I clasp my hands tightly in my lap to keep them from shaking. I try to keep my face neutral and calm.

"Francesca, there is no need to be frightened," she says, obviously intuiting my inner turmoil, and I try to relax. "While what I need to discuss with you is of great importance, there is still time for final decisions. However, with the upcoming salone presenting certain opportunities, I want you to be as prepared as possible."

I cannot find my voice and merely nod. My zia continues, "As I mentioned before, now that you are sixteen, it is time for you to think of your future. You are extraordinarily gifted, Francesca, which affords you more choices than other young women. You possess wit and beauty along with talent as a writer, all gifts which I believe would be for naught if you entered a convent. And while you claim that you do not imagine you would make a successful courtesan, I must disagree. I think you do have many qualities which would serve you well in this profession. . ."

Zia Veronica must see the skepticism flashing on my face.

". . . such as an agreeable personality, among other aspects which men of stature value," she emphasizes. "Also, I would hate to see all of your education and literary gifts go to waste because no matter how talented you are, you will not be able to pursue a literary vocation without the financial and moral support of a father, or in his absence, a father-figure. Since you do not have a father, it would be most beneficial to have at least one patron, but preferably more, who would not only assist you in your literary projects but would also provide you with protection and be willing to defend your reputation and your labor as honest and honorable." She pauses until I meet her gaze once again. "This is an essential distinction between a cortigiana di lume, whose only occupation is to provide men with sexual favors in exchange for money, and a cortigiana onesta, whose primary means of social advancement is akin to the artistry, literary talents, and musical abilities of the traditional male courtier. We Venetian courtesans of the latter variety are also expected to provide cultivated company and stimulating conversation, two skills which I have no doubt you will easily acquire."

I can feel my face grow red-hot with embarrassment at my zia's frank description of the common *cortigiana di lume*'s exploits. Once again, all I can do is nod.

"I also want to make you aware, Francesca, that I have saved up a significant dowry on your behalf, and as a *cortigiana onesta*, all of that money will remain in your hands. If you marry, however, your entire dowry will immediately become your husband's property, and he alone will have the right to invest it or squander it as he wishes." She reaches for my hands and clasps them between her own. "Francesca, I think of you as my own daughter and in honor of my dear sister's memory, I wish to do what's best for you and your future."

When I remain mute, she sighs. "Well? What is going on inside that bright mind of yours?"

Swallowing hard, I take a deep breath and hurriedly say, "Zia Veronica, Giovanni has asked me to marry him. He has plans to study at l'Università di Padova because he does not wish to become a glassmaker and prefers to study medicine instead, and both he and his uncle are confident that the authorities will allow him to leave Murano. Giovanni says l'università has begun accepting women, and he believes I could continue my education and become a published author, which could make it possible for me to pursue a literary career. Would that not solve the problem of not having a father figure or a benefactor to help me in that endeavor? I love Giovanni, zia. And whether it is in Padova or Murano, I want to spend my life with him. I am sorry I did not inform you of this earlier, but I did not wish to distract you from all of your planning for the upcoming festivities. And since Giovanni will not be leaving for Padova for another year, there did not seem to be any rush to tell you."

It is now my zia who remains quiet. I can see that she is trying to figure out how to respond to my news. Before she can say anything, I rapidly add, "Giovanni is a good man. You've known him since he was a young boy. You are well acquainted with his zio Lorenzo, so you already know that Giovanni comes from a respectable, hardworking, decent family. I know he will treat me well and I have full confidence that he will not spend my dowry foolishly."

"Oh, Francesca," my zia finally says with a deep exhale. "I am not surprised by this news, but it does make the situation a bit complicated."

"Why is it complicated?"

She regards me for a long moment with an expression I cannot interpret. "Francesca, you are young and idealistic." I wait for her to continue, uncertain where this is headed. "While the Republic allows for the daughters of glassblowers to marry the sons of noble families, that particular law, however, does not accommodate the opposite union, and you are still the daughter of noble lineage."

"But I am an orphan with nothing!" I cry out. "If it were not for you, zia, who knows where I would be now, or if I would even be alive. What difference does my lineage make to the Republic when everything my parents owned is gone? The authorities have no awareness of the dowry you have generously saved for me and as far as they know I am penniless. Why should anyone care *who* I marry?"

"I understand your frustration, Francesca, and I agree that Giovanni is a fine young man," she says.

I cannot even look at her, so full of vexation am I.

"I am not saying 'No' to your possible future as Giovanni's wife," zia continues. "And the fact that he will no longer be living as a glassblower on Murano will make the prohibitive marriage laws obsolete. But I want you to consider *all* options first before you make such an important decision."

"How exactly do you propose I do that, zia?" I ask in a tone much harsher than I intended.

"Please hold off on giving Giovanni your answer until after the salone. This will be your first time attending an intellectual, literary salone and the guest list consists of several important, influential associates of Domenico. I think it would be highly beneficial for you to meet them. You will have the opportunity to display your talents with the commedia you have written and at this age, you are in your prime for attracting the attentions of patrons for a possible long-lasting mutually beneficial relationship." After a short pause, she says, "You will, however, need to find some way of refraining from constantly blushing."

I cover my face and feel the intense heat on my hands, the coolness of my touch soothing my burning cheeks.

"Francesca, you are becoming a woman. It is time to acknowledge the age-old rituals between the sexes. It is nothing to be ashamed of. In spite of the Church's hypocritical restrictions and prohibitive laws, especially in regard to the comportment of women, it is all natural and human." I remove my hands from my face and stare at my zia in astonishment. What she has said is tantamount to blasphemy, but it is precisely this level of candor that makes her such a force. "Nevertheless, despite all of that *piety,* it is ironic that several of the city's convents are nothing more than cheap brothels, servicing a more common clientele consisting of sailors and other visitors of lower status. At least the cortigiana onesta has some level of freedom in deciding certain aspects of her life; primarily, that she maintains control of her own dowry and any subsequent wealth she might amass."

I have heard these rumors about certain convents, but the utter hypocrisy of the all-powerful Church strikes me especially hard at this moment.

"What exactly do you wish me to do, zia?" I ask, resigning myself to the inevitable.

"After the salone, you will have time to reflect on your experience upon meeting those men of prominence to help you decide what life would best suit you. As you said, Giovanni will not be leaving for Padova anytime soon. In the meantime, I want to expose you to all the options available."

I stand up and walk to the window.

Are there no options for women which do not involve acquiescing to someone else's complete control? Whether it be isolated, joyless, confinement in a traditional convent, or within a lonely, loveless arranged marriage, or at the mercy of a benefactor who only deems you suitable for his patronage as long as you remain young and beautiful, why have women always been little more than slaves to whomever holds the power and purse strings?

Looking out at the crisp autumn day, I feel a tremendous heaviness and dread overtake me. I know it is not my zia's fault that life is unfair, but I do not want this choice. Why does the possession of money or lack of it have so much sway over life's crucial decisions? And now, I suddenly fear for my zia's future. At her age, she is still alluring, but what will become of her when her patrons no longer find her desirable? After all she has done for me, do I not owe her my allegiance by allowing her to mentor me in her profession to ensure that any money I accrue will remain within our family, securing a comfortable future in her old age as well as mine?

Zia Veronica walks over to the window and stands behind me, placing her hands on my shoulders. "Cara ragazza," she says softly. "Do not fret. Everything will work out. All I am asking of you for now is that you keep an open mind and to trust that I will always do my best to guide and safeguard you."

"Signora Veronica!" Domisilla calls from outside the door. She opens it gingerly. "Signor Vecellio is here."

"I will be right there," my zia responds and gently squeezes my shoulders as she places a soft kiss on my cheek and steps away. "Andiamo," she says to her maid and follows her out of the room.

I remain at the window in solemn contemplation. The clear sky and billowy clouds are a reminder of the idyllic picnic I shared with Giovanni, which already feels as if it were a million years ago, and I wonder if there will ever come a day when a woman can be in complete command of her own destiny.

Chapter 9 — FRANKIE

Burano, Italy
Monday, August 5, 2019

I catch my first glimpse of the famous colorfully painted houses of Burano as our Number 12 ferryboat passes the small island of Mazzorbo, which is linked to Burano by a wooden bridge, known by the locals as Ponte Longo—long bridge. At one time, Mazzorbo was an important trading center, but these days it is primarily known for its orchards and vineyards. Similar to the tiny island of San Michele, which provides the main cemetery for Venice, Mazzorbo is the location of the Cimitero di Burano.

"Oh, my God! How cute!" I say, quickly snapping a photo of the brightly colored buildings.

"Just wait," says Luciana. "This is nothing. Wait until we are on Burano. You will be amazed."

I'm happy Luciana offered to accompany me on this all-day excursion to the islands of Murano and Burano. We both had the same day off from the Hotel Vendramin and when she asked if she could join me and volunteered to be my personal tour guide, I was thrilled to have some companionship after spending far too many days of solo sightseeing. We got an early start and spent the entire morning on Murano, where I located and bought an almost identical millefiori vase to the one I saw at the hotel on my first day in Venice.

Our 25-minute ferry ride from Murano arrives at the Burano stop. We disembark the ferry and even if Luciana were not with me, there would be no need to guess which direction to go. Follow the tourists! Burano is fairly isolated, being 45 minutes by boat ride from Venice. Generally, it is not as busy as Murano because most day-trippers only have enough time to make it as far as the glass island. Today, however, there are quite a few visitors who made the extra journey along with us. Nevertheless, Luciana informs me that it is not as crowded as it could be since we are here during what is generally the hottest month in Italy, the heat automatically reducing the number of tourists.

We head down Viale Marcello, a wide pedestrian walk, bordered on the right by a park with a water fountain, and on the left by a row of ordinary buildings, not yet the colorful houses I have come to expect. Burano, like its sister islands, does not accommodate any automobile traffic, but this walkway is unusually wide for such a small area and feels like a miniature Piazzetta. We pass by a fritto misto fish and chips stand, souvenir kiosks, and several tourists attempting to cool themselves off with a refreshing Italian ice or a gelato.

Luciana and I continue walking until the street tapers and soon becomes nothing more than an alleyway, merely wide enough to allow one person at a time to walk through. We arrive at the Fondamenta San Mauro along one of only three canals on this particular island. As I follow Luciana and step out onto the fondamenta from the confines of the narrow calle, I let out a whoop of delight.

"This is incredible!"

Luciana laughs. "See? I told you."

I feel like a little kid, discovering a treasure trove of gifts on Christmas morning.

"This is like walking through a storybook!" I say, thrilled by the tutti-frutti mixture of painted buildings in a sorbet variety of colors lining both sides of the canal. I am giddy with wonder while I take several pictures and then I follow Luciana as we turn right and walk along the Fondamenta di Cavanella.

"Thank you for being so patient," I tell her, pausing every few steps to take another picture.

"Not a problem. I understand. It is, um, how do you say? Fantasiose?"

Before we left Venice this morning, Luciana requested that she practice her English all day. I assured her that her English is already better than my Italian, and it was *I* who needed all the practice I could get, but I agreed, nonetheless.

"Fanciful?" I take a guess.

"Si! Yes, Burano's color houses are fanciful."

"Case preziose," I add. "Precious houses."

"Ecco!"

We resume our stroll and I notice that all the doorways of the homes are covered with striped sheets or curtains. I ask Luciana about them.

"Well, as you can feel, it is very warm," she explains. "All the doors behind those curtains are open. This way, it allows fresh air to blow through the house, while keeping a little privacy for the people inside because we tourists walk by very close."

"Of course," I concur. Leave it to the Italians to come up with a more imaginative solution than boring screen doors.

"What is that leaning tower?" I ask pointing to our left.

"Ah, si. Il Campanile Storto! You see, Pisa is not the only city with a leaning tower. That is part of the Chiesa di San Martino. It is the one church on Burano. And even though Mazzorbo is a smaller island, it has two—La Chiesa di Santa Caterina and San Michele Arcangelo."

"I'm amazed at the number of churches in Venice," I say. "I read somewhere that Venice is roughly 414 square kilometers, with a population of approximately 60,000 people, and there are 139 churches. There cannot possibly be enough parishioners to occupy all those churches at any given worship service. Why are there so many churches?"

"We Italians are odd," Luciana says with an exaggerated roll of her eyes. "It is not that we are sooo religious. It was all about power and politics. And competition. At one time, Venice was one of the most powerful cities in the world. All trade from the East had to go through Venice before it went out to the rest of Europe. And Venice was in great competition with Genoa, another powerful port city. So, it was not enough for Venice to build an enormous basilica to rival Genoa's Duomo, it also had to try for the *most* churches."

"Politics, money, power, and religion," I say, as I photograph the leaning tower in the distance. "Some issues don't ever seem to change, I guess."

"All the same issues that have motivated every war since the beginning of time," Luciana says, and I look at her in amazement because she has expressed my exact thought.

"How true," I agree, and add, "I thought maybe the Church felt it had to have an extra big presence in Venice to save all those fallen souls during the debauchery of the Carnevale celebrations."

Luciana lets out a surprising guffaw. "Si! That too!"

We turn left and cross over a bridge onto Via Giudecca. The canals are full of small rowboats and motorboats, but no gondolas, water taxis, nor vaporetti since it is a smaller island and, like Murano, the canals are narrower than the ones in Venice.

Despite its obvious touristic quality and no lack of souvenir shops where visitors can purchase various items made by the famous Burano lace makers, there remains a surprising authenticity to this place. Perhaps it lies in the fact that I see more locals going about their business or plainly hanging out, sitting, and conversing. Or maybe it's the group of small boys we pass, playing a pickup game of soccer in the tiny campo adjoining their houses, playing in bare feet, no less! Or it might just be that all the homes' main entrances, with their striped curtains, open directly onto the streets and fondamentas, which is not the case in Venice. There, from what I have discerned, most of the homes situated along the canals have a main entrance on the street level, which leads up to the higher floors, where the residents live. Here, the proximity makes the citizens and their way of life seem more . . . accessible, perhaps, because it is more observable?

"There is a very distinct vibe to Burano," I tell Luciana.

"Vibe?"

"Atmosfera."

"Ah, si! It is like Burano is back in time."

"It does feel lost in time."

"Yes. *Lost* in time. It is as it always has been. I imagine if we were here 500 years before, it would look and feel the same."

"I hope so," I say wistfully.

"Oh, what a shame," Luciana says as she abruptly stops in front of a bright blue building, with red-geranium-filled flower boxes outside each window. "This is the Trattoria al Gatto Nero, one of my favorite restaurants. But unfortunately, it is closed today."

"Now that you mention it, what should we do for dinner?"

"Well, I thought we would have a nice meal at this trattoria, but since it is closed, we could go to Via Baldassarre Galuppi, the main street, and find a place where we could have something light and small and later, return to Venice for dinner."

"Why not have dinner here?"

"In my opinion, the best time to eat here is mid-day because . . . well, you will see," she replies, knowingly. "By late afternoon, Burano begins closing down and becomes very quiet when there will be a mass exodus of tourists back on the ferry."

"Sounds nice. Even quieter than Venice?"

She nods.

"When I first arrived in Venice, it was one of the things that surprised me. For some reason, I thought Venice would stay up all night. You know, like New York. The city that never sleeps."

"That is mostly during Carnevale."

"Well, I must admit I don't mind it as much as I thought I would," I say. "Especially since I have to wake up early to work in the kitchen with Maria. Despite being more of a night owl, I've gotten used to the earlier hours."

"Anch'io," Luciana admits. "Me too, because I am already an . . . early person?"

"Early bird?"

"D'accordo!" she exclaims, and with a small pout says, "I am sorry I did not check ahead about the hours for il Gatto Nero. I wanted you to try it. It serves the best seafood!"

"That's alright. It's a good excuse to come back. I'll have to save the Lace Museum for another time as well, because I think it closes at four o'clock and it's already three. It's impossible to see everything in one day."

"This is true."

"Can we go to the Chiesa di San Martino first before heading over to the main street?"

"Yes," Luciana replies. "It is on our way. We can cross over the bridge up ahead and walk along the Fondamenta del Pizzo. There is a pretty park along the water, and we can enter the church from the Piazza Baldassarre Galuppi."

"Lead the way!"

We cross over a bridge where the street called Corte Novello turns into Calle della Provvidenza and on the other side of the canal, the Fondamenta della Pescheria turns into Fondamenta del Pizzo.

"What is it with the street names around here?" I exclaim. "It's the same in Venice, where it's even more confusing when the names change suddenly, because it's a bigger area than Burano."

Luciana laughs. "Sorry. I suppose we Italians enjoy variety. Or perhaps, we become bored easily."

"That's alright. I'll take it," I laugh along with her. "Your zest for life, your delicious food, your beautiful language, your art, and everything else about your culture makes the confusion worth it!"

"Brava! But obviously you have never experienced one of our frequent train strikes."

"No, but I did experience the air traffic controllers' strike the day I arrived."

"Mamma mia!"

Our promenade along the Fondamenta del Pizzo takes us around the southern tip of Burano, where we pass by several docked yachts too large to enter the tight canals on this island. We continue through the park Luciana mentioned earlier.

When we emerge on the other side of the park, at Piazza Baldassarre Galuppi, Luciana informs me, "Burano is divided into five areas, similar to the Venice sestieri. Originally, there were five islands separated by four canals, but at one time the fourth canal was filled in to create this piazza and the Via Baldassare Galuppi. The Rio Tera in Venice are also made from filled in canals. Rio Tera means buried canal and the water from the canal often still flows under the road. As the cities grew and the population increased, we needed more streets and common spaces."

"That's fascinating. You're a wonderful tour guide, Luciana. Thank you!"

"Prego," she answers with a delighted smile. "I am a proud Venetian from many past generations, and I love showing my city and all the islands on the laguna to visitors. It is why I enjoy my work at the Hotel Vendramin. I have been working there every summer for the past three years. You see, I will begin my last year at the University in Milano, where I have been studying in the School of Language Mediation and Intercultural Communication."

Luciana and I have been working at the same hotel for two months, but this is the most time we have spent together getting to know each other and I've enjoyed our entire outing. Her company reminds me of how much I miss Mayra and hanging out with my girlfriends.

"What do you plan to do with your degree after you graduate?" I inquire.

"I enjoy connecting with people and I want to continue with tourism services. Possibly in hotel management or tour guiding. I have studied French, Spanish, German, and now you are helping me with my English!"

"You're fluent in five languages?" I am flabbergasted. "That's amazing! I'm so jealous."

"You are almost there too," she graciously offers.

"Well, I'm getting there with Italian, thanks to you and everyone else at the hotel. Where I get into trouble is when people speak the Veneziano dialect. But now you have inspired me to continue with my French."

"Ah, yes. French can be difficult. It makes my mouth sore."

"Me too!" I laugh.

"Do not worry about the Veneziano. We have so many dialects in this country it would be almost impossible to learn them all, but as long as you are able to speak Dante's 'official' Italian, you will get along anywhere in Italy. Here is the entrance. After you," she says, opening the heavy door to la Chiesa di San Martino.

We step inside the 16th-century Roman Catholic Church. Under normal circumstances it would feel ornate, but in contrast to the numerous churches I have already explored in Venice, this one feels modest in comparison, but beautiful, nonetheless. After taking the requisite photos, I make some notations in my journal.

"I have to immediately write down an identifying feature so when I browse through my photos, I'll be able to tell which church I'm looking at," I inform Luciana, in response to her quizzical look.

"I understand," she nods. "They all look similar after a while."

I try to suppress a smile, but she catches it.

"Cosa?" she asks. "What is it?"

"Nothing. It's just funny to hear you say that because it sounds like something a typical boorish American tourist would say: 'All you see are museums, castles, and cathedrals, and they all look the same,' which would normally leave me feeling embarrassed for my fellow Americans. But there is some truth to it," I sheepishly admit.

"It is okay. We think so too," she laughs again. "Shall we find a nice place to sit and have a spritz? Maybe some crostini or fritto misto?"

"Yes!" My mouth is already watering. "Sounds perfect."

The afternoon heat is intense on the Via Baldassarre Galuppi as it radiates off the stone walkway, which is the main thoroughfare on this picturesque little island. It is also the most congested area on Burano, as it contains one souvenir shop after another, interspersed with restaurants and gelaterias.

"You have to be careful when you buy the lace products," warns Luciana. "In the same way as on Murano and Venice, there are many stores that sell cheap replicas brought in from China. The real Murano glass will always have a special sticker of authentication such as the one on the vase you purchased, and it is best to buy lace either at the Lace Museum or directly from one of the lace makers you see working on something. Those women will often sit and work outside their shop so you can see their handiwork in person, which they hope will inspire you to buy from them."

"Good to know. Before we leave, I want to buy something for my grandma."

"Martina Vidal, Emilia Burano, Dalla Lidia Merletti D'Arte, and Laces by Olga are a few places we can try to find something for your nonna."

"Great!" I say, and we stroll through the piazza joining the other tourists.

We select the Trattoria Raspo de Ua as our watering hole because I am captivated by the sign above the awning over the outdoor dining area, with its rustic mural of colorful seafood and the light fixture, which looks like a bunch of grapes hanging from a vine.

"I think you have an artist's eye, Frankie," Luciana tells me as we take a seat at one of the tables in the shade of the awning.

"Thank you!" I say appreciatively. "I actually am an artist, an actress, and a writer."

"How fascinating!"

"And I have always appreciated aesthetic details. I think I may have been Italian in a past life."

"Oh! Really?" Luciana says in a conspiring whisper, eagerly leaning forward in her chair. "Do you believe in past lives?"

With a slight hesitation because I fear that admitting to a belief in reincarnation can be interpreted as "out there" by some people, I say, "Yes. I do."

"Me too!" she exclaims, wide-eyed. "Ooooh, tell me more!"

"Well," I say, relieved that she doesn't think I'm crazy and encouraged by her childlike enthusiasm, "when I first began learning Italian, I thought it came easily for me because it's similar to Spanish. But, once I arrived here, I felt like . . . I don't know. Like I already belonged here. Italy, Venice, everything about this place feels so natural and familiar to me. Does that make sense?"

"Si!" she says and sits up straight, clapping her hands rapidly in front of her face like a little girl. "I, too, feel I have had past lives. My mother is a therapist, and she sometimes takes people into hypnosis for past life regression, and she would say that what you are feeling is *remembering.*"

"Really? That's interesting," I say and cautiously ask, "Is your family religious? I mean, I didn't think reincarnation was something most Catholics believed in."

"You are correct," she replies. "But no, we are not too religious. Oh, I do believe in God, but we, mi famiglia that is, we are not so much practicing. What about you?"

"Same. I was raised Episcopalian, and I too believe in God, but I don't believe that God and church must always be one and the same thing. I actually think they are two completely separate things. But the reason I enjoy seeing these historic houses of worship is because I always experience a strong feeling of great spiritual power because people have gathered there to worship for centuries. However, I don't believe that faith has to be some allegiance to a set of rules or doctrine that *men* made up millennia ago in order to control the masses and retain power over people."

Luciana is staring at me with a look of surprise. *Shoot. Have I offended her?*

"Oh, Frankie! You and I are made with the same material!" she says, and I am confused. In response to my perplexed expression, she continues, "Oh, Jesu bambino! My English! How do you say? Siamo tagliati dallo stesso panno. Oh, what is the expression? Um . . ."

"Cut from the same cloth?"

"Si!" she shouts, startling the waiter who arrives at our table. "Oh, mi scusi!" she says to him with an embarrassed giggle. "Shall we order? Would you like a spritz?"

I nod.

"Due spritz, per favore," she tells the waiter. "E un ordine di calamari fritti e crostini. Is it okay, Frankie?"

"Perfetto. Grazie."

"Grazie!" Luciana echoes and as soon as the waiter leaves, she leans forward once again, and with her elbows on the table, her face resting in her palms, she says, "My mother once had the opportunity to see the Dalai Lama. You know him?"

"Yes, I know *of* him."

"Ecco! He is a very spiritual man, no? He is believed to be the 14th reincarnation of the Buddha, and he said 'No religion. Religion is absolutely unnecessary. Just have some compassion in your heart.' Can you believe it? It is amazing, no? I think he is right. Religion, as an institution, has caused many of the problems in history."

"I agree. Wars have been fought, and horrible ideals have been justified by the misinterpretation of spiritual texts by men who claim to have the authority to tell us what they mean. Take slavery, for example. Passages in the Bible were cited for hundreds of years in order to defend that particularly heinous practice. And although slavery was finally abolished, the end result is still rampant prejudice and discrimination, especially in the United States. Not to mention the blatant sexism against women still in existence today!"

"Exactly!" Luciana nods. "Oh, my goodness! You are a feminist, Frankie. Me too!"

"I think women's struggle for equality originated with the story of Adam and Eve in Genesis that we have all been taught for centuries."

"Yes?" Luciana inquires. "Go on."

"Well basically, God made Adam, and Adam and God were best friends. Then Eve came along because Adam got bored and needed a companion. Which, of course, negates the fact that all life comes forth from the female. Instead, we were taught that Eve was created from Adam's body, his rib. So, right away there's one weird lie that automatically makes women inferior and denies the powerful creative force inherent in all females. It immediately strips women of the one thing that proves our alignment with the Divine or God or whatever you want to call it."

"So true!" says Luciana. "It would make more sense to say that Eve came first, and that Adam was created from her body."

"Yes! Anyway, everything was perfect when it was just God and Adam. But then, Eve couldn't be grateful with the way things were because she had the audacity to want more, and she went for it. Then all hell broke loose all over the earth and suffering was unleashed forever and it was all Eve's fault. Is it any wonder why women find it difficult to trust themselves? Almost from birth, we are given the message that we need to be compliant and behave, we can't trust our desires and ambitions because they are dangerous. Eve's biggest crime was not that she disobeyed God, but rather that her recklessness brought down Adam as well. Proof that women are not reliable. With that history, is it any surprise that women are so often denied positions of power and leadership? Then, we grow up and we have to contend with the impossible female example of the virginal perfection of Mary, mother of Jesus, and we are further thrown into a no-win situation. This has been the message to all girls everywhere for over two thousand years!"

"You are so right, Frankie! I never thought of Eve's story that way."

"Me neither until my Grandma pointed these things out to me. I owe all my feminist education to her. She also told me that before Christianity, ancient pagan religions often incorporated the Divine Female. I mean, just look at all the female goddesses in Greek mythology. The Native Americans, ancient Hawaiians, and Egyptians also understood the interconnected qualities of the male and female."

"Siiii," she exhales thoughtfully.

"But for me, the worst part about all this historical misogyny is that women have bought into it, which has often caused us to be our own worst enemies. And it drives me crazy how often we modern women sabotage each other."

"Can you give me an example?"

"Um, okay. Let's see. Oh! Do you know what cellulite is?"

"Si! It is the same word in Italian, but we pronounce it, che-lu-lee-tay."

"Well, cellulite is something most women have, and before 1972 it wasn't necessarily considered a flaw. For the most part, the appearance of cellulite was considered pretty normal and seen as merely a variation in flesh and a natural part of a woman's body."

"Just like all the women in Botticelli paintings!" Luciana says. "So round and voluptuous. It was considered beautiful to be soft and full of flesh, no?"

"Exactly! But then, in 1972 a woman named Nicole Ronsard, who owned a beauty salon in New York, first introduced the concept of getting rid of cellulite by selling procedures to help women eliminate it. She wrote a book about it and was featured in one of America's top fashion magazines in which she described cellulite as a 'disfiguring attribute.' As soon as American women read that, they suddenly had it cemented in their minds that these very common lumps and bumps were hideous, disfiguring defects. And she, Nicole Ronsard, became a millionaire by convincing women that they needed to be fixed. All by selling them the idea that they were fundamentally defective."

"Porca miseria," Luciana exhales, and I can't help but laugh because swearing in a foreign language always sounds funny to my ears and her potty mouth reminds me of Mayra.

"However, we can't continue to solely blame the patriarchy," I add. "Clearly, we women need to hold a mirror up to ourselves and take a good hard look at our responsibility in propagating sexism and misogyny."

The waiter appears with two glass goblets of spritz and our food. "Buon appetito," he says and leaves to attend another table.

"Salute!" Luciana says and we clink glasses. We both take a long sip of the prosecco and soda water combination, the perfect libation on a hot Italian afternoon.

I have been talking *a lot*. But Luciana doesn't look as if she's ready to flee, so I continue.

"The entire beauty industry is founded on making sure women remain feeling as inadequate as possible about every single aspect of their appearance. And even if we are aware of the manipulation, we have become so brainwashed and experience such a deep, underlying, pervasive, collective self-hatred that it has become an acceptable part of life. We judge ourselves and other women harshly in a way we don't do with men. Anyway, it's one of the main reasons I left social media. The whole selfie/Instagram culture just always left me feeling horrible about myself. Not to mention all the trolling, which has become so pervasive. Maybe someday I'll have a tougher skin and not let it get to me, but right now I feel too fragile."

"Oh, Frankie," Luciana murmurs. "I understand. And I did notice you do not seem to use your telefonino very often except to take photos."

"Every time I see an advertisement for cell phones, I'm reminded that there is a whole industry devoted to selling us the experience of connection: 'Can you hear me now?' But the truth is, not all connections sustain us equally. We can have a million people in our contacts list and yet not know a single person who will bring us some chicken noodle soup when we're home all alone, sick in bed. I'm starting to realize that I need to look more closely at the kinds of connections that I'm making. Do they bring joy? Do they bring meaning?" I waved my fork over the plates in front of us. "Do they bring food?"

"It is true!" Luciana agrees. "My mother says the reason online conversation is so difficult, the reason so many people say that reading comments on social media or an article makes them crazy, is that there is no context for that kind of communication. We also cannot see each other. As human beings we evolve not just to listen to a person's speech, but to process body language, faces, and voices. When you do not have any of that, and you also have a lack of relationship, then you have what can be toxic exchanges between people. This is why relationships and connections are so important for the future of society."

"Yes!"

"I have seen terrible posts on Facebook," Luciana continues. "One girl in my school when I was in scuola superiore, what you call high school, had some horrible people writing terrible things about her. They wrote, 'Too much pasta!' 'Put the pasta fork down!' 'More insalata, less gelato and biscotti!' Can you believe it? And the poor girl was driven to try suicide. But fortunately, she was not able to succeed, and she is much better now."

"That's so sad," I say, and we are both quiet for a long moment. "I honestly don't know a single girlfriend of mine who doesn't have some crazy issue with food and their weight. I've struggled with eating disorders for years and am only just recently able to have a healthier relationship with food. But it still seems to take up so much of my mental space and time every single day just to keep it under control. It's exhausting."

Luciana nods in sympathy. "I also am not on social media a lot anymore because my mother has convinced me it can be harmful to mental health. She says social media fuels narcissism and equates Twitter to a modern-day Colosseum or town-square hanging."

"Wow, your mom sounds incredibly wise," I say. "She and my grandma would get along great! It's amazing that your mother had the chance to meet the Dalai Lama."

"Yes, and my mother is also amazing. She is an interesting mixture of the scientific and the mystical. I am mostly mystical. My mother says I come from the fairies and I agree. I think it is why I have always felt . . . heavy in my body. You understand? It is as if my soul yearns to be light. Sometimes I feel I am on the wrong planet, maybe. Like my home is someplace else and my desire to be light is me wanting to return home. Do I sound *pazza*? It is crazy, no?"

Time. Stops.

I cannot believe what I have just heard. I have felt heavy in my body my entire life! As a little girl, I often felt like I was in the wrong life. At such a young age, I did not have the words to articulate the feeling of alienation. I merely chalked it up to my inability to fit in or belong, but maybe it had more to do with feeling misunderstood. Later, that sensation is probably what turned into suicidal ideation. At this precise moment, I am finally making the connection that what I desired was not to cease being, but simply to experience the lightness of being, as Luciana describes. Even words felt heavy and almost unnecessary. I would often wish that the adults around me would Just. Stop. Talking! Most conversations felt useless, inane, and utterly stupid. Couldn't we just communicate telepathically? It would be so much tidier and efficient.

As these thoughts race through my mind, I fear that I have been out of my body for a long time, but one look at Luciana's expectant expression conveys that all of these thoughts have taken place in a nanosecond. Okay, good.

"No! It's not crazy at all!" I say, amazed. "That's fantastic! Oh, my God, Luciana, I have always felt that way too! But I've never told anyone because I too was afraid people would think I was nuts. And I never imagined anyone else could possibly feel the same way!"

We both laugh and gaze at each other with open-mouthed, wide-eyed wonder.

"I can't believe this, Luciana! It's as if we're alien soul sisters!"

"Si!"

"I wonder if there are others who feel this. We might not be the only ones."

"Hmm," she says slowly and thoughtfully, "I do not know."

We continue to stare at each other in stunned silence. We both laugh and shake our heads in unison.

"What about your father?" I finally ask.

"Ah! He is a scientist who also embraces spirituality. He is a professor of Environmental Science at the Ca' Foscari University of Venice. And my older brother, Davide, graduated from the Sapienza University of Rome, where he also studied Environmental Science and is currently a research fellow at the university."

"Dang, Luciana, you have quite the impressive family."

"Si, grazie," she says with an impish grin. "I am very proud. My father and the university work closely with the Venetian authorities to try to help the situation of the acqua alta problem, which is getting worse every year."

"Yes, I've heard all about that. Is there anything that can be done?"

Luciana sighs heavily. "I hope so. My father believes the issue of global warming is a spiritual problem because we humans have lost our connection to the Divine, which is most obviously represented by Mother Nature. It is a difficult and complicated situation. There are several ideas, but as with many topics in Italy, and especially in Venice, there is a lot of bureaucracy and often the inability to agree. Also, there is unfortunately much corruption."

We are quiet for a few moments while we absorb all that has been said and savor our meal.

"Tell me about your family, Frankie," Luciana says as she wipes her mouth with a linen napkin and picks up her spritz to take a sip.

After all that has been revealed, I feel an incredible bond with Luciana and for the next ten minutes I tell her all about my history in El Salvador, my parents, the tragedy of losing all three of them, and my wonderful grandma whose love and unwavering acceptance made it possible for me to be here at this exact moment. Throughout my narrative Luciana's expression goes from surprise to incredulity to sorrow and disbelief.

"Oh, Frankie," she says softly. "I am sorry for all your loss. It is a very sad story, but you have triumphed and your nonna sounds amazing!"

"Yeah. My grandma is the best. I like to describe her using a quote by one of my favorite writers—Cheryl Strayed. Do you know her work? She wrote the book, *Wild?*"

"Ah, si! *Selvaggia.* I saw the film about the book."

"In describing her mother's love, Cheryl Strayed says that her mother held her with 'unconditional positive regard.' Isn't that beautiful? It's exactly what I feel from my grandma."

"Oh, it is lovely. I, too, feel that from my mother," Luciana beams, and I cannot help feeling that familiar twinge of envy whenever I hear of a young woman's close relationship with her mother. "Everybody should feel it. Can you imagine how the world would be different if everyone felt such strong love?"

"Heaven on earth," I answer, wistfully.

"Yes," Luciana says, and after a beat, "Frankie, I admire how brave you are. I wish I could be that brave."

"What do you mean?"

"Here you are traveling and spending the entire summer in a foreign country all by yourself. It is admirable. I do not enjoy being alone. But you seem good with it."

"Well, the truth is, I prefer being with other people, but as an only child, I grew up having to learn to be alone. So, I guess I just adapted."

"When my mother works with the parents of her young clients, she becomes frustrated when she hears the parents say, 'children are resilient' because she says it is often used as an excuse by adults to relieve their guilt and to justify putting children through difficult situations. My mother says it is not so much that children are resilient, but that they obviously have no choice. Whatever they do to adapt, it is all in order to simply survive."

"Mm-hm. I think she may be right," I say. "Anyway, I'm glad you decided to join me today. This has been much more fun than sightseeing all by myself."

"I am sorry. I should have offered before. I assumed you preferred to travel alone. But now, I am available for more companionship whenever you want," she declares with a radiant smile.

And I realize at this exact moment how lonely I have been most of my life. While my depression has certainly been a real thing, perhaps what I have most suffered from is actually loneliness, and *that* is what has been at the root of my perpetual sadness. My therapist would often tell me that there is such a stigma to loneliness, and it's easier for people to accept depression than loneliness. I think I finally understand what Grandma has been trying to teach me about asking for help. If loneliness is the disease, then we are all the remedy. We can be the medicine that each other needs. We can be the solution other people crave. We are all doctors, and we are all healers. The question is: Do we have the courage to reach out to others when we feel they may be in need? More importantly, do we have the courage to tell others we need them?

"I would love to have you join me!" I tell her.

"Fantastic! Allora, shall we go see where we can find something nice for La Nonna?"

"Andiamo!"

We settle our tab as the church campanile strikes five o'clock and ask our waiter to take a picture of us.

While walking along the Via Baldassarre Galuppi toward one of the lace shops we passed earlier, I notice there are fewer tourists about.

"Wow. You're right," I observe. "There appears to have been a mass exodus of tourists already. What time does the last ferry leave for Venice?"

"We still have a couple of hours, but we probably shouldn't take too long."

"Well, lead the way. I'll trust your judgment on the best place to find something for my grandma."

After stopping in several linen stores, we end up at a small shop on a side street off the main drag, close to the ferry stop, where I find a delicate table-runner I know my grandma will love.

We are the final customers to leave the shop and the women who run the store wish us a "Buon viaggio!" as they close for the day.

We board the awaiting ferry and find a spot toward the back so we can lean against the rail and continue looking at Burano when the ferry takes off. Luciana surprisingly takes my hand in hers and swings our arms together the way I remember doing with my best friend as little girls. Luciana's light-hearted glee is contagious and fills me with a desire to be more carefree and less serious. I both envy and admire her easy-going personality and wonder what kind of homelife and parents contributed to her self-confidence and joy. How much of her effervescent exuberance is nature and how much is nurture? And would I, with my past, be able to ever attain that level of self-assuredness?

"I found my alien soul sister!" Luciana laughs, and her giddiness is irresistible.

"Addio, Burano!" I shout as the ferry begins moving.

"Addio?" Luciana inquires. "I thought you said you would return."

"Oh! You're right," I laugh. "Not addio. Arrivederci!"

"Brava!" she declares and intertwines her right arm with my left arm. We both use our free hands to wave goodbye to Burano and cry out in unison, "Arriiivederrrciiiiiiii!"

Until next time.

Chapter 10 — FRANKIE

Venice, Italy
Tuesday, August 6, 2019

"Where is Papi?" I ask Mami. "¡Sinverguenzo!" she grumbles. Papi stumbles in the front door. He has bruises and scrapes all over his face. There is dry blood on his lip and on his shirt. He looks scary and smells like beer and throw up. "What happened, Papi?" "He crashed the car!" shouts Mami. "He's going to kill someone!" . . . "What's the matter with you?" Mami says. "Why do you always have a long face. My friends are asking me what's wrong with you. It's embarrassing!" . . . "Why aren't you eating?" "I'm not hungry," I say, but I am starving . . . I stand on the scale and I'm so frustrated! I only lost two pounds yesterday. Just water and a salad today! I want to make myself invisible, so she'll stop screaming at me. I want to disappear.

I felt heavy in my body. Luciana's revelation from yesterday echoes through my mind and the serendipity of our shared phenomenon continues to mystify me as I wipe down the tables in the dining room after the breakfast service has ended. I glance up from my task and catch Luciana's eye while she sits at the front desk attending to one of the hotel guests. She smiles and waves my way and I smile back.

"Frankie," Maria calls out to me as she enters from the kitchen.

"Hmm?"

"Ti piace l'opera?"

"Um, I do not really know. I have never been. But I love musical theatre, and I am sure the opera would be interesting. Why?"

"Well, I have two tickets to the opening night at La Fenice, but unfortunately, that evening falls on the same weekend that my husband and I will be out of town. You know, at the end of this month when you and Luciana will be covering for me? I was wondering if you would like to use the tickets?" Maria says all this in rapid Italian, and I give myself an imaginary pat on the back for becoming proficient enough to follow it without having to ask her to slow down, the way I did when we first started working together.

"Oh! Yes! Thank you. That would be wonderful!"

"Good! The show is on August 31ˢᵗ. Do you have someone who can go with you?"

I glance over at the front desk. "I will ask Luciana if she would like to go."

"Perfetto! I will bring you the tickets tomorrow morning."

"Grazie, Maria. I am excited. What is the show?"

"It is Puccini's *Madama Butterfly.*"

"Great. Grazie ancora!" I'll need to do some research, so I can follow the story.

Maria and I complete our clean-up and preparation for tomorrow's breakfast service, and while she goes back inside the kitchen to retrieve her purse before she leaves for the day, I walk over to the front desk.

"Hey, Luciana," I say.

"Sì? Dimmi."

"Are you available on August 31ˢᵗ to attend the opening night at La Fenice? Maria has just offered me two tickets to see *Madama Butterfly*."

"Oh, che divertimento! Yes! That would be delightful! I love *Madama Butterfly*. My parents used to be yearly patrons at La Fenice, and they took my brother and me to the opera often when we were growing up. I used to complain about going, but now I am glad I was exposed to it at such a young age. You also enjoy opera, Frankie? That is another thing we have in common!"

"Actually, this will be my first time attending any opera," I confess. "At least it will be in Italian, so hopefully I'll be able to understand it. If not, you can help me."

"Certamente! You will love it. Maria!" Luciana calls out when Maria appears from the kitchen. "Thank you so much for the tickets!"

"Prego. Think nothing of it," answers Maria. "See you tomorrow. Ciao!"

"Ciao, Maria!" I wave.

"Ah domani!" says Luciana. "What fun!" She beams at me. "We will get all dressed up and make an enchanted evening of it." She had switched back to English to address me. Her ability to shift so quickly and seamlessly between the two languages is a superpower.

"Definitely!" I say. "I can't wait to tell Grandma and my theatre friend, Mayra, that I will be seeing an opera at the historic La Fenice!"

"Si! My parents will be surprised when I tell them that I will be returning to that theatre after so many years. Oh, and speaking of my parents, Frankie, we would like to invite you to our home for dinner. Are you able to come this Saturday evening?"

"Oh, wow, Luciana! Yes! Thank you. After hearing so much about them, I'd love to meet your parents."

"Bene. Then I will let my mother know that you will be joining us. Do you like risotto?"

"Do I like risotto?! Are you kidding? It's one of my favorite Italian dishes."

"Perfect! Then you are in luck because it is one of my mother's specialties."

"Oh, I can't wait! I think I'll treat myself to some shopping this afternoon, so I can have something nice to wear on our opera date. I'll see you later! Ciao!"

"Ciao!"

I run upstairs to my room where I move the desk chair onto my balcony and settle down with my laptop to write a long, detailed email to Grandma and Mayra. I attach several photos of yesterday's trip to Murano and Burano and tell them all about the La Fenice opportunity and my new friend. I'm so excited and I wish I could call them right now, but it's three o'clock in the morning in California.

I do a Google search on *Madama Butterfly* and discover that it was the inspiration behind the musical, *Miss Saigon.*

Oh, wow! How did I not know that?

Composer Claude-Michel Schönberg was motivated to write *Miss Saigon* after seeing a picture in a magazine. The photo was of a young girl and her mother at the airport in Vietnam. The girl's mother had been looking for her ex-lover, an American

G.I., and she wanted to send the girl to the United States for a better life. Schönberg and his writing partner, Alain Boublil, were struck by the uncanny similarities of this true story to Puccini's famous opera and decided to write a musical set during and after the Vietnam War.

Huh. Well, there ya go. So many works of art are borrowed from previous sources.

* * * * *

I saw the Broadway revival of *Miss Saigon* with my grandma on a trip to New York City in 2017. She had seen the original production back in the early 1990s and was eager to share it with me. I was captivated by the beautiful music and the epic scope of the production, but also unnerved by the portrayal of the female characters in the brothel scene at the top of the show. I wondered if my discomfort with the scantily clad actresses engaging in hyper-sexual choreography, in what I can only describe as an adolescent boy's wet dream, had more to do with the current Me Too movement, or my concern for the actresses themselves at having to perform in that number, eight shows a week. I couldn't help but ponder, as a fellow performer, how I would feel in their place.

When I voiced these misgivings to Grandma during the intermission she said, "Yeah, I agree. I'm not sure this show ages very well."

"I can't quite figure out why that scene made me feel so uncomfortable," I said. "Am I just a big prude or what?"

"No, of course not. There is a difference between choreography that is sexy or even sexual, and simulated sex,"

Grandma explained. "The latter feels very close to watching pornography, and when it's live theatre, it's a little *too* close."

"Exactly!" I agreed. "Whenever I've seen a production of *Chicago* or *Cabaret,* which always incorporate a lot of sexy choreography, it never feels . . . icky."

"That's because Bob Fosse's choreography is very stylized, which I think helps remind you that you are watching something theatrical. Whereas the stuff in that opening number we just saw felt a little too graphic and that it was done mostly for shock value. And I agree with you that in this Me Too and Time's Up era, it's hard to watch those actresses doing something that looks so demeaning. The Me Too Movement has been apocalyptic in the truest sense of the word, which is to say revealing, to uncover. It's not that all of a sudden there's been an uptick in sexual harassment. That has been going on for a long time, but we're asking the wrong question. What we should be asking is why do we have a sexual harassment and rape culture to begin with? In my opinion it all comes down to heresy."

"Whoa," I said. "What do you mean?"

"The definition of heresy is anything that has all the trappings of Christianity but that actually violates and defies its essence. So, when girls are told over and over again that it's God's will that men dominate women, that is the theological underpinning for a sexual harassment and rape culture. And if boys grow up believing that a man is the spiritual head of the household, then surely he is also the spiritual head of his offices, businesses, and corporations that are filled with women. When there are messages delivered in God's name, they go down to a very cellular level within all of us. Those stories become a part of our DNA without our permission. And you don't have to even be religious, believe in God, or have any knowledge of the Bible to be influenced because those messages are ingrained across countries, cultures, and societies. They live in us. It's in the air we breathe."

Leave it to Grandma to turn an ordinary outing into a lesson in theological history. Once again, I was blown away by her ability to explain things to me that are normally so difficult to understand in such a matter-of-fact way. For a woman of her generation to speak candidly about topics that would normally be considered taboo—well, that's what makes her so fierce. She's amazing!

"I wonder if the creators of *Miss Saigon* were writing it today, as opposed to back in the late 1980s, would they approach the material differently now that we're all supposedly more woke," I mused.

"Great question," said Grandma. "And a perfect example of why it's so important to have a diversity of perspectives inside the rooms where decisions are made."

"What do you mean?"

"It's really hard to say whether or not the creators of *Miss Saigon* would have the insight to write it differently today, but one thing is for sure, having women in the room would most likely force a shift away from the typical 'male gaze' perspective," Grandma explained.

* * * * *

I continue perusing the internet and quickly fall inside a rabbit hole of the *Miss Saigon* controversy that erupted during the original Broadway production back in 1990. It turns out that when *Miss Saigon* opened in London's West End in 1989, British actor Jonathan Pryce played one of the show's leading men, a scheming Eurasian pimp called the Engineer, and he was slated to continue that role when it moved to Broadway. Jonathan Pryce is a white actor who wore prosthetics to alter the shape of his eyes and makeup to alter the color of his skin. Asian American actor B.D. Wong brought up the complaint to the Actors' Equity Association that by casting a white actor in a role written for an Asian actor, the production supported the practice of "yellow-face," equating it to the "blackface" minstrel shows of the 19th and 20th centuries, a convention that relies heavily on physical and cultural stereotypes and makes broad commentaries about racial identity.

Wong asked the union to compel the producer of *Miss Saigon* and all future Broadway producers to cast their productions with racial authenticity. Actors' Equity initially agreed to support Wong's complaint, but ultimately rescinded its decision after receiving pressure from various sources, and *Miss Saigon* opened, as cast, at the Broadway Theatre on Thursday, April 11, 1991.

The entire dispute, however, did eventually lead to some profound changes. By the time the show reached Broadway, Jonathan Pryce had abandoned the use of the eye prosthetics and yellow-toned make-up. After he won a Tony Award for the role and left the show, the producers finally changed their approach, and in the years since, they have chosen only actors of Asian heritage to play the Engineer, both on Broadway and on the United States tours.

All at once I understand what Grandma had been talking about! This issue could have been avoided if the creators, producer, casting director, and director, all white males, had taken it upon themselves to include some Asian people in their collaboration. Enlisting the opinions and voices of the people whose story you are telling is one solution to preventing the problem that arises when you have only one perspective telling a story targeted for an audience of the same perspective. *Duh!*

Despite its controversial history, there are a lot of people, including several Asian American actors I know personally, who are big fans of *Miss Saigon.* For many Asian American performers *Miss Saigon* is still one of the few shows that offers opportunities for prominent roles on a Broadway stage, a problem that is, unfortunately, all too familiar for artists of color.

Well, all of this background information should make for an interesting evening at the theatre.

I turn off my laptop, grab my purse, and head out to find a fabulous outfit.

Chapter 11 — FRANCESCA

Venezia, Italia
Martedì 21 novembre 1550

"What terrible luck to have such horrible weather today," says my zia.

"Perhaps it will clear up by the time the guests arrive," offers Domisilla.

Or perhaps I will be fortunate, and the entire masquerade will be cancelled, I think as I watch Zia Veronica pace back and forth in front of the large window in the portego.

"Well, there is nothing to be done," my zia declares. "It is much too late to cancel, and all the preparations are at hand. We will simply make the best of it."

"Si, signora," answers Domisilla. "I will check on Bortola and see how the meal is coming along, and then I will come to your chamber to help you get ready."

"What a shame," says my zia after Domisilla leaves for the kitchen, staring out the window, with her back to me. "Ah, well," she turns to face me. "We will make it a joyous evening, nonetheless! And you, my dear, will look absolutely enchanting in your new gown."

"Grazie, zia Veronica. It is truly the most beautiful thing I have ever owned."

Despite my trepidation about the evening ahead, my new frock of lush burgundy velvet, embellished with gold thread embroidery, will be a delight to wear.

"Francesca, there is something I need to inform you about this evening," she pauses for a moment then says, "I regret to say that I received news earlier today that your dear father's delinquent brother, Maffio, will be making an appearance tonight."

"My uncle?! Why? How?"

"Unfortunately, it appears that he has not only made his way back to Venezia but has also managed to become quite friendly with certain members of i Signori di Notte and has secured a position as chancellor, of all things."

The Council of Ten is composed of noblemen who set themselves up as the supposed guardians of Venezia's morality. It is rumored that they comprise a spy system, serving as a secret service throughout the city.

"What?" I am incensed. "How is that possible? After all his misdeeds? Why do they not arrest him for failing to pay off any of his debts?"

"I completely understand your outrage, Francesca. I imagine that your family's noble lineage, especially on your father's side, belies all of your Uncle Maffio's reckless behavior. What hypocrisy! He, who himself wasted countless hours and money frequenting the brothels in Castello, is coming to *my* home to spy on me!"

"Is there any way to prevent him from coming?"

"I am afraid not, Francesca. And unfortunately, he will have the advantage of hiding behind a maschera, so we may not be able to identify him. At least not right away. We will simply have to comport ourselves as if he were any other guest and kill him with charm," Zia Veronica mutters bitterly, and then under her breath says, "Perhaps we will get lucky and this storm will cause him to drown in one of the canals on his way over tonight."

Dalle tue labbra—from your lips, I say to myself.

Her half-smile twists with regret and a bit of chagrin. "Mi dispiace, Francesca. I am sorry. Your uncle is a complete disgrace, but in honor of your father's memory, let us put our best foot forward and get through the evening without any problems. The guest list consists of refined people of great intellect. He will not even be noticed."

"What do you think he'll do when he discovers that I am living here?" I ask, fearing now that this evening will be a catastrophe.

Zia Veronica gives me a sympathetic look. "You will also have the advantage of wearing a mask, carissima. He may never discover your identity. And even if he does, what of it? He left you with nothing, so there is no reason for him to expect that you have anything now."

"But what of my dowry?" I ask, fighting off the rising feeling of panic. "I have no rights! He might assert claim to me and assign himself as my guardian, taking over for my deceased father just so he can have access to it. He could easily retain a large portion of it and sell me off to one of his cohorts just so he could elevate his own position in society."

* * * * *

I remember a time when, as a very young child, I had been playing hide-and-seek with Beatrice, my nursemaid, and concealed myself behind the heavy drapes of the large window in the sitting room of my ancestral home. I heard my father and uncle arguing upon entering the salotto and held my breath, fearful that I would be punished if discovered.

Through a tiny slit in the drapes I saw and overheard my father berate his brother.

"Maffio, this life of delinquency must stop! You appear to be under the delusion that there is an unlimited supply of money at your disposal. I absolutely refuse to give you an advance on your allowance. Do not ask this of me again!"

"Perhaps if you did not permit yourself to be fooled by the cunning gold-diggers you have allowed into our family you would not deny me what is rightfully mine!" Maffio hissed. "That sister-in-law of yours is nothing but a fraudulent, immoral trickster who extracts money from men through her seductive schemes. She brings shame to our family by association. You should have married better."

"Watch yourself," my father warned.

"Your wife couldn't even manage to give you a son," he had the nerve to say to my father. "Now our inheritance will be further squandered by having to provide a handsome dowry on that useless girl,"

It was the one and only time I ever saw my father lose his temper. He stood nose to nose with Maffio, taking the lapels of his cloak in both hands, and in a dangerous tone said, "I defy you to repeat your vulgar accusations at the risk of grave physical harm." Perhaps because my father was normally so mild mannered, this uncharacteristically violent outburst was enough to silence Maffio. For the time being.

* * * * *

I shudder at this unsettling memory and tremble with apprehension.

"Shhh," my zia whispers, placing her arms around me, trying to soothe my hysteria. "There is no reason to believe that he has any knowledge of the dowry I have saved for you. As far as he knows, I am a self-serving puttana, whose only concern is for myself. And if all else fails, we will convince him that you are my apprentice who will be following in my footsteps in this world of debauchery."

With her hands remaining on my shoulders, she holds me at arm's length and looks deep into my eyes, "Have I not always taken care of you?"

I stare back at her. "Yes, of course, zia."

"Bene. Then trust me. All will be well."

"Signorina Francesca?" Bianca, the young woman who has trained as my personal maidservant, enters the portego and curtsies. "I will help you dress now."

"Go," my zia tells me. "I will see you in a couple of hours. It will be a marvelous evening, Francesca. I promise. Take good care of her, Bianca. Make her radiant!"

"Si, signora," answers Bianca. "It will not be difficult. Are you ready, signorina Francesca?"

"Si, Bianca. Andiamo," I say, and follow her to my bedchamber.

"I have added lavender oil to your bath, signorina," Bianca informs me as we enter my chamber, and I immediately inhale its delicate fragrance. She helps me undress and I cautiously step into the large basin brought upstairs earlier by the other servants.

The water temperature is perfect, and I sink into it, emitting an involuntary moan, and close my eyes as I recline against the side of the basin.

"I will take your garments downstairs to be laundered and return shortly to assist you with your bath," says Bianca. "The lavender will help you relax and soften your skin. Enjoy, signorina. I will be back subito."

"Grazie, Bianca," I say, grateful for all Zia Veronica's loyal servants who make my life far easier than I feel I deserve. Perhaps my zia is right. I have been spoiled by this life, and perchance I would be useless as Giovanni's wife or anyone else's wife, for that matter. How much would I miss all of this pampering and intellectual stimulation? Giovanni's life and mine have been vastly different. Will those differences eventually make us incompatible? Shouldn't I be grateful for what I have and not be so brazen as to desire more? Why allow myself to feel unsatisfied, when what I already have is so much more than most girls my age?

The storm outside continues to rage and I can hear the wind rattle the shutters.

"Signorina?" Bianca calls out before opening the door and re-entering. "Is the water still warm?"

"Sì."

"Bene," she says and picks up the small linen cloth and bar of olive oil soap sitting on top of the short stool beside the basin, then sits down on the stool.

For the next hour Bianca gently scrubs my body and combs out the powder, which was left in my hair from the night before to cleanse it. The scent of lavender fills the entire room and every pore in my skin feels saturated with the luxurious oil. Bianca dries me off with a large piece of linen and proceeds to help me dress.

I sit at my dressing table, where I stare at myself in the gift from Signor Vendramin for this special occasion, a smaller version of the Murano looking glass, similar to the one in my zia's chamber. All the while Bianca works on my hair, my mind drifts elsewhere, preoccupied with the dread of coming face to face with my Zio Maffio after all these years. I vaguely notice when she creates two braids, intertwining them with gold ribbons, and coils the plaits, encircling the crown of my head. The rest of my hair flows loosely down my back and she adds a bejeweled billiment, perfectly matching my gown. Then, as the finishing touch, Bianca inserts my mother's pearl earrings in my earlobes and fastens the matching bracelet around my wrist.

"Ecco qua, signorina Francesca. Tutto finito!" Bianca triumphantly announces.

I snap back to the present moment and my unfamiliar reflection causes me to inhale sharply. In the looking glass I see my transformation from girl to young woman. And despite my small bosom, which does not fill out my dress the way my zia's voluptuous figure fills out hers, I appear mature, sophisticated, and elegant.

"You are pleased, signorina Francesca?" Bianca asks, sounding unsure.

"Yes, Bianca! Very pleased." I take her hands in mine. "Thank you."

She smiles shyly and gently removes her hands from my grasp, averting her eyes, and for the first time I realize how close in age we are. Yet, our circumstances are worlds apart.

How ridiculous I am! Why have I been so thankless? If not for providence, I could have easily ended up a scullery maid or worse, had Zia Veronica not rescued me. In my zia's employment, Bianca is better off than a mere scullery maid, but even so, she will never have the opportunities with which I have been graced.

"The guests should be arriving in another hour or so, signorina Francesca. If you do not require anything further, I will see if Domisilla needs my assistance."

"Yes, of course, Bianca. I am fine. You may go."

Bianca curtsies, picks up the wet and soiled linens, and walks toward the door.

"Thank you very much, Bianca," I call out before she exits, and she answers me with another bashful smile before closing the door behind her.

I continue to stare at my reflection. I look deep into my own eyes and resolve to maintain my composure no matter what occurs this evening. Looking over at the portrait of my parents, which hangs on the opposite wall from my bed, I offer up a prayer of courage and strength to their images. The Church would have me penalized for idol worship and heresy if they knew. What do I care! No doubt my sins are already incalculable; I live under the roof of Venezia's most celebrated courtesan, and I am female. No amount of penance would ever satisfy the all-powerful men who possess control over all the citizens of our fair city. How much longer must we women continue to be punished for Eve's transgressions?

There is only one thing for me to do. I will make my Zia Veronica proud.

I rise from my chair and walk to the door. It will soon be time to receive the guests. I will see if Zia Veronica is finished dressing.

I step out of my bedchamber and walk down the hallway that leads to the portego, and when I step into the room, my heart stops.

"Francesca!" Giovanni says breathlessly.

He is standing in the middle of the room, carrying a large sack, his hair and clothes wet from the rain. True to his word, he has returned with the candelabras my zia ordered and has braved the storm to bring them just in time. His hair looks darker because it is damp, resulting in his exquisite eyes appearing more luminous than ever. Bianca stands to the side, having shown him upstairs upon his arrival.

"I will let signora Veronica know you are here," she tells him.

"Francesca," Giovanni repeats after Bianca leaves. "You are . . . iridescent."

And in this exact moment, I know precisely where and with whom my future rests. In his eyes I see my truest reflection and understand that what he speaks of is much more than my physicality. I know that he sees *me*. Truly sees me, and in that short statement he acknowledges my intellect, my talent, my dreams, my ambitions, and my spirit. So yes, I will put my best self forward tonight, and I will indeed make my zia proud, but I will not require any time after this evening to help me decide what kind of future would best suit me. I have already made up my mind. Punto e basta!

"Giovanni," I finally find my voice. "You must be freezing. Why on earth did you come out in this storm? The candelabras could have waited. My zia would have understood."

"Certainly right!" my zia proclaims, stepping into the room. She is wearing the same green gown she wore for her portrait and somehow manages to look even more dazzling than the first time she donned it. "Giovanni, why did your zio Lorenzo insist on having you come? You will catch your death!"

"Buona sera, signora d'Aragona," Giovanni says with a bow. "Please do not blame my zio. It was I who insisted. My zio managed to complete them in time and I wanted to make sure you could enjoy them this evening. I know how much you have been planning and looking forward to this particular gathering."

We hear a gust of wind and the rain pelts against the leaded-glass panes of the windows. A thunderclap startles us all.

"Mio Dio!" Zia Veronica exclaims in response. "Bianca, would you please make sure all the shutters are secured?"

"Of course, signora."

Zia Veronica returns her attention to Giovanni. "Your actions are incredibly noble, Giovanni, but I cannot have you return to Murano in this! No, you must remain here tonight."

"Signora d'Aragona! I cannot possibly impose," Giovanni protests.

"Not a word! Francesca is correct. You will freeze to death and it is far too dangerous. I hope your family does not worry too much when you do not return this evening, but tomorrow morning we will send you on your way as soon as it is safe. In the meantime, we must get you out of those wet clothes before you succumb to la grippe. My uh . . . special guests have been known to leave articles of clothing behind from time to time. I am sure we can find you something dry to wear," my zia playfully teases him with a coquettish wink and Giovanni's face becomes bright red.

"Again, I do not wish to impose," Giovanni stammers, avoiding my eyes.

"Nonsense! Francesca, will you please take Giovanni to the kitchen and ask Domisilla to find clothes for him?"

"Certamente, zia."

"Grazie, signora! But first, please allow me to show you what my zio has created for you." Giovanni extracts from the large sack two candelabras of bronze. Each one capable of holding three candles with the base, column, knop, capital, sconce, and drip pan up the center, and two arms on each side with their own sconce and drip pan. From each of the drip pans dangle four intricate glass leaves.

"Madonna!" exhales Zia Veronica. "Maestro Lorenzo has done it again. What genius!"

"I am so happy you are pleased, signora," Giovanni says. "May I place them on the dining table for you?"

"Si. Per favore, Giovanni!"

Giovanni and I follow Zia Veronica into the dining room, and he places the candelabras on the long table, spacing them apart so that they create a perfectly balanced tableau.

"Che perfezione!" my zia breathes. "I am profoundly grateful to you and your zio. And now," she says abruptly turning to look directly at him, "We must get you out of your clothes!"

Once again, Giovanni and I both blush uncontrollably at my zia's choice of words.

"Incredibile!" She lets out an exasperated breath when she sees our flushed countenances. "What am I going to do with the two of you? Go! Find someone who will help you dry off and warm up, per l'amor del cielo!"

"Si, signora! Grazie!" answers Giovanni.

"Si, zia! Andiamo ora!" I say, and Giovanni and I run off together, unable to control our laughter as we go in search of Domisilla.

Pausing outside the kitchen entrance, Giovanni and I lean up against the wall in the hallway, breathlessly trying to stifle our giggles.

"If I didn't know any better, I would think your zia enjoys embarrassing me on purpose," Giovanni says.

"Yes, Giovanni. She is an incorrigible flirt! But she is absolutely correct in insisting that you remain here tonight. You cannot possibly go back outside in this tempest. Besides, I am so relieved to have you here. I must admit, I am quite nervous, and your presence will make this evening all the better."

"Francesca, I have no doubt that you will impress everyone, and I appreciate your zia's hospitality, but I will not intrude. After I dry off, I will remain out of the way."

"No, Giovanni!" I protest. "Do not be silly. You must join in the festivities. Why not? Otherwise, what will you do? You certainly cannot remain tucked away in the kitchen."

"I will go back downstairs," he says. "No doubt Alfredo will need help with all le gondole, because he informed me when I arrived that his assistant, Marco, has fallen ill and will not be in attendance this evening. The boats will require special mooring throughout the duration of the storm."

I am disappointed, but of course he is correct. And what better person than Giovanni to assist Alfredo this evening? He is as knowledgeable as Alfredo when it comes to watercraft.

"Oh, very well," I concede. "Hurry! We must get you dry and warm and I will ask Bortola to prepare a plate of food for you before you go downstairs."

Giovanni follows me into the warm kitchen, and we are immediately greeted with mouthwatering aromas.

"Signorina!" cries Domisilla upon seeing us. "May I help you?"

"Per piacere, Domisilla. My zia says that you may know of extra clothes for Giovanni. As you can see, he is soaked through."

"Ah, yes. But of course!" she says. "Follow me, signor Giovanni. I will set you up in one of the guest chambers and bring you some garments."

"Grazie," Giovanni says and waves to me as he follows her out.

I walk over to the large, rough-hewn, wooden table next to the stone hearth, where Bortola, the cook, and her helper, Luisa, stand preparing an antipasto of boiled octopus with parsley.

"Would you please prepare a plate of that polpo bollito con prezzemolo for Giovanni when he returns?" I ask, pointing at the antipasto.

"Si, signorina Francesca," Bortola responds and motions for Luisa to arrange it.

"I will return in a few minutes," I say, and leave the kitchen to find my zia.

As I approach the portego, I hear a familiar voice and am greeted with a hearty, "Buona sera, Francesca! My, what a vision you are! I remember when you first came to live here at Ca' Vendramin. You were but a bambina, and now look at you!"

I step forward and curtsy. "Grazie, signor Vendramin. It is a pleasure to see you again."

Although Domenico Vendramin has been my zia's long-standing benefactor and I have lived here for several years, as a child, I was not given privilege to interact with him or any of the other guests who frequent the regularly held intellectual salons he jointly hosts with my zia.

"Thank you so much for your generous gift," I continue. "The looking glass is stunning."

"Ah, prego. It is nothing," he responds breezily.

Zia Veronica, who has been standing next to her patron, comes to my side and places her arm around me. "We are so looking forward to seeing your commedia erudita, are we not, Domenico?"

"Certainly," he agrees. "And I have hired an extraordinary troupe of actors to help you present it."

"Grazie ancora," I say.

"Your official debut into society will have all of Venezia talking tomorrow morning after everyone has had the opportunity to witness your talent," Zia Veronica says, hugging me and bestowing me with kisses, one on each cheek. "Has Giovanni been taken care of?"

"Yes, Domisilla is seeing to it and I asked Bortola to prepare a plate of food for him. He says he will remain downstairs with Alfredo this evening and help him with le gondole."

"Ah. Yes, that is a good idea. Povero Alfredo will certainly have his work cut out for him tonight."

"What's this?" interjects Signor Vendramin.

"Giovanni Briati, the nephew of Maestro Lorenzo, the mastermind behind the two looking glasses and this gorgeous chandelier," explains my zia, indicating the light fixture directly above us. "Bravely, but also perhaps foolishly, came all the way from Murano to deliver the matching candelabras his zio just completed, in order for us to enjoy them this evening. The poor boy was soaked through and the servants are providing him with dry clothes, a meal, and I insisted that he stay the night rather than risk drowning while crossing the laguna back to Murano."

"Of course," responds Signor Vendramin, looking a bit distracted and uncomfortable discussing such rudimentary domestic issues.

"That reminds me," Zia Veronica says. "I must pay Giovanni."

"Allow me!" says Signor Vendramin, extracting six Ducati and several scudi from his leather money pouch. He hands them to me. "I am including a little extra to compensate him for his journey through this storm."

"Grazie, signor," I say. "I am sure your generosity will be appreciated by both Giovanni and Maestro Lorenzo."

"Come into the dining room, Domenico," my zia says. "I will show you the candelabras and we can enjoy a glass of wine while we await the arrival of our guests."

"If you will excuse me," I say to both of them. "I will check on Giovanni and get him settled with Alfredo, then I will join you."

"Va bene," Zia Veronica says and takes Signor Vendramin's offered arm as they proceed into the dining room.

I re-enter the kitchen at the same time as Giovanni, who looks like the dashing son of a nobleman, dressed in the forgotten clothing of one of my zia's wealthy clients. I smile when I see him, and he returns my smile with an embarrassed grin.

I walk up to him and place the coins in his palm. "This is your payment from Signor Vendramin."

He regards the money with surprise. "This is too much!"

"Signor Vendramin wants to compensate you for braving the storm. Accept it, Giovanni. You and your zio deserve it."

"Signor Giovanni," says Bortola. "Please sit down and have something to eat."

She sets down a bowl of antipasto, another bowl of anchovies with onions and olives, a plate of pheasant, cooked with chard and fennel, and lentils with salted pork. Giovanni sits and Luisa brings over wine served in one of Maestro Lorenzo's colorful glass goblets.

"Mio zio does have a gift," Giovanni says, picking up the goblet admiringly before taking a long drink.

"Signorina Francesca, may I get you something as well?" asks Bortola.

"No, grazie. I will be dining with the other guests later. I only wish to keep Giovanni company while he eats, and then I must rejoin my zia and Signor Vendramin."

"I do not wish to keep you, Francesca," says Giovanni, between bites. "You must return—I will be all right."

"There is plenty of time, Giovanni. It is fine. I cannot tell you how relieved I am to have you here even though you will be downstairs. Just knowing you are near will calm my nerves."

"Francesca, you need not be anxious. I have no doubt that you will dazzle everyone with your brilliance. From what I have already heard of your commedia when you read me part of it, it is full of wit and humor. I am sure the guests will find it highly entertaining."

"No, Giovanni, it is not just that. My zia informed me that my Uncle Maffio has returned to Venezia and will be coming tonight. That tyrant sold my home and squandered all of my family's money, not to mention leaving me homeless on top of already being orphaned."

Giovanni stops eating, wearing a concerned expression. "Why on earth is he making an appearance here tonight?"

"Apparently, i Signori di Notte have deemed him worthy of joining their ranks and my zia believes he has been appointed as a spy this evening."

"O, mio Dio," he exhales.

"Si! I absolutely dread seeing him after all these years. And I fear that since my commedia has not been sanctioned by the Church, he has the authority to use that against my zia—as well as bringing trouble upon my own head. Perhaps I should convince my zia, before the guests arrive, that it may not be a good idea to present it."

"Hasn't she already read it?"

"Yes, but this latest development has me thinking that we shouldn't take any risks."

"Don't you think she would have advised you against presenting it if she considered it too perilous?"

"Yes, I suppose so."

"And what did your zia say in regard to your uncle's presence tonight?"

"She believes he is such an ignoramus that he will be overshadowed by all the other guests and find himself alone and ignored, and we should carry on as if he does not exist. I know she does not want to give him the satisfaction of allowing him to see her intimidated by his newfound position of authority. And she probably has confidence that Signor Vendramin will defend her and me, if worse comes to worse. But I am still afraid."

"Yes, I see," he says slowly. "I do not blame you for being concerned, but I would trust your zia. She certainly has had experience dealing with all kinds of ill-tempered and ill-mannered associates. If anyone can handle such a scoundrel, I am sure she can. In any case, Francesca, I will be right here, close by, and I will not allow any harm to reach you."

"Oh, Giovanni, thank you! Just having you here does give me great comfort."

He reaches for my hand and squeezes it before bringing it up to his lips. Bortola and Luisa pretend not to notice.

For the next several minutes we talk softly while he finishes his meal.

When his plates are practically licked clean, he stands up and says to Bortola and Luisa, "Grazie mille, signore! Tutto era delizioso!"

They both nod appreciatively, while they continue their preparations. We leave the kitchen and take the stairs to the lower level.

"Alfredo!" I call out upon reaching the ground floor.

"Signorina Francesca!" he exclaims, emerging from the storage room. "What can I do for you?"

"Alfredo, Giovanni will be staying the night. There is no way he can return home in this storm."

"Si, certamente," Alfredo agrees.

"I wish to be of service," interjects Giovanni. "I would like to remain down here with you during the festa and help with le gondole."

"Ah, si! That will be immensely appreciated. The guests will require extra help disembarking. The winds are strong. And I could certainly use help securing the vessels, so they do not smash against each other and the fondamenta."

"Perfetto. Va bene," says Giovanni. "And now, Francesca, you must go upstairs. It is cold down here and you do not want to soil your gown and shoes. It appears that we may be in for an acqua alta this evening." He points to the rising tide just outside the water entrance and gently leads me toward the stairs, and whispers, "Do not worry, Francesca. Everything will be fine. If you need anything, I will be right here."

"Che Dio ti benedica, Giovanni," I whisper back. "Grazie, Alfredo! Ciao."

Alfredo nods and Giovanni sends me off with a wink and a smile.

I climb back upstairs to rejoin Zia Veronica and Signor Vendramin.

Chapter 12 — FRANKIE

Venice, Italy
Saturday, August 10, 2019

I arrive at the address given to me by Luciana on Calle del Capitelo and locate the last name, Nardi, next to the doorbell on the right side of the ornate, arched, wooden door. I press the button.

"Frankie?" I hear Luciana's cheerful voice over the intercom. "Sei tu?"

"Si, sono io," I reply.

"Oh, good! Come in."

The buzzer sounds and I push the door open. I enter a small foyer of exposed brick walls. Directly to my right is a large plastic bin where umbrellas and tall rubber boots in various sizes are stored. Straight ahead is a narrow marble staircase with a wrought iron rail.

"Come on upstairs!" cries Luciana from up above.

As I reach the landing at the top of the stairs, Luciana stands just inside the open door of her family's apartment and greets me with her customary kilowatt smile. We exchange the double kiss, and she steps aside to let me in.

"Welcome to Casa Nardi! Mamma! Papà! Frankie has arrived."

"Here you go," I say, handing her the bouquet of flowers and bottle of red wine I picked up before coming over.

"Oh, grazie, Frankie! What beautiful fiori di Dalia," she gushes, just as her parents appear behind her.

"Mamma, Papà! Look how lovely," Luciana says displaying the flowers and wine. "This is Frankie, whom I have been telling you all about. Frankie, this is my Mamma and Papà."

"It is a pleasure to meet you, Professore e Dottoressa Nardi," I say, using their professional titles and the formal *Lei*. "Thank you so much for inviting me."

"Welcome to our home, Frankie," Luciana's mother says as she leans forward to do the kiss, kiss. "Please, call me Giulietta," she continues, implementing the familiar *tu*.

"For me as well," says Luciana's father, shaking my hand and also doing the double kiss. "Call me Bruno. So, we finally get to meet the famous artist, Francesca!"

"Papà!" interjects Luciana. "I told you, she goes by Frankie."

"No, no, it is fine," I say. "I actually really like the name Francesca. It is what Paolo called me the first night I arrived at the Hotel Vendramin. Perhaps I should adopt it."

"Splendid!" says Bruno. "Allora, won't you come in."

"Si," says Giulietta. "Please come in. Bruno, why don't you open up that bottle of prosecco? We can enjoy the wine Frankie brought with dinner. Thank you, Frankie."

"You are welcome. I hope this wine will go well with whatever you are serving tonight."

"Oh, yes. Il vino will be perfect with the risotto. Do you like prosecco?"

"Yes, prosecco would be wonderful."

"Va bene. Luciana, take Frankie to the terrace while I put the flowers in water, and we will bring out the prosecco."

"Si, mamma. Do you need any assistance?"

"No, no. Your father and I will take care of it. Go out and enjoy. We will join you subito."

Giulietta and Bruno head for the kitchen and Luciana takes me by the arm as she leads me through their living room. It is a cozy, inviting, and eclectic room with terrazzo flooring, white walls, and exposed dark wooden beams across the vaulted ceiling. The home has obviously been remodeled and updated, but retains a nostalgic, authentic flair with a mixture of both modern and antique furnishings, heavy damask draperies, expensive looking area rugs, and interesting, colorful artwork.

We walk out to the terrace through large double glass doors and my jaw drops open. I immediately go to the iron rail that looks out over an expanse of greenery, a sight so rare in this city. At this northern end of Cannaregio, the buildings are not as tall as the ones near Piazza San Marco and along the Grand Canal, so from this height I catch a glimpse of the lagoon between some of the buildings.

"Wow! Look at this view!"

"That is the Parco Villa Groggia," explains Luciana, indicating the greenery below us. "It is not the biggest park in Venezia, but it is nice, no?"

"Oh, my gosh, yes! This is so beautiful. Have you lived here all your life?"

"Si. My brother, Davide, and I were both born at the hospital in Mestre on terraferma, the mainland, but we have lived in this house our entire lives. Of course, now Davide lives in Roma ever since he began attending l'università. Remember when I told you that Mamma says I come from the fairies? I have spent many hours playing down below, pretending that it was my very own fairy queendom! When we were little, Mamma and Papà also used to take my brother and me to Parco Savorgnan, Giardini Papadopoli, Parco delle Rimembranze, and a few others that have small playgrounds."

"What a fascinating place to grow up," I reflect. "It is such a unique city."

"Ah! Here we are," Bruno announces, holding a tray of glasses filled with bubbling prosecco, followed by Giulietta carrying the dahlias in an exceptional lime green Murano glass vase, which she sets down in the middle of the patio table. Bruno walks over to where Luciana and I are standing by the rail and we each take a glass.

"Grazie," I say.

"Grazie, papà."

"Prego," he replies. "Giulietta?"

"Grazie," Giulietta says, as she takes her glass.

"Allora," announces Bruno, setting the tray down and lifting his glass. "A toast. To friends, to family, to laughter, to love, and to many years to enjoy them all. Salute!"

"Salute!" we all cheer and clink glasses.

The prosecco is cold and delicious. At this time of day, the setting sun is low enough that the entire terrace is in the shade and a slight breeze has picked up, bringing with it the promise of cooler temperatures this evening.

"Francesca," Bruno says after taking a sip. "May I request that we speak in English?"

"Um, sure," I say, both surprised and relieved. While my Italian has undoubtedly improved, it is still much easier to express myself in English. And since Luciana has told me so many intriguing things about her parents, I am eager to converse with them without any constraints.

"Wonderful!" Bruno immediately proceeds in English. "We all can use the practice."

"Yes, always," agrees Giulietta, although it is abundantly evident that their mastery of English needs no assistance. "Shall we sit down for a bit? Everything is ready. I only need to finish the risotto right before we eat, because risotto must be served fresh off the stove."

"You have a beautiful home," I say as we take our seats around the table.

"Oh, you are so kind," says Giulietta. "This home has been in my family for many generations.

"Tell Frankie the history of the house, Mamma," Luciana urges.

"At one time, my ancestors owned and lived within the entire building. But as the years went by, people died, they moved away, and little by little the building was subdivided and sold into separate units until it became what it is today. My parents lived in the apartment next door all the years they were married, and my sister and I grew up there. But when my father died, my mother moved to Verona to live with her own sister, whose husband had also passed away. Now they are two little old ladies, living together and happy. I miss my mother, but it was becoming too difficult for her to continue living here in Venice. The cost of living has become very expensive and the winters can be brutal at times for older people, especially during the acqua alta."

"Oh, me too, Mamma," says Luciana. "I miss Nonna . . . and Nonno." She looks at me and continues, "We were fortunate to have them so near during the years Davide and I were growing up."

"It's nice that you and your brother grew up having such a close relationship with your grandparents," I say to Luciana.

"Yes, just like you and your nonna, right? And Davide and I were even further lucky to also have our other grandparents close by. They still live here in Venice, but right now they are at our family vacation villa in Recco for the entire summer."

"Where exactly is Recco?" I ask.

"It is along the Italian Riviera. North of Portofino. How far would you say?" Luciana inquires of her father.

"It is roughly fifteen kilometers from Portofino," replies Bruno.

"It sounds nice," I say. "How long have you had your vacation home?"

"It has been in my family for, oh . . . about four generations," says Bruno. "My parents are also getting older, of course, and will eventually move to Recco permanently for all the same reasons that Giulietta just described, as well as their desire to get away from the yearly invasion of tourists. While Venice relies on tourism for much of its economy, it is a threat to a sustainable way of life for locals, who are quickly disappearing. Many of the buildings have been turned into tourist lodging, and housing is becoming scarce and unaffordable. As more and more souvenir shops and high-end retail stores are replacing small locally owned businesses in order to appeal to tourists, there are fewer and fewer fruit and vegetable markets, hardware stores, and other businesses necessary for the locals to survive. Oftentimes, during the summer months, the tourist population easily outnumbers the local population."

"Wow. I had no idea that tourism was creating such a hazard to the city," I admit.

"Yes, most tourists are unaware of the destructive problems facing our city," says Luciana. "That is why I believe strongly in educating our hotel guests. Along with enjoying the beauty of Venice, I wish to convey an appreciation and respect for how delicate it is and the importance of protecting it for future generations."

"A security guard at the Basilica shared with me why so many Venetians have moved out of the city because of the increasing problem of the acqua alta," I say.

"The security guards are now becoming tour guides?" Bruno laughs. "They are going to give you competition, Luciana."

"Oh, Papà!" Luciana responds, dismissively waving her hand at him as if swatting a fly.

"I don't think you have anything to worry about," I assure her, and she shoots her father a playful smirk. "No, I was just asking him about the watermark line on the walls inside the Basilica," I say to Bruno. "And he gave me a lot of interesting, but disturbing, information about the acqua alta situation. Luciana tells me you are working with the Venetian authorities to come up with a solution."

"Well, solution is a generous word," Bruno balks. "Educating, convincing, warning, cajoling, even threatening seems like a more accurate description of how I spend my days as a consultant for the MOSE Project."

"What is that exactly?" I ask.

"It is a reference to the biblical Moses, who parted the seas, and stands for Modulo Sperimentale Elettromeccanico, or in English, Experimental Electromechanical Module," he explains. "The project consists of rows of mobile gates at the Lido, Malamocco, and Chioggia inlets that will be able to isolate the Venetian Lagoon during the high tides. If all goes as planned, soon the MOSE will protect Venice and the lagoon from tides of up to three meters."

"That is assuming the corruption, which has greatly interfered so far, does not continue to disrupt and delay the project," says Giulietta.

"Yes," agrees Bruno. "Unfortunately, the delays in the project have been largely due to the misappropriation of funds."

"How so?" I ask.

"Pay-offs," he says. "Of the five to six billion euros spent on the project, a significant portion has gone to local and regional politicians and other businessmen. Thirty-five people were arrested in the scandal, including our own former mayor and governor of the region."

"That's terrible," I say. "Is there no place on this planet where corruption doesn't exist?"

"Believe me, I understand your frustration," Bruno says. "But the real problem is *global oblivion.* These types of climate issues must be dealt with on a global level, otherwise it won't matter what we do specifically here in Venice because the problem is worldwide. We have to dismantle a world that has been built out of an unjust economy that has had profound environmental implications."

"But that's part of the dark side of human nature, isn't it?" says Giulietta. "If only we had heeded the warnings. But we don't like to heed warnings, do we? We only want to do things that make money and give power. It is blind greed that drives our politicians along with an unrelenting thirst for power. It's a corporate takeover of everything. We are treating the natural world as though we are having a bargain sale. We are liquidating our natural resources as though we have somewhere else to go."

"Si, cara mia," Bruno says, lifting his glass to her as if in a toast. "As always, you are absolutely correct." He winks at her, takes a sip of prosecco, and she smiles back at him. "Human beings are the great determiners of ecology, and we are becoming an invasive species all over the planet."

"And where exactly are we supposed to go?" asks Luciana. "Mars?"

Bruno chuckles lightly and says, "Poverty is the fuel that drives environmental destruction and degradation. If we don't help people find ways of making a living without destroying the environment, we can't even try to save all the endangered species, much less a city that is sinking into the Adriatic. Unfortunately, the greatest threat to many of the world's leaders is economic collapse, and they fear an economic unraveling more than anything else including, but not limited to, public health and safety."

"So, what can be done?" I ask. "I mean, besides recycling, 'going green' and voting for the people who care about climate issues, how can we bring about change before it's too late?"

"That, my dear Francesca, is the million-dollar question, no?" Bruno says.

"But honestly, Papà, what *can* we do?" inquires Luciana in as serious a manner as I have ever witnessed in her.

"We have taken so much for granted," he says. "We need something that will force us to withdraw from our habitual ways of being in the world so we can look inward. Something that will compel us to redefine what is important. It needs to be something big to get us to reshape society in a way that is more just, more loving, more compassionate, and more respectful of all living beings on the planet. Sometimes a thing has to completely collapse. It has to be in enough pain that it actually breaks down, so that a whole new way of doing things can be birthed."

"I can't imagine what it would possibly take to get everyone around the world to do that all at the same time," I say. "Especially right now when my own country feels like it's imploding with the kind of leadership, or lack of leadership we have."

"Yes, your president is quite something, isn't he?" says Bruno.

"Ugggh!" I scoff. "I can't even bring myself to call him by that title. My grandma and I just refer to him as Agent Orange."

"Yes!" interjects Luciana. "Why is he so orange? Is that supposed to be a tan, or does he have some strange form of jaundice?"

We all laugh.

"Oh, my God, he's horrible!" I continue. "Agent Orange's blatant racial demagoguery places a direct target on anyone with black and brown skin, and yet, orange appears to be his color of choice?" This causes everyone to laugh louder. "I know none of our presidents have been perfect and they've all had their flaws, but the list of reasons why this one is so awful feels infinite, not least of which is the fact that he refuses to acknowledge science!"

"Che stronzo," Luciana says, and once again, her cursing makes me laugh.

I take a sip of prosecco and add, "The most frightening part is that although the U.S. is certainly not the only country with questionable leadership, the biggest problem is that Agent Orange is not only intellectually unprepared, personally unqualified, and ethically unfit to serve as President of the United States, but I believe he is also a sociopath. And that makes him dangerous!"

"Unfortunately, I must agree, Francesca," Bruno says. "The President of the United States has typically been the most powerful leader in the world and that makes him dangerous to all of us."

"Actually, I think a more accurate diagnosis would be that he is in fact a psychopath, which is even worse," says Giulietta. "Also, he is obviously a narcissist who will do and say anything to advance his own ambition. A very dangerous combination, indeed."

"How in the world do these people get elected?" asks Luciana.

"My grandma says that it's a combination of our society's obsession with celebrity worship and toxic social media that is partly to blame, which has resulted in the glorification of idiocy and a celebration of stupidity."

"Ah-ha!" says Giulietta. "Well put! But we mustn't be too quick to criticize another country's leadership. He is certainly not the first out-of-control narcissist who has risen to power. Italy's political history and its leaders have not been flawless either."

"You are right, Mamma. Anyone remember Mussolini, by any chance?" asks Luciana.

"Yes," agrees Giulietta. "He and Julius Caesar are only the two most obvious examples. There certainly have been many others."

"I believe what is required is a politics of deep cohesion," says Bruno, "because history has proven that every system of oppression depends on the silence, the paralysis, the confusion, and the compliance of those it seeks to destroy or control. What is needed is something that will inspire people all over the world to demonstrate solidarity on a grand scale, across gender, race, and class distinctions, in defense of those who are marginalized and in support of the collective good. All around the globe the structures of wealth, power, and abundance should be tilted in favor of the weak, the vulnerable, the widowed, the orphaned, 'the foreigner among you', as the Bible states. We must follow the tenets of the Beatitudes rather than live through fear, which always results in the oppression of a people because fear stems from a belief in scarcity. When the core belief of a civilization is *abundance*, then you build a safety net for everyone who is in trouble instead of causing more subjugation. Just look at the countries that, in general, have thrived. They are always countries with strong safety nets such as good health care and education for all. They make sure that justice flows to everybody."

"Is this now a sermon, Papà?" Luciana teases.

"Ah, yes," Bruno responds. "Pardon me, I forgot that I am not standing at the lecture podium."

"Papà was going to be a priest before he decided to become a scientist."

I look at Bruno in surprise. "Really? How fascinating."

"But can you imagine if he had gone through with taking his vows?" asks Luciana melodramatically. "I wouldn't be here!"

Bruno and Giulietta both shake their heads and laugh at Luciana's feigned horror.

"Oh, carissima!" Bruno chortles. "My life is abundantly better with you, your mother, and Davide in it. There is no doubt that I made the correct choice."

"Thank goodness for that!" Giulietta says with exaggerated relief.

"You see, Francesca," Bruno explains, "I decided that I could better serve humankind by becoming a scientist rather than a priest, because as a scientist I wouldn't have to shy away from declaring the blatant, bold-faced, unapologetic truth."

I must have a dumbstruck look on my face because Bruno laughs again when he sees my reaction to what he's just said.

"Allow me to explain," he continues. "The prophet, historically, is the one who cannot overlook injustice and there is a long history of killing prophets when they speak out against authority. Although, some scientists have had a bit of the prophet in them, like Galileo, who was imprisoned for daring to speak out against the beliefs of the Church. But for the most part, scientists are left alone. Usually, the worst thing that happens is that we are ignored and not believed, as is the case with the climate crisis—and also the warnings about rampant vector-borne diseases that have arisen in direct correlation to global warming."

"Really?" I say, surprised that I have never heard about this correlation before. "How are they affected by climate change?"

"One example is malaria, which is carried by mosquitoes in climates along the equator. As the global temperature increases, the mosquitoes' habitat will expand to greater latitudes, thus, transmitting infectious pathogens to a wider population. The challenge for health organizations is to be able to predict what populations will be most at risk, because prevention is always superior to reaction."

"Oh, wow. I never even thought about that," I say dismayed, recalling how much the mosquito population has already increased in the urban areas of California over the past few years, which until recently have been largely mosquito-free.

"But that is the gift the prophets give us," Bruno adds. "They are ruthlessly honest when things are broken. What happened in Jerusalem around the year 33 is as important, if not more so, than almost anything else in history, including The Enlightenment, World War II, the splitting of the atom, and the weaponizing of science. It basically determines how we tell time. But mostly it's important because Jesus was, himself, a prophet and, what you Americans call, the 'poster child' for protest, no?"

"Yes, that's true," I say. "And like Martin Luther King Jr. and others who believed in peaceful protest, he was killed."

"Ah, but that is only one part of the misinterpretation of the Jesus story that has been greatly warped," Bruno says.

"What do you mean? How has it been warped?" I ask.

"Well, first of all by the portrayal of Jesus as somewhat bland and emotionless. It is true that Jesus believed in the peaceful demonstration of righteousness, but even he lost his temper when faced with situations he deemed unacceptable," Bruno explains. "Which is why he chased out the moneylenders and all the others who were defiling his Father's sacred house. But I ask you, in the entire history of the world has there ever been a revolution that did not involve civil unrest? Even in your own country, before the American Revolution when all that tea was thrown into the Boston Harbor, that was most certainly considered an act of anarchy and the destruction of property. If it were possible to achieve massive change for the betterment of all human beings without social upheaval, then we would truly be experiencing heaven on earth. But we humans are not that evolved yet."

"Yes, I see what you mean," I say.

"The other misinterpretation of Jesus' story is that all of us were taught that the reason Jesus had to suffer on the cross was as a sacrifice for our sins. We humans all required atonement for our inherently evil souls, and God demanded the supreme sacrifice in order for us to be worthy of receiving his forgiveness."

"Why are we humans so silly?" inquires Luciana to no one in particular. "Why do we insist on believing in a God that is so punitive, vengeful, and even hateful? It makes no sense!"

"That is because we have created a God that takes the worst impulses of human beings and then project them as big as we can, and believe that must be what God is like because that's how we think we would behave if we had unlimited power. We humans still do not seem capable of understanding that God is that which exists beyond form. God is simply the placing of a name upon that of which nothing greater can be conceived. Perhaps now you can begin to understand the existential crisis I was having in my early twenties. Also, I met your mother and decided I did not want to live without her in my life, so there you have it."

Bruno takes hold of Giulietta's hand and kisses it. They gaze adoringly at each other, and for a moment I think they may have forgotten that Luciana and I are still here.

"Okay, you two love birds!" interrupts Luciana. "Please, Papà, continue with your explanation."

"Oh, yes, uh. Where was I?"

"The Jesus story became warped because . . ." Luciana prompts him.

"Ah, si! By making the story about sin and sacrifice, the people in power could control the masses through guilt, shame, and ultimately, the fear of not being able to enter the Kingdom of Heaven."

I knew it! I think to myself. My brain is on fire! This man is so eloquent and knowledgeable. Aside from Grandma, I have never heard any adult in my life speak so boldly about such things, EVER.

"But the truth is," Bruno proceeds, "that Jesus was a highly evolved, enlightened being who came to teach us that sacrifice was completely unnecessary for us to access divinity. And yet, ironically, his story became all about him being the *ultimate* sacrifice. Nevertheless, he understood his authentic nature, which was that he came from the Divine, and he traveled around spreading the message that we are all the sons and daughters of God. But this message was much too empowering and threatened the authority structures. Jesus of Nazareth was executed for being an enemy of the state because he stood up against the injustices of the day. He was a threat to the commercial, military, religious complex that marginalized the poor and had kept power in the hands of a few wealthy people."

"Let's not leave out how stories about women were also warped to propagate sexism and inequality!" adds Giulietta. "The roles that women played in the stories throughout the Bible were both minimized and often maligned. But it is obvious that the women must have been important if it remained in the Jesus story that it was the women who discovered that his body was missing from the tomb."

"It was also the women who remained with Jesus at the cross while all the men scattered and hid," adds Bruno with a hearty laugh.

"Not to mention that Mary Magdalene has always been horribly misrepresented," says Luciana. "She was not a prostitute! Her importance as one of Jesus' trusted companions was downplayed by claiming that she was a fallen woman, who repented and was saved by Christ's teachings. But now, there is the belief that she may have . . . Um, how do you say? Lei lo ha finanziato."

"She bankrolled him?" I say.

"Ecco!"

"Those stories are just another method that has been used throughout history to keep women silent," says Giulietta. "Even today, women and women's interests continue to be dismissed as unimportant—and that attitude goes across all areas of society. Just look at how differently men's health issues are addressed as opposed to those of women. When men have a medical problem, it is considered biological. But when women have the same complaints, they are considered psychological. And they are sent home with a pat on the knee and told to go on holiday, take a bubble bath, or have a glass of wine. We are not that far from the time when women were routinely committed to psychiatric hospitals for *hysteria*."

If my brain was on fire before while listening to Bruno, now it is a cascade of fireworks. I glance at Luciana who is nodding enthusiastically at her mother. Bruno has a proud smile on his face as he relaxes in his chair and sips his prosecco.

"All of these ideas perpetuate the notion that women cannot be trusted, and they cannot trust themselves," Giulietta proceeds.

"We were taught to believe that questioning a structure or authority is very bad and completely frowned upon. The need to belong is very strong in humans. So, when our questions threaten acceptance in the group, it is the perfect motivator to ensure that we behave. But I tell you, women will never fully thrive or be considered equal if the cost of belonging and acceptance is our silence. We can make it work for a while until the cost of our integrity becomes too high. Then we will explode like Mt. Vesuvius!"

"Si! Brava!" shouts Luciana and they high five each other. "Keep going, Mamma."

"Women are taught to be grateful for what is 'good enough' and to believe that if they do want more, it is dangerous," continues Giulietta. "But it is not dangerous to women, themselves, or to the common good. No! It is dangerous to the status quo and male-dominated institutions. If women were to fully own and unleash their power, civilizations would be transformed. The world as we know it would disintegrate if societies were motivated by, what have traditionally been considered women's values. Children would be fed, clothed, and educated, corrupt governments would collapse, and wars would end."

"There you go, Francesca!" says Bruno. "Perhaps that is precisely what needs to happen to bring about a new world order. Maybe that is the answer to your question."

"Frankie!" exclaims Luciana. "This is just like what you told me the other day. How women need to step forward and hold up a mirror to themselves and society to stop the madness!"

"Yes," I exhale slowly, in a dreamlike reverie as all the pieces fall into place. "Wow, Bruno. No offense," I say to Luciana and

Giulietta, then turn back to Bruno, "but I kind of wish you *had* gone into the clergy, because the world needs ministers like you to help us heal from all the destruction and bloodshed caused by toxic religious beliefs. The institutions are too potent to be left in the hands of those who use it to control people."

"Ahhh, but I believe we can all be ministers without having to be ordained," Bruno says. "We can achieve that purely through the example of how we live our lives, because actions speak louder than words, and love is not something you feel, but rather something you do. We can also interpret for ourselves the lessons of the Bible. Your intuition will always lead you to the truth."

"Sooo, maybe Eve was never supposed to be used as the example of what we did wrong that resulted in all the suffering of the world," I say. "Perhaps the true lesson of that Genesis story is that we owe it to ourselves and the future of humanity to have the courage to bite that apple! Eve's story is not our warning. She was actually our *role model*!"

"Ha, ha! Brilliant!" shouts Luciana.

"We need to stop allowing people who claim Christianity and use Divine Authority to justify and sanction all manner of atrocities and terrible policies," I say. "It is so opposite to the compassion, mercy, grace, and love that Jesus taught us. Over and over again fanatic, whackadoodle, fundamentalists quote the Bible and the words of Jesus to hurt and disrespect people, while claiming that the suffering they cause in others is God's will."

"Precisely," Bruno says. "Most people who leave the Church, don't leave because they stop believing in the teachings of Jesus. People leave Christianity because they believe the teachings of Jesus so much, they cannot tolerate being part of an institution that claims to be about anything that doesn't reflect his message of absolute love."

"Yes!" I exclaim. "That is so true! Even though I don't attend church anymore, I still consider myself a Christian, or perhaps more specifically—I am a Christ-leaning spiritual-seeker."

"Oh, that is wonderful," says Giulietta. "I like that!"

"Me too!" cries Luciana. "I might have to borrow that, Frankie."

"I can see that you are a philosopher as well as an artist," says Bruno admiringly. "But of course, those two often go hand in hand."

"Thank you, but you give me too much credit," I demur. "The work both you and Giulietta do is so important. And you too, Luciana. And Davide! I feel like I've wasted the last four years of my life studying theatre, when I should have picked a major that was more civic-minded, or some kind of social activism. I feel like my choices have been so frivolous."

"Oh no, Frankie!" Luciana protests.

"We need artists to reflect our humanity and goodness back to us, especially during difficult times," adds Giulietta.

"Francesca," Bruno says in a gentle, but serious tone. "Giulietta is absolutely correct. While science may be the thing that gets us out of a difficult situation, art will be what helps us through the situation because art is to the community what thoughts are to the individual. Art provides the community a forum where we reflect on who we are, where we hope to go, our strengths, our failures. Through art as our mirror, we decide what our values are and then we can act on them. That is the role of art. Entertainment? That is just a byproduct."

Quiet descends, allowing Bruno's statement to sink in. We all sip our prosecco.

"The sensitivity of the artist is crucial for the survival of humanity," Giulietta finally says after our contemplative pause in conversation. "Many artists are empaths. Throughout history people like you, in most cultures, were set apart from the tribe. They were considered to be a bit eccentric but also essential to the tribe's survival because they were the Shaman, the medicine men and women, the artists, and the poets. They are people who can see things that other people can't see and are willing to feel things that other people can't feel. And through the expression of their work, they teach the rest of us all those truths. There is a lot to being a prophet when you possess that kind of sensitivity."

There is a sharp pain in my head as the threatening sting of tears behind my eyes and the tightness in my throat from the effort of trying to suppress them feels like a million tiny daggers. I grew up in a family where my sensitivity was treated as high maintenance, and I was often shamed and labeled as difficult because my emotions were too big to handle for the adults around me. The term empath has become such a buzzword lately, and it isn't until now that I understand what it implies.

I inhale deeply and finish off the remainder of my prosecco to avoid dissolving into a blubbering mess. "Thank you," I am finally able to say. "That means a lot."

"Luciana is also an empath," Giulietta says. "I believe it is the reason she was always such a good sleeper and she would take daily naps up until she was about ten years old. Empathic children are often exhausted by all the emotional stimuli they receive from everyone and everything around them. They take in so much."

"I still enjoy taking naps!" says Luciana. "Frankie, maybe that is why we both feel like we belong on another planet. This one is just too much overstimulation."

"As each year passes and I grow older, I too feel the need for a daily nap. Does that mean that I am becoming an empath or just an old man?" Bruno laughs.

"You, caro mio," says Giulietta, standing up from her chair, "have always been a highly evolved being and you grow more handsome and distinguished with each passing year." She leans over and kisses him on the cheek. "Are we getting hungry? I think it is time to cook the risotto."

"Yes! I'm starving," says Luciana. "Can we help you, Mamma?"

"No, there is nothing to be done, but you can come inside and keep me company. Bruno, let's open the wine Frankie brought."

"Certamente," he replies.

"You two go on," says Luciana. "Frankie and I will bring in all these glasses. Should we bring in the flowers?"

"They can stay on the table," Giulietta replies. "It is still very warm, and we can eat on the terrace."

Giulietta and Bruno leave the terrace while Luciana and I place the champagne flutes on the tray. She picks up the tray and begins walking toward the door.

"Luciana, your parents are amazing! I'm sure you already know this, but you are so lucky."

"Yes, I do know," she says softly. "I realize that not everyone is so fortunate. And they like you too. I can tell that they are very impressed with your intelligence and curiosity. Those are powerful gifts, Frankie."

Damn it! I feel like I want to cry again.

These people are so gracious it overwhelms me. Ironically, in their presence my emotional scars feel more pronounced. Is it solely the cultural differences between Luciana's and my countries of origin, which produced the deficit in my upbringing that created my insecurities? Was it having parents who came from a country where religious doctrine combined with a machismo culture caused years of negative influence, resulting in internalized female self-hatred? And was that projected self-hatred the reason my mom was so hard on me, often treating me with such disdain and disappointment that I wanted to make myself as small as possible in order to circumvent her disapproval and anger?

El Salvador is not a country with a society known for its respect of women and girls, and females are often treated as though their only worth is in the sacrifices they are expected to make on behalf of everyone else. Nor has the culture traditionally valued the education and advancement of females, often assigning the eldest daughter in a family the daunting responsibility of caretaking her younger siblings, effectively and immediately ending her own childhood and further propagating the belief that a female is deserving of love only to the extent that she is willing to martyr herself.

Then again, Italy is also a country founded on religious doctrine and is literally the birthplace of the Roman Catholic Church. No. I do not have the answer to this unanswerable question, and it frustrates me. Perhaps it boils down to accepting the idea that there are both enlightened and unevolved people everywhere in the world, and our reason for being is to become self-aware in order to elevate humanity, as Bruno and Giulietta suggested.

"Are you okay, Frankie?" Luciana asks, turning to look at me just before entering the house.

"Yes, I'm fine," I say, trying to control my voice through the constriction in my throat. "I'm just trying to absorb all the important things we talked about."

"I'm sorry. My parents can be a little intense sometimes."

"No, no, it's okay," I assure her. "I find them incredibly fascinating and everything they said makes so much sense. I love having deep conversations. It's so validating to hear others say what I have been suspecting all my life."

"Good. Because I'm sure they are not done," she rolls her eyes. "My parents can discuss philosophy, politics, and social issues forever. So, you will not be disappointed." She smiles broadly and I follow her inside.

The delicious smell of sautéed garlic and onions permeates the air throughout the entire house.

"Oh, my gosh! It smells wonderful in here," I say.

"Um-hm," she replies. "Risotto ai gamberetti. My mother's specialty."

We enter the kitchen where the cooking aromas make me immediately salivate. Bruno has just uncorked the wine bottle, he pours himself a small amount in a glass, swirls it, then takes a sip. He hands the glass to Giulietta who drinks, closes her eyes, and nods.

"Um. Very nice," she says, and Bruno fills the glass, leaving it on the counter next to the stove where she can reach it.

"May I pour you two some wine?" he asks us.

"Si, per piacere," says Luciana, setting the tray down on the counter next to the sink and rinses off the champagne flutes.

"Here you go, Francesca," he says handing me a glass of wine.

"Grazie," I say and walk over to where Giulietta is standing by the stove, stirring the contents in a pot. "May I watch how you make your risotto?"

"Of course! It is simple. But you must stir it constantly and add the broth and wine a little at a time to the olive oil, garlic, and onion mixture."

"That's different from the way we make our rice," I tell her. "Arroz con frijoles negros, black beans and rice, was always one of my favorite dishes growing up. But I like the creaminess of risotto."

"Me too!" says Luciana. "It is my favorite. I will set the table."

I watch Giulietta add the Vialone Nano, the type of rice used in the Veneto region, to the soffritto.

"This step is called tostatura," she explains. "It means toasting. It is extremely important, and you should never skip it."

"We do the same with our rice," I say.

"Here is the part that is probably the most different," Giulietta says and for the next 25 minutes she slowly adds the chicken broth and white wine, stirring frequently, whereas the rice I was taught to make involves bringing it to a full boil, turning the heat down to low, covering the pan, and allowing the rice to absorb all the liquid.

When the rice is fully cooked, Giulietta adds butter and Parmigiano-Reggiano, the step she calls the mantecatura, giving the risotto its unique creaminess.

"And now, for the final step," she announces. "I gamberetti." She tosses in the cooked shrimp that was set aside on the counter in a small bowl. "Allora, dinner is ready!"

"It looks wonderful!" I say.

"Frankie, will you please help me carry out the salad and bread?" asks Luciana.

"Of course!"

"I will bring the bottle of acqua minerale and wine," says Bruno, and the three of us file out to the terrace.

After all the items are set on the patio table and we sit down, Giulietta appears, carrying a steaming bowl of risotto and places it right in the middle.

"It looks delicious, Mamma. Grazie." says Luciana.

"Prego," Giulietta replies taking her seat. "Buon appetito!"

"Buon appetito," we all murmur and begin passing the plates of food around the table.

The caprese salad consists of the reddest, juiciest tomatoes I have ever seen in my life, and the aromatic fresh basil makes me want to roll around in a field of it and engulf my body in its perfume. I take a piece of bread, so crunchy on the outside and soft on the inside and can't believe how good something so simple can taste. Then, I bite into a forkful of risotto and have to force myself not to moan.

I am so grateful that I have achieved progress in making peace with my eating disorder and body dysmorphia so that I can fully enjoy this scrumptious meal. My therapist once told me that eating disorders are not necessarily about weight but are more often about control, which explains why females are disproportionately afflicted by this disorder because we frequently feel that our lives are not in our control.

After all that Giulietta shared earlier, I now see how pervasive and destructive are the forces that continue to work against women having full agency over our lives. The distraction created and disseminated by society and the media to keep women constantly obsessed with their bodies and weight is a deliberate tactic to keep women marginalized. As long as all our energy is being directed toward fixating on what we look like, we won't have any energy left to fight for true equality. If we were to completely stop denying our feelings by starving or stuffing ourselves, women might finally begin to come to grips with the emotion most denied to us: anger. But those in power do not want women to be angry because the Patriarchy knows that when women get pissed off, they *demand change.*

"Oh, my God," I say. "This is the most delectable thing I have ever tasted. If there is such a thing as heaven, this is the only thing I want to eat for all eternity."

Luciana laughs and Bruno says, "Good choice, Francesca. Agreed!"

"I am pleased you like it," says Giulietta, humbly. "I think we Italians do well with our cuisine. Our food is usually pretty good."

"I'll say!" I laugh. "It's more than just 'good.' It's some of the best food in the world!"

We continue eating, talking leisurely about my adventures in Venice so far. They ask me about my family and my life back in California. When I tell them about my parents, Giulietta and Bruno express the same sorrow as Luciana had during our day in Burano.

After a slightly awkward pause, Bruno asks, "What made you decide to come to Italy, and Venice in particular?"

"I fell in love with the language," I explain. "And I've seen so many movies that take place in Venice, I was intrigued."

"And is it what you expected?" he asks.

"Oh, my gosh, it's so much more!" I say. "Sometimes its beauty is overwhelming."

"California is also supposed to be very beautiful," says Giulietta.

"Yes, it is," I say. "And the climate is very similar, especially in Southern California, although we don't have the kind of humidity you do here. And even some of the terrain looks a lot like parts of Italy, but the beauty of this particular city is so distinctive. Unfortunately, global warming has wreaked havoc on California as well, resulting in massive, uncontrollable fires throughout the state, beginning in late summer through the fall. Each year it seems to be getting worse."

"Our summers are also becoming hotter and more uncomfortable with each passing year all throughout Europe, just like the acqua alta situation is becoming worse," says Luciana. "That is why most Italians go on holiday for the entire month of August to escape the heat. Normally, we would all be in Recco with my grandparents during this time, but Mamma and Papà have made the sacrifice of staying here with me, so I am not all alone."

"It is not a sacrifice, carissima," Giulietta says tenderly.

"You see," Luciana explains, "for the past three summers while I have worked at the Hotel Vendramin, I could not go away during the month of August, so my parents have skipped their summer holiday to stay here with me. We go to Recco for a couple of weeks at the end of September, instead, just before I go back to university."

"It is a small concession, Luciana," says Giulietta. "We know you do not like being alone, so why endure loneliness if you do not need to?"

The remarkable differences in our upbringings and the parenting styles of Bruno and Giulietta strike me with such intensity as I listen to them converse. Again, I wonder if my parents' hard-scrabble life as immigrants hardened them and thus resulted in their unreasonably high expectations of me. My mother would often tell me that my life was so much easier than hers had been, and therefore I had no reason to ever feel sad or upset about anything, which led me to swallow and negate my emotions. I was often left to fend for myself and figure things out on my own, and I'm pretty sure my parents would have considered loneliness an emotion of indulgence.

"Well, at least they will be going to join my grandparents in Recco for one week at the end of this month," Luciana tells me. "Davide and his fiancé, Chiara, are there right now because they will be getting married next summer at our villa, and they are getting all the preparations ready. By then, I will have graduated from university and I will be free to go for the entire month next summer." She beams triumphantly.

"Wow, a wedding at a villa on the Italian Riviera?" I exclaim. "That sounds like a dream!"

"It should be quite lovely," agrees Giulietta. "Bruno and I will just need to help Davide and Chiara with some of the catering options."

"Ah, yes!" Bruno declares. "A full week of eating at the best restaurants in order to choose wisely. I cannot wait!"

"Fortunately, Frankie and I will be seeing the opera during the time you two will be gone, so it gives me something to look forward to," Luciana says.

"Oh, that reminds me," I say. "I want to be able to understand *Madama Butterfly* as much as possible. Do any of you know of a book on Puccini that you could recommend?"

"Oh! We should go to the Belli Libri dell'Acqua Alta! I'm sure there are tons of books about all the Puccini operas," Luciana says. "Luigi, the proprietor? His wife works at La Fenice."

Small world, yet again, I think to myself.

"That's a good idea," I say. "I've been wanting to go back there."

"Great! Let's stop by there this coming Monday. We both have the day off again."

"Perfect," I say.

"You see?" Bruno says to Giulietta. "These young ladies will be having the time of their lives while we are away. Luciana will not even notice we are gone."

"Oh, Papà!" Luciana says feigning exasperation.

"Yes, I am glad," says Giulietta, then after a pause, "Actually, Luciana, why not invite Frankie to come stay here with you during that week?"

"Oh, Mamma! That's a wonderful idea!"

"Frankie," Giulietta says, "would you consider it?"

"Yes! Please, Frankie!" Luciana insists before I even have a chance to respond. "You can have Davide's room. It's just been sitting there, empty, since he moved away. And since we both have to report for work early, we can walk to the hotel together every morning. Oh, it would be so nice! What do you say?"

I look around at all their expectant faces and am touched by their hospitable invitation and trust, especially after having just met me.

"That . . . sounds like fun!" I finally say. "It's awfully nice of you to offer. Are you sure?"

"Of course!" says Bruno. "Giulietta and I would both feel better knowing that Luciana has some company."

"Yes, why not?" agrees Giulietta. "You two girls will have a fantastic time. Così divertente!"

"Okay, then!" I say and Luciana grabs my hands, laughing with unbridled delight.

"Allora, would anyone like some caffè?" asks Giulietta.

"Or grappa?" asks Bruno.

"None for me, thank you," says Luciana. "It is still too warm. Can we go straight to the gelato?"

"How about you, Frankie?" asks Giulietta.

"Gelato sounds great for me too, grazie."

"Va bene. I will start the caffè and then we can bring out the gelato." Giulietta says as she picks up the serving dishes and heads for the kitchen.

The rest of us collect the remaining dishes and bring them inside. Bruno extracts a bottle of grappa from the antique liquor cabinet in the corner of the living room, while Giulietta pours expresso into two small porcelain cups and places them on a tray along with a sugar bowl, spoons, and napkins. Luciana scoops out the spumoni into four glass bowls and I help her carry them out to the terrace.

The gentle breeze continues making the temperature delightfully comfortable under a starlit sky. Giulietta lights several candles in various areas of the terrace. We enjoy our dessert in relative silence with the only sound being that of the occasional motor of a vaporetto in the distance. I want to remember this evening forever.

Just as we complete our gelato, the nearest bell tower chimes. Eleven o'clock.

"Oh, wow!" I say. "I had no idea it was so late. I'm so sorry. I feel like I've overstayed my welcome. I should probably go."

"Nonsense!" says Giulietta. "It was our pleasure having you. There's no need to rush off."

"No, I really should be getting back. I'm working early tomorrow morning. Thank you so much for everything!"

"It was a delight to meet you, Francesca," says Bruno. "We look forward to seeing you again soon."

"Yes, I am so happy you've agreed to come stay with me," says Luciana. "We'll have to plan lots of fun things to do!"

"Let's just bring all these dishes inside and we'll walk you back to the Hotel Vendramin," says Giulietta.

"Oh, no," I protest. "That's not necessary. It's already so late. I'll be fine."

"It will be our pleasure," Bruno insists. "Besides, I need the exercise to get ready for all the eating in Recco."

Luciana laughs and calls after him as he enters the house, "Si, papà! You will have to swim extra laps at our beach during this next trip."

"Your villa has its own private beach?" I ask.

"Yes. It's in a little cove."

"This place sounds like a slice of heaven!"

"It is!" she says, and then whispers, "I'm so happy you will be staying here with me, Frankie. It will put their minds at ease, and they can enjoy themselves without worrying about me."

I look at her and wonder about the age-old question of nature versus nurture. I once heard someone say that our DNA loads the pistol, and environment pulls the trigger. Luciana's unabashed enthusiasm and joy for life is undoubtably her nature, yet she admittedly dislikes being alone with such fervor that her parents go out of their way to help her avoid this phobia. Are Bruno and Giulietta overly solicitous because Luciana is so sensitive or is Luciana sensitive because her parents raised her so cautiously? Bruno and Giulietta certainly don't strike me as having been so-called helicopter parents, but perhaps they were. Or maybe they are just highly conscious parents who are keenly attuned to their daughter's needs and don't see the benefit of having her suffer unnecessarily. Nature versus nurture. Why is being human so complicated?

"Yes, it'll be fun!" I tell her.

* * * * *

As we walk through the quiet, empty neighborhood of Cannaregio, our footsteps echoing off the buildings along the narrow streets, I am reminded of my first night when I arrived in Venice almost at the exact same hour of night. It feels like eons ago. So much has happened and that lonely girl who showed up, lost and confused, is now walking arm and arm with her friend, while her friend's parents walk arm and arm behind us.

Our late-night stroll takes us through all the tranquil residential streets as we avoid the wider and busier, at least during the daytime hours, Rio Tera. From the front door of their building all the way to the Hotel Vendramin, Luciana continues a non-stop stream of conversation, describing all the things we will do and the places she will show me during our *settimana dell'amicizia* and I add my own ideas for our friendship week.

After crossing over the bridge on Calle Zancani, we turn left at Fondamenta de Ca' Vendramin and arrive at our destination.

"I cannot thank you enough for such a wonderful evening," I say softly so as not to disturb the neighbors and the sleeping hotel guests in the rooms above. "The food was delicious. Everything was amazing!"

"You are so welcome, Frankie," Giulietta says as she double kisses me.

"It was a delight spending the evening with you, Francesca," says Bruno. "Buona notte." Kiss, kiss.

"I'll see you on Monday, Frankie. Ciao." Luciana hugs me.

"Buona notte," I whisper.

The three of them link arms as they turn around and walk back toward Calle Zancani and turn right, disappearing from my view.

The church bells all over Venice chime the midnight hour as I walk up the ancient marble stairs to my room inside the Hotel Vendramin.

Chapter 13 — GIO

Ooof! Another hot day.

Business has been excruciatingly slow all day, the heat keeping even the most ardent tourists away. I wish Luigi would close the bookstore after the noon meal for a couple of hours, but he insists on staying open because he says that most of the tourists, especially the Americans, are not used to businesses being closed mid-day and we would lose the majority of our customers. I disagree. I think we should change our hours of operation and stay open later in the evening, after the sun is down when the temperature is finally bearable. Ah well, the sun is sinking low now and the people will begin showing up soon, hopefully, on their way to dinner. I sit on top of a milkcrate next to the wheelbarrow in the front courtyard while I wait for customers.

"Luciana!"

"Ciao, Frankie!"

Frankie? What?!

I look toward the entrance of the courtyard, where I heard the voices. *Mamma mia! It is her!*

La Signorina Bellissima has returned and she is speaking to another signorina, who looks familiar. . . ah, yes! Luciana! Of course. Cristina's friend from school. I have not seen her since Cristina's graduation party from scuola superiore before leaving for l'università. Oh, no. I must not let Luciana see me. She is a talker and will want to engage me in conversation. This is not how I wish to meet La Signorina Bellissima for the first time.

Che porca miseria! I was not expecting this. Why was I not prepared? I quickly slip inside the store before they see me.

"Gio!" says Luigi, spotting me as I run inside. "There you are."

Ciao! I call out, rushing past him toward the back of the room, and make myself look busy. I remain hidden behind a volcanic mound of books inside a bathtub where I have a clear view of Luciana and Frankie entering the store.

"I think I remember all the books about music being in this first room," I hear Luciana say.

"Luciana! Bella ragazza! What a nice surprise to see you," Luigi exclaims at the sight of her.

"Si, Luigi. It has been a long time. How is Cristina? She texted me a couple of months ago to let me know that she was not coming back to Venezia again this summer. It has been ages since I have seen her."

From my hiding place, I hear Luigi's regretful sigh before responding.

"She does not enjoy the summers here in Venezia at all, and she now has a new job as an assistant for a powerful attorney in Padova. She is hoping they will offer her a permanent position in the law firm once she passes her final exams. Sofia and I will go to visit her in Ottobre once the tourist season is over and I can close the bookstore. And how is your famiglia?"

"Everyone is well, grazie," Luciana says. "Davide is getting married next year! Mamma and Papà will be going to Recco in a couple of weeks to help Davide and his fiancé with their wedding plans. The wedding will be at our villa."

"Little Davide is getting married?" Luigi laughs. "All of you ragazzi have grown up so quickly."

"Luigi, have you met my friend, Frankie?"

I peek out from my hiding spot and see La Signorina Bellissima smile and offer her hand to Luigi.

"I was here a few weeks ago," Frankie says.

"Si! I remember. You work at the Hotel Vendramin with Luciana."

"Yes. Wow, good memory! I've been wanting to return and now I have the perfect excuse."

"Oh?" Luigi inquires. "Is there something specific you are looking for?"

"Frankie and I will be attending the opening night at La Fenice!" says Luciana.

"Ah! That is wonderful," Luigi exclaims. "Sofia and I will also be in attendance. We will look for you."

"Oh, good!" Luciana addresses Frankie. "You will get to meet Luigi's wife, Sofia, who is the Marketing Director for the opera."

"What interesting jobs you both have," I hear Frankie tell Luigi.

"Frankie is an actress, herself, and has studied theatre at l'università," explains Luciana.

Ah-haaaa, I think to myself. *No wonder she is so luminous. She is accustomed to being on the stage.*

"Aaand, she is also a writer," Luciana adds.

Of course! That is why she is so observant . . . and a romantic!

"You make me sound much more interesting than I actually am, Luciana," Frankie says.

She is also humble.

"I absolutely adore your bookstore!" Frankie tells Luigi. "It makes me feel like I have died and gone to book heaven. I could literally spend hours here!"

Dear God in heaven, did you hear that?

Luigi smiles broadly. "I am so pleased that you like it. I enjoy the pleasure it brings to our customers," he says.

"I can't imagine how you keep track of it all," Frankie says. "It seems like a lot of work."

"It looks like you've amassed an even bigger collection since the last time I was here," adds Luciana. "It has been so long ago; I cannot even remember when that was."

"It has gotten a bit out of control," Luigi admits. "I've been thinking of hiring some extra help to organize it, but I am not sure who would want to take on such a task. Ah! Basta! That is a problem for another day. What can I help you find?"

"Luciana thought you might have some books on Puccini," Frankie tells him. "Maybe something specifically about *Madama Butterfly* so I can study up on it before we see it."

"Certainly!" Luigi tells her, getting off his stool behind the cash register and walking around to the front of the counter to point directly at me!

Merda! I slink down, taking refuge underneath a table piled high with magazines, and busy myself looking through several crates full of paperback novels.

"Isn't this wild?" comes the shrill nasal voice of an older woman as she leads a group of portly American tourists inside the store.

I take advantage of this distraction to make my way over to the adjacent room, where I remain close to the adjoining door so that I can continue listening.

"Welcome!" Luigi calls out to the Americans and then addresses Luciana and Frankie. "Mi scusi, signorine. The afternoon rush of tourists is finally here. Just go toward the back and you will find all the books on music inside that bathtub and on those two bookshelves next to it."

"Grazie, Luigi!" Luciana and Frankie say in unison and they both walk to the exact spot I just vacated.

"Bjorn girno!" I cringe as the American woman thoroughly butchers my language. And Luigi wonders why his daughter, Cristina, doesn't want to return to Venezia in the summer? *Cazzo di turisti!*

It is easy to keep up my surveillance unnoticed amidst the large number of customers who all seem to have chosen this afternoon to descend upon us. For the first time I do not mind the incessant selfie-taking throughout the store, because the crowd provides me with enough coverage so that I can remain in close proximity to Frankie and Luciana without them seeing me.

They seem to be enjoying themselves in their excavation of the bathtub. I watch them step into the gondola outside the "Fire Exit" and peruse through several books.

"Oh, look at this one, Frankie!" says Luciana handing her a paperback. "It has an entire chapter on *Madama Butterfly.*"

"This is perfect!" says Frankie, leafing through it. "And it's not too big. I like books that I can fit into my purse. That way I always have something to read. What a great suggestion, Luciana. This place is magical!"

"Yes, even in a city like Venezia, which is full of interesting locations, this one is quite exceptional."

"I have always loved bookstores," Frankie says. "I find being around books so . . . relaxing. There's something meditative about roaming through the shelves and fingering the spines as I read the titles."

"Even this one?" Luciana sounds surprised. "I understand what you mean about the feeling of relaxation, but I must admit that I find all of this a bit overwhelming. It is a little crazy, no?"

"I think that's part of its charm," says Frankie. "But yeah, I know what you mean." After a pause she says, "Well, I think I found what I was looking for," indicating the paperback Luciana handed her.

"Brava," says Luciana. "Shall we go find someplace for dinner?"

"How about pizza?"

"I know just the place!" says Luciana.

I feel heavy-hearted as I watch them disembark the gondola and step inside the water entrance in preparation to leave the store.

Che stronzo! I am such a fool. What is the matter with me? Now she is departing, and I have missed another opportunity to make her acquaintance. Who knows when, or if, she will ever return?

"Did you find what you were looking for?" asks Luigi when Frankie reaches the cash register.

"Yes! I found the perfect book!" she says, handing him her credit card.

"Va bene, va bene," he replies. "I must say that I am surprised that someone of your generation didn't just look up *Madama Butterfly* on the internet."

"Yes, I did do a bit of research online," Frankie says. "But I still love reading books. And I believe in patronizing local businesses whenever possible."

"Well, I am very impressed," Luigi says. "And grateful for your business. I hope the book will help, but you will also have the advantage of subtitles."

"Subtitles?" Frankie says with surprise and looks inquisitively at Luciana who shrugs her shoulders.

"Si! Il Teatro La Fenice provides subtitles in English," explains Luigi.

"That's fantastic!" says Frankie.

"Si!" agrees Luciana. "That was not the case all those years ago when Mamma and Papà were yearly patrons."

"Now I'm really excited!" Frankie says, placing the book in her purse. "Grazie!"

"Prego," Luigi answers, then turns to Luciana. "Allora, it was wonderful to see you again, Luciana. Please give your family my regards."

"I will!" she replies and then looking around asks, "Is Gio here? I haven't seen him."

Uh-oh! Fortunately, Frankie is already outside looking through the bookmark bins on the table and out of earshot.

"Si, he is around here somewhere," Luigi replies. "He is probably outside in one of the courtyards. That's usually where he likes to hang out." Then in a furtive whisper, Luigi adds, "He keeps an eye out for shoplifters."

Luciana laughs lightly and says, "We will see you soon at La Fenice!"

"Ci vedremo presto!" he replies.

"Arrivederci!" calls Frankie from the courtyard.

"Ciao, ragazze! Come back again."

"Definitely!" answers Frankie. "I'll be here until the beginning of ottobre, so you'll see me again."

Thank heavens! I am so relieved that Frankie will return, but next time I must be better prepared.

"Um, excusi me?" Ugggh. That woman and her friends are still here. "We'll be heading to Bologna in a couple of days," the woman says to Luigi. "How long is the train ride from Venice to Bologna?"

"Hey, I could go for a nice boloney sandwich right about now!" says her loutish companion.

God help me!

I immediately exit through the side door to the back courtyard before my ears are further assaulted by their inane gibberish.

I climb the book staircase and sit on top of the wall. I feel unbearably disappointed in myself. Ah well, this will motivate me to figure out a way to introduce myself to Frankie the next time she comes by.

"Ciao!" I hear the shrill nasal voice again. "Arrevadurcci!"

"Chow mein!" calls out her companion, followed by raucous laughter from the rest of their group.

Idiota!

The clouds are assisting the setting sun in producing another glorious kaleidoscopic light show, accompanied by the reflection on the water, creating a living prism. Is there any other city that has more beautiful sunsets? I doubt it. This daily phenomenon almost makes putting up with the tourists worthwhile. Almost.

Chapter 14 — FRANKIE

"*Tu? Tu? Tu! Piccolo iddio! Amore, amore mio.*" The English subtitles above the stage translated: You? You? You! Little idol of my heart! My love, my love.

This IS *Miss Saigon*!

Mesmerized, I watch Vittoria Yeo, the soprano who plays Cio-Cio-San, the lead role in *Madama Butterfly*, fiercely embrace her little boy one last time before she commits seppuku in the final scene of this opera.

"*Guarda ben! Amore, addio, addio! Piccolo amor!*" Look well! Little love, farewell! Farewell, my little love!

All the comparisons to *Miss Saigon* are front and center for me while I sit inside this lavish, neoclassical-style, historic theatre, watching a renowned piece of opera, which is set in Japan, with a cast of mostly white performers. In the past, the title role has been played by many of the world's greatest opera divas, none of whom were Asian. At least this production stars a soprano from South Korea, so I guess that's an improvement, but still . . .

Cio-Cio-San urges her little boy to go play. After he leaves, she picks up a dagger, and plunges it into her heart. Offstage we hear the mournful cry of her lover, Lieutenant Pinkerton, for his

Butterfly. The orchestra crescendos and culminates with a thunderous combination of timpani and cymbals. Blackout.

The audience erupts in applause. When the performers come onstage for the curtain call, I glance over at Luciana, seated to my left. She is openly weeping and stands up along with the other patrons who are rising from their velvet upholstered chairs. I am applauding and also stand up, but not because I am moved to great emotional depths as Luciana obviously is, but out of appreciation for the talent I have just witnessed.

But I feel a little guilty for my preoccupation with the *Miss Saigon* comparisons, my enjoyment a bit tainted by thoughts about the relentless racism in all aspects of life, including the arts. What makes the inequality within the arts so disappointing is the fact that artists often consider themselves to be people who possess a deeper understanding of the human condition, and yet that doesn't exclude the arts from operating out of the same deeply ingrained biases as all other institutions.

What was it that Bruno said the other night? "Sometimes a thing has to completely collapse so that a whole new way of doing things can be birthed." Here I stand in La Fenice theater. Like the mythical immortal bird, the Phoenix, able to soar out of its own ashes, this renowned landmark has literally been reborn after three devastating fires since it was first built back in 1755. Does something that drastic need to happen within the entire world of the arts?

"O, mio Dio!" Luciana sniffles, rummaging around in her little beaded purse for a tissue. "That was magnificent. Did you like it, Frankie?"

"Yes. Very much," I assure her, not wanting to spoil the experience by confessing all my dark thoughts about the hopelessness of the world. *Jeez, I need to chill out.*

Whenever I become despondent over how little things have changed and the excruciatingly slow march of progress, I try to remind myself what I have heard long-distance runners say when describing a marathon race: In order to believe that you will complete a marathon, you must encourage yourself the entire way and visualize the finish line because that is the only way you'll make it through to the end.

"It's unbelievable that human beings can produce such glorious sounds," I say.

"I *know!*" Luciana says, dramatically placing her hand on her heart. "Their voices are incredible. Thank you so much for inviting me, Frankie. I had forgotten how much I love *Madama Butterfly*. It is definitely my favorite opera."

I paste a smile on my face in response.

We gather our things and wait for the couple who were sharing our box, friends of Maria and her husband, to exit through the door.

"Buona notte," they say to us as they step out into the hallway.

"It was so nice spending the evening with you," Luciana tells them and I wave.

"These were great seats," I say. "I'll have to buy something nice for Maria as a thank you for allowing us to use her tickets."

"Good idea," Luciana says. "Let me know what you find, and I will pay you for half of it. I wish now that my parents had not given up their subscription to La Fenice. These box seats are hard to come by and the productions sell out very quickly. It makes me appreciate all those times they brought Davide and me here. If you are interested, Frankie, they offer tours during the day. You'll be able to go inside the Royal Box, the ballroom, and see the Maria Callas exhibition. Did you know that she began her career here at La Fenice? And if you are lucky, there might be a rehearsal in process during your tour, which you can listen to."

"Yeah, I might check into it," I say. "That would be a great activity to do with my grandma when she joins me in October."

Before we exit the box, I sneak one last glimpse at the lush interior decorations throughout this space. Everywhere I look, we are surrounded by gold leaf and mirrors. I follow Luciana out to the hallway where we join the rest of the exiting patrons, walking past the mint-green doors that lead to the other box seats, and make our way to the two stone staircases in the foyer, which are surrounded by frescoed white moldings, peach-colored walls and terrazzo floor, large marble columns, and crystal chandeliers. The entire building exemplifies the luxury and opulence that must have surrounded the lives of the Venetian aristocracy.

We eventually find ourselves outside, descending the stairs onto the Campo San Fantin. Just as our feet hit the street level, we hear, "Luciana! Frankie!" We both turn around and look back up toward the theatre's main entrance. We spot Luigi at the top of the steps, waving to us. He is accompanied by a woman in a stylish black dress, her hair done up in an elegant chignon. That must be Sofia.

"Luigi, Sofia!" Luciana says as they approach us. "I was afraid we had missed you."

"Ciao bella!" Sofia says bestowing Luciana with kisses.

"Ragazze!" says Luigi. "Did you enjoy the opera?"

"Sì! È stato glorioso!" Luciana gushes.

"Did the book help you, Frankie?" asks Luigi.

"Definitely," I say. "And together with the subtitles, I understood everything!"

"Sofia, this is my friend, Frankie," Luciana introduces me. "She is from America and working at the Hotel Vendramin this summer. She is an actress!"

"Ah," says Sofia, looking appreciatively at me. "How wonderful!"

"It must be so interesting to work at one of the most famous places in the history of Italian theatre," I say, extending my hand to her.

"Sì," she answers. "And attending opening night is always one of my favorite parts of the job. But unfortunately, I have a very early morning tomorrow, so we will not be able to join the cast members in celebration. If we were staying, you could have joined us and met the performers."

"Oh, that is too bad," says Luciana, "but perhaps it is just as well because Frankie and I also have to get up early tomorrow. We are covering for Maria this weekend while she is out of town. That is why she let us use her tickets. And Frankie is staying at my house this week while Mamma and Papà are in Recco. I promised them that we would behave and not have too many parties," she adds with an impish giggle.

"The author, Laurel Thatcher Ulrich said, 'Well-behaved women seldom make history,'" Luigi says with a wink.

"Oh, Luigi!" Sofia playfully scolds him. "Don't be a trouble-maker."

"The production was wonderful, and we had a great time," I say.

"Bravissimo." Sofia says. "Allora, I'm afraid we must be going. It was a pleasure meeting you. Buona notte!"

"Piacere," I answer.

"Ciao!" says Luciana. "It was good to see you again, Sofia."

Sofia begins walking away, and as Luigi passes us he whispers behind the back of his hand, "Between you and me, I am happy to go home to my bed and not have to make small talk with those divas and divos."

Luciana and I smile at him, conspiratorially.

"Buona notte," he says, and catching up to Sofia, offers her his arm as they head down Calle Drio la Chiesa.

"He's quite a character," I laugh.

"Si," Luciana says. "His favorite thing to do when we were growing up was to embarrass his daughter, Cristina, especially when we were teenagers. He was relentless, but always made everyone laugh!" Then after a pause adds, "I'm sorry. I made the decision to end our evening already without asking you. Did you want to go get a drink somewhere?"

"No, it's fine," I say. "We do have to get up early tomorrow."

"Va bene. Let's catch the vaporetto at the Sant' Angelo fermata."

We walk northwest, in the opposite direction as Sofia and Luigi and wind through the streets of the San Marco sestiere arriving at the Fondamenta del Teatro just as a vaporetto pulls up. After scanning our cards, we board the vaporetto and find two seats in the front.

Our vaporetto glides past the government offices housed in the apricot-colored Palazzo Cavalli, under the imposing Rialto

Bridge, and past the rose-colored Palazzo Fontana Rezzonico, the birthplace of Pope Clement XIII. Under the bright moonlight, the Grand Canal shimmers at the foot of all the splendid palazzi.

"I can't get over how surreal this city is. What is it like living in in a place that feels so lost in time?" I ask as our journey takes us by ornate overhanging balconies and intricate Moorish windows. "Does it ever become ordinary?"

"No," says Luciana with a beatific smile. "We Venetians love our city. It is never surprising to us when we hear it called the most beautiful city in the world because we already know it."

I nod in complete comprehension.

"And although it has become increasingly harder for people, such as my grandparents, to live here, most veneziani would like to continue welcoming tourists because without them, the city cannot survive. However, my personal complaint is with those horrible monstrous cruise ships!"

"I agree!" I say. "That collision that occurred at the beginning of June, just before I arrived, must have been awful."

"It was! Not to mention all the erosion and damage they create for the foundation of the city. They are a huge menace with large numbers of tourists disembarking and overtaking the city for just a couple of hours before disappearing without spending any money, which is quite annoying for all the merchants. There have been many protests to stop those ships from coming. I hope eventually they will be banned from entering the laguna altogether. I know that must sound ironic coming from me when my education and livelihood is centered around tourism, but I am also an environmentalist. This way of life is not sustainable for the future of my beloved city."

"I totally understand."

"The other problem that large groups pose is waste management," Luciana continues. "There are times, at the height of tourist season, when the waste bins in Piazza San Marco require emptying *every half hour*! Can you imagine?"

"It's like your father was saying the other night, that we humans take too much for granted and don't stop and think about the effect of our carbon footprints."

Luciana merely nods in agreement and we sit in silence until we reach our stop at San Marcuola Casino. We disembark and walk north toward Rio Terra Farsetti, along the border of the Ghetto Nuovo, the historic Jewish quarter, then continue through Cannaregio to Casa Nardi, Luciana's home.

"Why is *Madama Butterfly* your favorite opera?" I ask as we cross over the bridge at the rio della Misericordia.

"Many operas center around a tragic love story, which after a while, I find tedious," says Luciana. "And although *Madama Butterfly* is also a tragic love story, the best part is the love of a mother for her child."

"Why do you find tragic love stories tedious?" I laugh.

"I am so tired of stories with the message that the most important thing you can ever do in your life is find your one perfect person to be with for all eternity. Ugh, so boring!"

I laugh even harder and quickly cover my mouth when I hear my laughter echo off the walls along the empty, quiet streets. "I never took you for a cynic, Luciana!"

"I know," she laughs softly. "But haven't we women had enough of being told that our ultimate goal in life is to find a good mate so we can finally get married and settle down? Isn't there more to life than just being a wife and mother? I'm so tired of women only being valued as reproductive beings. I'm not even sure I ever want to have children."

"Really? Why?" I am genuinely surprised.

"I guess it's the result of growing up with two environmental scientists and a therapist," she says. "I find it hard to justify bringing new life into this world we are quickly destroying. What kind of future are we leaving for the next generation? Also, because of the work my mother does, I know all too well the many ways we can damage our children."

"I see what you mean," I concur.

"But back to your question about why I like *Madama Butterfly*," she continues. "That story actually makes me reconsider having children."

"Huh?" Now I'm thoroughly confused.

She titters at my reaction. "I know, I am not making any sense," she says, stopping at the top of the wooden bridge over rio di San Alvise, a short distance from her house. "Knowing that I feel reluctant about having children, my father always tells me that the best reason, and in his opinion the *only* reason, for having children is to experience the capacity of God's love."

"How so?" Now I'm intrigued.

"He says that there is no comparison to the love of a parent for their child. It is the purest form of love that we humans can experience because it is completely selfless. Or should be, anyway, if one approaches parenting from an evolved place. But that's the problem, no? My mother says that most humans are not very evolved, so parenting becomes about ego fulfillment and the child is used as a reflection of the parent's sense of self."

"Okaaay," I say, once again feeling my head spinning at the deep level of Luciana's and her parents' philosophical views about life. "So how exactly does a parent's love for their child bring us closer to God than other forms of love, like romantic love or the love between friends?"

"Because we humans always expect something in return in those other kinds of relationships, don't we? It is only in a parent's relationship with their child that we can come anywhere close to experiencing the kind of love that God has for us because we are God's children. A parent loves completely, without requiring anything from the child. A child could misbehave terribly and even tell the parent that they hate them, and still the parent's love would remain true. Isn't that what many of the Psalms are? Human beings having temper tantrums and railing against God? So, it is that sacrifice the mother in *Madama Butterfly* makes to save her son that illustrates what my father has always told me, and I realize he is probably right. That kind of love is the closest we can ever get to understanding how much God loves us. That is why it is my favorite opera and why it makes me rethink my decision about having children. It always brings me to tears."

You who I cradled in my arms.

"Frankie? Frankie!"

There is a keening—raw and mournful.

"Dio, mio! Cosa succeded? Frankie, what is wrong?"

The howl is guttural. Animalistic.

I swear I'll give my life for you.

The whine is the caterwaul of a feral cat. But the wailing does not emanate from anything feline. The sound is me.

"Frankie!" Luciana cries. "Are you hurt? What is the matter?"

I am in a heap, having fallen onto the wooden slats of the bridge, my two hands desperately holding on to the wooden rail, as if, were I to let go, I would continue falling to the earth's molten core. *What if I did? Maybe I should.* Body-racking sobs make it almost impossible to breathe.

It's so odd—I have spent years perfecting the art of resisting tears and behaving like someone who has come out the other side of grief, and so often, my guilt, shame, self-doubt, and confusion were easier to handle than grief. But then I hear a song, see a movie, read a story, or engage in conversations with people who echo the deepest truths I have always carried within my soul . . . and everything collapses. It's curious that I didn't cry at the end of *Miss Saigon* or *Madama Butterfly*, but Luciana's description of her father's astute insight has completely undone me.

"Frankie," Luciana says, sinking down to my level, placing her arm around me. "You are scaring me. Are you injured? Can you answer me that?"

I take in a ragged breath and manage to shake my head—no.

Luciana exhales a sigh of relief and says, "Okay, shhh. You're alright. Can you stand? Here, let me help you. We are very close to home. Shhh, shhh, it's okay. I have you. Be careful on the steps. Hold on to me. You're okay. Shhh."

With one arm around my shoulders, the other holding my hand, Luciana guides me down the stairs and onto the Fondamenta Riformati. She leads me along the walkway as I continue sobbing, blinded by my tears and rapidly swelling eyes. The entire way, Luciana coos softly, as if comforting a lost child.

We reach the door to her house, and I lean against the wall of the building while she retrieves the keys from her purse and unlocks the door. My crying has subsided somewhat, but my eyes remain closed and my breath comes in gasps.

"Come on, Frankie, we are home now," Luciana places her arm around me again, guides me inside, closes the door behind us, and leads me up the stairs to her apartment.

At the top of the landing, she keeps her arm around my shoulders while she unlocks the door with one hand. She turns the knob, pushes the door open, and tenderly leads me inside.

I have stopped crying, but my eyes are painfully swollen. I keep them closed and stand still while she closes and bolts the door to lock it, then turns on a light switch.

I am so tired. So very tired.

"Come sit down, Frankie," she says and leads me over to the sofa in the living room.

I sit, and hear her leave the room and go into the bathroom and then the kitchen. She returns, and I feel her take a seat next to me on the sofa. She places a tissue in my hand.

"Here," she says. "Have some water."

My eyes are raw, burning slits but I manage to open them enough to see the glass of water she hands me. I take two long gulps and set the glass down on the coffee table, then blow my nose on the tissue. After setting the used tissue on the table next to the glass, I lean back on the sofa, eyes closed, and let out a deep exhale.

"Frankie?" Luciana says tentatively. "Is there anything I can do for you?"

At her gentle request, new tears spring forth and I lean forward, placing my wet, puffy face in my hands.

"Oh, Frankie. I am so sorry. Do you want to talk about it?"

Oh, Luciana. Where do I even begin?

I am weeping for the traumatized little girl who watched her parents tear each other apart with their rage—at times they almost literally killed each other. I lament all the times she felt scared and alone, yet her fears were met with scorn and resentment for daring to require so much attention.

I mourn for the girl who, no matter how hard she tried to be good, her efforts were often met with disapproval and scolding.

Mostly I feel tremendous sadness for the young child who kept a terrible secret: that before she was five years old, she was sexually molested by two different people. She never told anyone because she was afraid that she would get in trouble and be blamed, or worse—she wouldn't be believed. She still hasn't told anyone. Not even her therapist.

And finally, I grieve for the parents who loved me as best they could, but who still came up short, and with whom I will never have the opportunity to reconcile. The art of living seems to reside somewhere in the delicate balance of forgiving and letting go of the past and holding on to love and hope for the future. It seems that I have felt off-balance my entire life.

Is that why I feel so heavy?

"Frankie, would you like me to draw a warm bath for you? Perhaps it will help you relax, and you will feel better, hmm?"

I nod feebly and whisper, "Okay. Thank you."

I lean back on the sofa again, keeping my eyes closed, while Luciana turns the water on in the bathroom. I have a splitting headache.

"Come," Luciana says, and I feel her take my hand. With her assistance I stand and allow her to guide me toward the bathroom.

We step inside and a subtle floral scent envelops the room.

"I added some lavender-scented Epsom salts," Luciana tells me. "I hope that's okay."

"Thank you," I repeat.

"Take your time, Frankie. Let me know if you need anything." She shuts off the water and gently closes the door, leaving me alone.

Every movement is an exhaustive effort as I slowly undress, avoiding the mirror and my swollen reflection. I step into the tub and the water greets me with soothing amniotic warmth.

I want to remain here and drift into nothingness. Living, feeling . . . it's so hard. I don't want to feel anymore . . .

* * * * *

My eyes fly open and I gasp. I must have fallen asleep. I don't remember dozing off. I have no idea how long I've slept, but the water is starting to chill. I remove the stopper and allow the water to drain while I reach for a towel and begin drying off. I wrap the towel around my body and brush my teeth, still avoiding my ragged reflection in the mirror above the sink. I pick up my discarded clothes off the floor and walk down the hall to Davide's room, where I am staying. The apartment is quiet, but I notice a light emanating from the living room.

After I finish getting into my PJ's, I hang up my towel in the bathroom and return to the living room. Luciana is seated on the sofa, wrapped in a light blanket, eyes closed. As I approach, she opens her eyes and smiles.

"Oh! I guess I fell asleep."

"I'm so sorry," I say. "I didn't mean to keep you up so late. You didn't need to wait for me. Please go to bed."

"No, it's okay," she insists. "I made some tea. Would you like some?" She indicates two porcelain cups and a matching teapot covered in a colorful, paisley cozy sitting on top of the coffee table.

I am beyond exhausted, but after all the care she has bestowed upon me, the least I can do is stay up with her a little while longer. I owe her an explanation.

I nod and sit down next to her. She pours the tea into the cups.

"It's herbal," she says handing me my cup. "So it won't keep us awake all night. Also, here are a couple of aspirin. In case you have a headache."

"Luciana, I don't know how to thank you."

"Fa niente, Frankie. Are you feeling better?"

"Yes," I say wrapping both hands around the delicate cup, feeling the warmth, and take a tentative sip. Chamomile. "Um, it's good."

She smiles and drinks her tea.

I take another sip and set my cup down on the coffee table. I position myself on the sofa so that I can look directly at Luciana with my legs tucked underneath me and take a deep breath before I begin speaking.

"Luciana, I'm sorry I scared you. I had no idea I would fall apart like that. It surprised me as much as you. Maybe more so because I thought I had gotten over it."

"What happened, Frankie?"

"You know how I told you about my parents and how they died?"

She nods.

"Well, that was only part of the ordeal. While they were alive there was immeasurable sadness and so much that I regret. And now I will never have the chance to make things right. Or to let them know that even though they made terrible mistakes and hurt me deeply, that I forgive them. I feel so lost and I don't know how to move forward. Sometimes I feel fundamentally broken."

Tears well up again and I take a tissue from the box on the coffee table. Luciana places her cup on the table and pats my thigh lightly while I blow my nose.

"What you told me about your father and his explanation of parental love made me realize that my parents did the best they could with what they knew," I continue. "And if they had known better, they would have done better. But we are all victims of victims because everyone is damaged and afraid. My parents simply were unable to do better because they themselves had been deprived of security and love during their formative years. I just wish I had had that knowledge earlier. And I wish I had appreciated all the sacrifices they made for me while they were still alive."

"Oh, Frankie," Luciana says softly. "Mi dispiace tanto. I am so sorry."

"My parents were very fearful and shame-based. With immigrants there is often incredible hardship in getting to their new home, and it affects how they see the world. I know now that that is why they had such unrealistic expectations of me, but at the time all I felt was that I was unlovable, unworthy, and a constant disappointment. And when you are the child of addiction, you have to grow up too fast and your heart gets broken a lot. You have to act like an adult while you still have the mind and needs of a child."

"I wish my mother were here so you could talk to her, Frankie. She would know just the right and perfect thing to tell you and advise you. But I can tell you this—my mother always says that in therapy there are only two people we all need to deal with in order to heal: our parents. She even encourages Davide and me to go into our own therapy because she believes that the only people who do not need therapy are the people who had perfect parents."

"That probably rules out about 99% of the world," I say.

"Exactly. But I know how fortunate we have been because the greatest gift my parents gave Davide and me was recognizing us as individuals. They allowed us our temperament and did not impose their expectations on us. My mother says the most important thing is to parent the child you *have*, not the child you *want.*"

"Oh, my God," I say. "That makes so much sense. I always felt that I was the wrong child for my parents. I was too feisty, too gregarious, too loud, too emotional, too sensitive, just . . . too much of everything that they disliked or made them uncomfortable. And I also felt that my father would have been happier if I had been a boy, so I tried to be athletic and sporty to please him, but I am no athlete. My mom always wanted me to become a nurse because that was what she wanted to be but could never afford to go to school. I was always happier reading, drawing, writing, dancing, singing, and playing pretend. I strongly suspect that had they lived, they would have felt that getting my degree in Theatre Arts was a waste of time and money."

"My mother often quotes Carl Jung, who said that the greatest tragedy of a child is the unlived life of a parent. That is the thing that often gets in the way of a parent seeing their child's own uniqueness, no?"

I stare at Luciana wordlessly, so impressed by this young woman's understanding and infinite compassion.

"Grazie mille," I say and squeeze her hand.

From an open window we hear the nearest church bells pealing, followed by others farther away.

"Oh, my God!" I say, realizing how late it is. "We should go to bed. I'm sorry I kept you up so late. Thank you so much for listening, for the tea, the bath, for everything!"

"Fa niente. Are you sure you are okay?"

"Yes," I assure her and pick up the two aspirin from the table. I down them with the remainder of my lukewarm tea and carry the two cups into the kitchen while Luciana follows with the teapot.

"Just leave everything in the sink," she says. "We can deal with them later." She goes to the refrigerator and takes something out of the freezer. "Here," she says, handing me a small white bundle. "I wet and froze a wash cloth. You can place it over your eyes while you fall asleep. It should help with the swelling."

"You're the best, Luciana."

We both walk down the hall to our respective bedrooms and at the door to Davide's room, Luciana surprises me with two effusive, well-planted kisses, instead of the usual air-kisses, and a warm hug.

"Buona notte, Frankie. I hope you sleep well. Sogni d'oro!" She walks to her room.

"Sweet dreams to you too," I answer back, then just before I enter my room I call out, "Luciana!"

She turns to look at me.

"I have no doubt that whatever you decide, it will be the perfect choice for you. But for what it's worth, I think you would make a wonderful mother."

Placing a hand on her heart, she smiles sweetly, and says, "Grazie."

We each close our doors and I slip into bed. I reach over to my phone sitting on the nightstand and am about to turn it off when I see a text from Mayra:

> How was Madama Butterfly?

I reply:

> Good. La Fenice is breathtaking! I'll fill you in
> tomorrow. Going to bed. Ciao!

She still has trouble taking into account the nine-hour time difference. I turn off my phone and seem to fall asleep before my head hits the pillow.

Chapter 15 — FRANKIE

Venice, Italy
Sunday, September 1, 2019

"Hi there," the policeman says. "Are you okay?" I am hiding under the kitchen table. I put my hands over my ears, but I can still hear the yelling. Mami and Papi are fighting again. Papi hit Mami really hard. Mami is holding the big rock we use to keep the door open. She yells at Papi to stay away or she will throw the rock at him. Another policeman is talking to Papi. "Hey, you're alright," the policeman says to me. "Do you want to come out and sit with me?" "I'm scared," I say. "I know," he says. "It's okay." Mami and Papi are still yelling, but I come out from under the table and sit on one of the chairs next to the policeman. He is nice. He lets me wear his police hat and it is too big for my head. It makes me laugh. "Do you like to play games?" he asks. "I like to draw," I say. "Wow, that's neat. I bet you're really good at it." I smile. Mami and Papi have stopped yelling, but Mami is crying. "Can I go home with you?" I ask the Policeman. "No, sweetie, I'm sorry. You need to stay here." "But I'll be really good, I promise!" The two policemen are leaving. I watch them through the window getting into their police car. I bang on the window to get their attention. The nice policeman waves goodbye. I keep banging on the window.

Bong-bong-bong-bong-bong!

The cacophony of bells announces that it is five o'clock in the afternoon. I reluctantly open my eyes and see soft amber light filtered through the shutters. I have napped for three hours!

Exactly twelve hours ago, Luciana and I dragged our weary bodies out of bed and hastily got ourselves ready to report for work. We walked in sleepy silence through the empty streets, arriving at the Hotel Vendramin at 6 a.m. on the dot, giving us plenty of time to partake in strong cups of caffè latte and a cornetto, the Italian version of a French croissant, before we began preparations for the breakfast service.

Today marks the beginning of the off-season and already the hotel is only at 75% capacity, making our job easy to handle in Maria's absence. After Luciana assisted me in laying out all the food for the hotel guests, she took her place at the front desk, recently vacated by Paolo after working his night shift.

"Mamma mia!" Paolo had declared when we first walked in. "You two look like you have been celebrating all night at Carnevale!"

Luciana mumbled something about the opera letting out late and he knew better than to inquire or tease us further.

Our shifts completed at 1 p.m.; we wasted no time coming back to Luciana's house where we both headed to our rooms for a much-anticipated pisolino, but I only intended to nap for a half hour or so.

I indulge in a long luxurious stretch and realize that I am hungry, having forgone lunch for the much-needed siesta. The apartment is very quiet. I wonder if Luciana is still asleep?

I walk out of my room and notice that Luciana's bedroom door is open and peek inside. No Luciana. I continue down the hall, into the living room and see her seated out on the terrace.

"Ciao," I say, stepping outside.

"Ciao bella! Did you have a good nap?" She holds a cup of caffè normale since it is well past noon and the Italians only drink coffee with milk in the morning.

"Yes! I can't believe it's so late. Have you been awake long?"

"No. I just got up about a half hour ago. Would you like some caffè?

"No, thanks," I say, still not having gotten used to the Italian habit of drinking coffee into the afternoon and evening hours. "If I have coffee now then I'll be up all night and I'll never get back on schedule."

"Si," Luciana laughs lightheartedly. "Are you hungry?"

"I'm starved!"

"Me too! Let's go to Osteria alla Vedova. I'm in the mood for some spaghetti con vongole.

"Sounds yummy. Give me just a few minutes and I'll be ready to go."

"Va bene," she says airily, and I head for the bathroom while she takes her empty coffee cup into the kitchen.

In the bathroom I brush my teeth and try to comb my tousled hair into some semblance of presentability. I gather it in a low ponytail, then rinse my face with cold water. The nap and cold water seemed to have done the trick and my face looks almost normal again after my "ugly cry" last night. How do those actresses do it? The ones who manage to look beautiful while crying on camera. If I had to do more than one take, I would need to receive cortisone injections directly into my face. Maybe that's why they all inject themselves with Botox.

I grab my purse from my room and encounter Luciana waiting for me in the living room.

"Pronta?" she asks.

"Ready!" I answer, and we head out.

We walk down to Fondamenta dei Ormesini before it inexplicably turns into Fondamenta Misericordia and pass by a long succession of restaurants and bars, the crowds already noticeably diminished now that many of the tourists have returned home. Fondamenta Misericordia takes us over Ponte Chiodo, a historic canal footbridge, unusual for its lack of balustrades. We walk over one more bridge across riello de Santa Sofia and shortly arrive at Osteria alla Vedova. This casual eatery is definitely off the beaten path and a true local hangout.

Luciana and I find a table near a window at the rear of the narrow, intimate dining room. The waiter hands us our menus and leaves. The leisurely pace of Italian waiters compared to their American counterparts is something I've grown accustomed to, but at this moment, famished as I am, I want to order and eat NOW!

"Do you mind if we order soon?" I ask Luciana. "I'm really hungry since we missed lunch."

"No problem," Luciana says and signals our waiter as if she were hailing a cab. He approaches our table, and she asks me, "Would you like something to drink?"

"Un vino rosso per favore," I tell the waiter.

"Due," Luciana adds, "E una bottiglia di acqua minerale naturale. Grazie!"

He leaves with a nod and a smile.

I peruse through the menu, but Luciana lays down her menu without looking at it and declares, "I already know what I want."

"What do you recommend?" I ask.

"The spaghetti con vongole and con gamberetto are my favorite," she says, pointing out the items on my menu. "I will have the spaghetti con vongole."

"Okay," I say ceremoniously closing my menu. "Then, I will have the spaghetti con gamberetto."

"Molto bene," Luciana replies.

Our waiter reappears with two glasses of red wine and a large bottle of mineral water. He pours some of the contents of the bottle into the two water glasses already on our table. He takes our order and our menus, swiftly making his way to the kitchen. We were among the first customers to arrive at the restaurant just after it opened for dinner, and now it is becoming busier, with several locals sitting in the bar area for an aperitivo and cicchetti, a small snack or side dish, before dinner.

"Oh!" Luciana exclaims. "I forgot to tell you. Mamma and Papà called while you were still asleep. They are all doing well and asked how we enjoyed the opera. I told them we saw Luigi and Sofia and that our box seats were incredibly close to the Royal Box. They said Maria and her husband must have been patrons for a very long time in order to obtain such premium seats. Each year, subscribers get to move up just a little closer to the center."

Although Luciana has not mentioned my breakdown at all today, I am feeling a little embarrassed, with that insidiously familiar feeling of shame starting to creep in. I often picture shame as the Grim Reaper, scolding me by wagging its evil, wretched, cadaverous finger.

"Luciana, thank you again for all your help last night," I say. "I really appreciate your understanding and all your kind words of advice. I feel a little guilty, though, because it was a lot of heavy stuff to dump on you, especially since we really haven't known each other very long."

"Do not worry, Frankie," she says gently. "We are friends. It does not matter that we have only been friends for a short time, because I can already see that you are a good person. I feel honored that you trusted me with the pain of your past. And that is what creates true connection because I think a person must earn the privilege of hearing another's story. I believe that our painful experiences are not a liability but a gift because it awakens our empathy and compassion. Also, my mother often warns me that we must be careful to not judge ourselves harshly when asking for help, because if we cannot ask for help without seeing it as weak, then we will not be able to offer anyone else help without considering them weak."

"Oh, my gosh," I say. "That is exactly the kind of thing my grandma tells me all the time. I so wish you two could meet. I'm bummed that you'll be back at school by the time she arrives in Venezia. Not to mention the fact that I'll miss you terribly when you leave. Your friendship has been one of the best things about this trip!"

"Aw, for me too, Frankie! What is your itinerary for your trip with your nonna?"

"We don't actually have one, other than we'll be concentrating on the northern half of Italia. Since ottobre is off-season, we figured we could be somewhat spontaneous. I think we'll decide where to go and make hotel reservations a couple of days beforehand. We'll have the entire month, so we can kind of take our time."

"In that case, why don't you come visit me in Milano?" Luciana asks with a huge grin. "It is my second home, and I can give you the grand tour! There is a nice pensione on the same street as my apartment. I would invite you to stay with me, but the second bedroom will be occupied by my roommate, Gabriella, who will be back from her home in Trento. My parents own the apartment and during the summer when my roommate and I are gone, they rent it out through Airbnb. There are so many interesting sights in Milano—Parco Sempione, Castello Sforzesco, and my favorite pizzeria, Pizza OK."

"Pizza OK?!" I say. "Are you serious?"

"It's a silly name, I know. But the pizza is the best! And I'll introduce you to the finest waiter, Max. He will treat you and your nonna like royalty. And the Duomo! Oh, you must see it. If you enjoy visiting all the churches here in Venezia, wait until you see the Duomo di Milano!" She leans forward, sneakily looks around, and in a low voice says, "Don't tell anyone, but I think it rivals our own Basilica San Marco."

"Luciana!" I say in mock horror. "If any of your fellow veneziani hear you, they will have you locked up for treason and blasphemy."

She leans back in her chair with a smug look. "Yes, I know. But I cannot tell a lie." She leans forward again and snickers, "No, but seriously, it truly is magnificent."

Our waiter arrives with our meals. Luciana's plate of spaghetti is topped with a generous number of clams in their shells and mine with two giant prawns, complete with head and abdomen. He leaves both of us an extra plate for all the discarded shells . . . and body parts. This is something else I have grown accustomed to. Here in Italy, even pizza con frutti di mare is served with all the shellfish still in its shells. Perhaps if we Americans got used to eating seafood dishes this way, it would force us to slow down and eat at a much more leisurely and enjoyable pace.

The waiter wishes us, "Buon appetito," and disappears for the remainder of our meal, so unlike American servers who constantly interrupt with, "How is everything?"

"So, what do you say?" inquires Luciana after we have both taken our first bite. "Will you come to Milano? My parents and I will be returning to Recco in a couple of weeks and we will stop in Milano first, where they will help me move back into the apartment before school starts. Then, on our way back home from Recco, together with my grandparents, we will all stop in Milano again, where we will have one final family dinner and the four of them will continue on to Venezia. So, I will be back in my apartment by October 1ˢᵗ, when classes begin. Even if I am busy with classes, I will give you and your nonna lots of suggestions on where to go and I can join you in the later part of the day. Obviously, if you are there during a weekend, then I can accompany you the entire time. What do you think?"

"Luciana, how can I possibly say 'No' to you? Of course!"

"Meraviglioso! Just give me a couple of days' notice, so I can make reservations at the pensione for you. I can probably get you a discount."

"You're fantastic!" I lift my wine up to her and we clink glasses.

"I assume at least Roma is on your non-existent itinerary, no?" she inquires.

"Yes, Roma and Firenze are definitely on the must-see list."

"Good! Then I will give you Davide's phone number and address where he and Chiara live. I know they would be happy to host you and show you some of the sights in Roma. And I'm sure my parents would love to have you over for dinner once more so they can meet your nonna. See, Frankie? You have a whole new family here in Italia."

This time I don't even try to suppress the tears and allow them to tumble freely down my cheeks.

"Grazie, my alien soul sister," I manage to choke out while wiping my face with my napkin.

"Sorelle forever," she smiles back.

*　*　*　*　*

Two hours later, our appetites thoroughly satisfied, we emerge from the restaurant and begin walking home.

"How about a gelato?" Luciana asks.

"Well, if you insist . . ."

Luciana laughs. "There is always room for gelato, no?"

"Naturalmente!"

We wind up back on the Fondamenta dei Ormesini at Gelato Artegianale, where I order a scoop of pistacchio, and Luciana orders bacio, a chocolate/hazelnut combination. After receiving our cones, we step outside the gelateria and sit down on the edge of the fondamenta, dangling our legs and feet over the water.

"Oh, Luciana," I sigh, relishing the quiet tranquility of another glorious Venetian evening, "I wish I could stay here forever."

"Why don't you?" she asks in all seriousness.

I stare at her. "How? I don't know where I would find another job. And even if I could, I don't know how I would go about getting a job permit and extending my visa. The only thing I know for sure is that I really do not want to go back home."

"Why is that?"

"Oh, my God, there are so many reasons," I groan. "I'm having serious doubts that I'll ever be able to make it as a professional actress. And right now, the United States is so screwed up I can't stomach going back to that mess. The worst part is that although there have always been different political opinions, never before has there been such hateful division. I mean, people on different sides of the political spectrum can't even have a civil conversation anymore. Everyone just yells at each other. No one listens. All objective reality and truth has gone out the window, along with subtlety and nuance. Everything is either black or white. You can't even count on the TV news coverage to give unbiased reports because crazy conservative media conglomerates no longer even resemble true journalism, but instead spend all their time kissing our so-called leader's ass just so they can get higher ratings. The talking heads they prop up in front of their cameras do nothing but spew lie after lie and spread all kinds of ridiculous conspiracy theories. And people actually believe them! But you should see the facial expressions on those news reporters when Agent Orange comes on, ranting and raving. Even *they* have a look like, 'What the fuck?!' It's so ludicrous."

"E pazzesco!"

"Yes! It is crazy!" I say. "But the worst part is the cowardice and unethical conduct of the members of his own party in

Congress who, for some unfathomable reason, will not hold that bastard accountable! I swear, his number one henchman, the Senate Majority Leader, will go down as one of the most evil bastards in history. I just don't get it. It is absolutely reprehensible. And I hate to say it, but I know people who voted for Agent Orange and I can hardly stand being in their company because I just don't understand how they can still support him after all the evidence that proves his utter incompetence."

"People can be very blind," Luciana says. "Especially when what they believed turns out to be false. People, in general, have a hard time admitting when they are wrong."

"But that's just it—he's not only incompetent, he's an absolute narcissistic maniac, completely devoid of empathy who cares about nothing and no one but himself! But he knows exactly what he's doing to fuel the fire of his supporters. How can people not see that? It's so obvious!"

Luciana shakes her head. "If it makes you feel any better, I don't think Americans are the only ones who fall for such dishonesty. We humans seem to be vulnerable to deception. I think it starts with believing in Saint Nicholas, Father Christmas, Santa Claus, or whatever you wish to call him. We are taught as children to silence and ignore that critical part of our brains for some reward."

I stare at her completely dumbfounded. "You are so right! I never thought of it that way. I guess as a kid I thought believing in the Easter Bunny and the Tooth Fairy was fun, but that is how it starts! It sets us up for disregarding our intuition and that voice we all have inside us that says, 'Wait a minute, that can't be true!' It's no wonder people are willing to kill themselves in order to pull off a terrorist attack if they believe they'll immediately enter eternal paradise."

"Not to mention being surrounded by seventy-two virgins, or whatever it is they believe," Luciana says.

"Oh, my God!" I moan. "Why are we sooo gullible? Pretty soon we will have another presidential election and I cannot tell you how scared I am that he will be re-elected."

"But how is that possible?" Luciana asks. "If he is so awful, surely he will be replaced, no?"

"Throughout his campaign, many people couldn't have envisioned that such an idiot would ever succeed in rising to the most powerful position of leadership in the world, and yet, here we are. It's unbelievable! His entire presidency has already been a nightmare. I can't imagine how much worse it will be if he gets re-elected. Not to mention that I don't feel safe in my brown skin even though I am a full-fledged American citizen."

"Really?" she asks with a look of shock. "Why?"

"Because he is a blatant, unapologetic racist! And his supporters just cheer him on. You should see the videos of his rallies. It's like they've all been drugged or brainwashed or something. Right now, he is attacking undocumented immigrants, but I know it is just a stepping stone to what he's really after, which is to rid the entire country of anyone who isn't white."

"He sounds like Hitler."

"Oh, my God, yes! And ICE, the U.S. Immigration and Customs Enforcement, has become like the SS. It has been torturous watching people get thrown into cages like animals with children and babies being ripped away from their parents at the U.S. immigration detention centers."

"Throughout Europa, we are also experiencing a massive arrival of migrants, refugees, and asylum seekers. It is a very big challenge, and no country has figured out how to deal with the problem. But putting people in cages and tearing children out of parents' arms is inhumane."

"Precisely," I say. "There is no excuse for treating people that way, especially when they are leaving horrible situations in their homelands and literally fleeing to save their lives. What happened to basic decency and compassion? I've often thought that I should be out there with them, doing something to help, but I feel so helpless and useless."

After a few moments of silence, Luciana says, "No one gives birth alone. The job of the midwife is, perhaps, just as essential as the body that is doing the creating."

I gawk at her. "Luciana, you sound like a fortune cookie."

She guffaws uproariously, almost spilling her gelato into the canal.

I laugh along with her. "What on earth are you talking about?!"

She composes herself and after wiping her mouth with a napkin explains, "We can't all be down there amidst the blood and the guts. Sometimes we are there marching and fighting along with the others, but it is also important to tell the stories of the ones who are in the middle of the stories. There is a place for the people who are telling the stories as well. Maybe that is you, Frankie. Perhaps it is through your astute observation and your art that you can help create change."

I gaze into the water, watching the moonlight playfully reflect on the surface as a small motorboat slowly passes in front of us. I know she has a point, but I can feel myself starting to become discouraged as my self-doubt creeps in. How could I possibly make a difference?

I try to shake off the negative thoughts and bring myself back to the present moment when Luciana says, "What about the Belli Libri dell'Acqua Alta?"

"Huh?"

"The Belli Libri dell'Acqua Alta!" Luciana repeats. "Didn't Luigi say he was thinking of hiring someone to help him organize the bookstore? And you, yourself, expressed how much you love bookstores. It's perfect! You are meant for each other, no? And what better place to inspire a writer?"

"Do you really think he would hire me?"

"Of course! Why not?"

"Well," I say, "wouldn't it be easier for him to hire someone local? I mean, the fact that I am a foreigner who requires a work permit and visa makes hiring someone like me way more complicated than he probably wants."

"Yes, but you are forgetting something," she insists.

"What?"

"His wife, Sofia, works for La Fenice," she declares triumphantly.

Bemused, I don't even bother to hide my confusion and dryly ask, "Luciana, *whyyy* are you speaking in riddles?"

"Sofia works with foreigners all the time at the opera because they bring in artists from all over the world. If anyone knows how to obtain work visas and permits, it is her!" Luciana responds with a self-satisfied expression.

"Oh, wow."

"I'm sure it is just a matter of applying at the Commissariato San Marco, the State Police. Sofia will certainly know how to navigate all the bureaucracy."

"Oh, my God, Luciana, that would be so awesome!"

"Where there is a will, there is a way, Frankie. Always."

I let out a squeal of delight and give her a hug. I'm trying not to get ahead of myself, but this idea, if it works, would be a dream come true. "I'm gonna call my grandma tonight. I'm sure she'll be more than thrilled to have me pursue this plan, but I want to let her in on it before I approach Luigi. I should probably talk to him as soon as possible, don't you think? Didn't he say they were going to be out of town sometime in Ottobre?"

"Si, they will be visiting Cristina in Padova."

"I should go see him first thing tomorrow morning since I have the day off because if, by some miracle, he decides to hire me, I'll need time to get everything organized before they leave for Padova and my grandma arrives. I may need her to bring some extra clothes and other items for me."

"I agree."

"This is so exciting, Luciana! Once again, you have come to my rescue."

"I assure you that it is purely self-serving," she states dramatically. "I don't want you to leave Italia either, so there!"

We finish our gelato, and I am floating on air as we walk back to Luciana's house.

As soon as we arrive, I race into my bedroom and call Grandma.

"Frankie! How are you? Is everything okay?"

"Hi, Grandma! Yes, everything's great. How are you doing?"

"Oh, I'm just fine. Had some friends over on Saturday for a barbeque. The weather has been lovely. What's going on with you? It must be pretty late over there."

"Yes, I'm about to get ready for bed, but I had to tell you some exciting news! I may have found an opportunity for another job so I can stay here in Venice."

"Oh, Frankie! That's wonderful! Tell me all about it."

"You remember that fantastic bookstore I wrote you about?"

"Yes. The one that floods?"

"Belli Libri dell'Acqua Alta. It's not a for-sure thing yet, but the proprietor wants to hire some extra help and Luciana thinks his wife can help me with permits and visas. I'm planning on going there tomorrow and talk to him about applying for the job, but I wanted to let you know first."

"Frankie, that sounds perfect! What about a place to live? You can't stay at the hotel, can you?"

"No, I haven't gotten that far yet. I guess I'll have to rent a place. I'll cross that bridge when I get to it," I titter. "That expression takes on a whole new meaning here in Venice. Anyway, let me first see if I can even get this job."

"Well, you know you have my total support."

"Thanks, Grandma."

"How long do you plan to stay there?"

"Ideally, I would love to stay a full year. I think it would be great to experience Venice through all the seasons. Already, it feels so different than it did just a week ago when it was still crowded with tourists."

"Well then, I guess I'll have to go out there for Christmas. Unless you're thinking of coming back to California for the holidays. But wouldn't it be fun to spend Christmas in Europe? Oh! We could travel to Germany and go to all those Christmas markets they're famous for! Wouldn't that be something? And of course, I'll have to come visit you during Carnival! What fun!"

"Grandma!" I laugh. "You might as well move in with me. Won't all that flying back and forth get expensive?"

"Frankie, you know what they say—you can't take it with you. I'm so excited for you, sweetheart. Let me know as soon as you find out."

"I will. I'll call you tomorrow right after I speak with Luigi."

"So . . . how is everything else?" Grandma asks, somewhat tentative. "Are you doing alright?"

"Yeah, Grandma. I'm good," I assure her.

"Oh, good. Good." Then after a peculiar pause, "I can't wait to see you. Do you need me to bring you anything?"

"Well, if I land this job, I'll probably need you to bring me some extra clothes and a winter coat."

"Of course."

"Oh! And Luciana has offered to be our personal tour guide in Milan! She also says her brother and fiancé can show us around Rome!"

"That's great! I can't wait to meet them."

"Well, I should probably get some sleep," I say. "I've been getting to bed late the last couple of nights. I want to get to the bookstore when it first opens tomorrow morning so I can talk to Luigi before the store gets busy."

"Okay. Good luck! I love you."

"I love you too, Grandma. Ciao!"

Chapter 16 — FRANCESCA

Venezia, Italia
Martedì 21 novembre 1550

My foot touches down on icy water.

"Dio!" I exclaim, scrambling back up the steps. It is dark and my eyes have not yet adjusted. Why are the torches not lit?

"Alfredo? Giovanni?" I call out, but my voice is muted by the howling wind. Where are they?

My eyes are starting to adapt, and I can now see the water entrance and the torrential rain just outside it. As I continue peering through the darkness, I notice that the water from the canal has risen over the fondamenta and is covering the entire floor of this lower level of the palazzo in roughly three centimeters of water. The acqua alta has arrived.

The wind kicks up again and blasts through the water entrance, spraying me all the way back on the stairs with cold rain. No wonder all the candles have blown out. But where are Giovanni and Alfredo? Earlier this evening after all the guests arrived, their oarsmen and gondolieri were invited to remain upstairs in the dry warmth of the kitchen, since Giovanni and Alfredo determined they did not require further assistance safeguarding all the vessels.

I remove my leather slippers and hold them in one hand while I lift my gown with the other. I inhale sharply as my feet make contact with the chilly water and I gingerly walk across the wet stone floor. I reach the door to the storage room and push it open. "Alfredo? Giovanni?" There is no one inside, but the floor in here sits a bit higher than the other room and is still dry, so this is where I will wait for them. During the wet season, the door becomes heavy and swollen with water and does not remain open on its own. I locate the large rock Alfredo uses to prop it open and place it up against the rough wood, leaving the door wide open so I can continue watching the water entrance for Alfredo and Giovanni.

There is a flash of lightning and a thunderclap makes me jump. Mio Dio, this storm is fierce!

* * * * *

Just a few hours ago, when I left Giovanni down here with Alfredo, I rejoined my Zia Veronica and Signor Vendramin upstairs in the dining room, where I discovered them trying on their maschere and I found myself in the whimsical company of Arlecchino and Colombina. Signor Vendramin's Arlecchino was a leather half-mask with a short, wide nose, arching eyebrows, and a bump on the forehead. Zia Veronica's Colombina was also a half-mask, covering her eyes and cheeks in silver and gold, and elaborately decorated with a spray of feathers emanating from the top.

Masks have been a part of our history for two hundred years. Venezia has one of the most rigid and elaborate set of social classes, and masks are a method of not only hiding one's identity, but also of hiding one's class. For many years, Venezia has enjoyed the position of an important meeting site for writers of northern Italia due to the proliferation of publishing houses. Literary salons such as the ones hosted by Signor Vendramin offer poets, especially those from the terraferma, an intellectual forum in the absence of a centralized court. Writers often travel great distances to consult with Signor Vendramin about their literary projects. Holding a masked affair makes it possible for writers of all classes to participate without discrimination.

"Ah, Francesca!" my zia exclaimed when she saw me. "Come see the beautiful mask Domenico has brought for you."

I approached them, smiling at their childlike glee and the playful delight they were taking in their disguises.

My zia picked up a small bundle off the dining table and carefully extracted my mask from the cloth it was wrapped in. "For you, cara ragazza," she said, presenting it to me, "Il gatto!"

The cat mask represents the city's feline friend, which is considered our hero and the greatest ally in the fight against the Plague because it ensures the rats that frequently come off the ships in our port are held at bay. This particular mask was decorated in the Scacchi style, based on the diamond shapes of a chess board with each of the individual diamond shapes bordered with a lovely gold relief pattern. This mask is also known as the Gnaga, after the Veneziano word, "gnau," which is the sound a cat makes. It is often part of the costume worn by men who wish to disguise themselves as women.

When my zia handed me the mask, she did so with a wink, letting me know that this was part of the plot to confuse and keep my identity hidden from my corrupt Uncle Maffio tonight. We both hoped that together with my slight frame and underdeveloped figure, the Gnaga would add an extra level of protection.

"Of course, only a blind fool could ever mistake you for a boy, Francesca," she told me. "But we are dealing with a fool after all, so we will employ all the tricks we have at our disposal."

The musicians and acting troupe arrived with a large trunk in tow and they began setting up their performance space in one corner of the salone. Two weeks prior, my commedia had been delivered to the lead player, Fabrizio, who also serves as their director, so that the actors would have time to memorize their parts and rehearse.

We all returned to the portego to await the arrival of the guests. While the four musicians played, I stood by the actors and was treated to a display of their various costumes and fanciful masks. I was so captivated by the troupe and all their accoutrements that I nearly forgot about my Uncle Maffio, until Fabrizio jokingly said, "Ah, I see our villain is here."

I followed the actor's glance and felt my stomach lurch. Having just ascended the stairs and stepping into the room was a sinister figure dressed in black from head to toe, wearing a Tabarro cloak, a wide-brimmed leather hat, and the white beaked mask of il Medico della Peste. In commedie, the Plague Doctor is characterized by his egotism and pride, often conflicting with his actual stupidity and ineptitude. I immediately discerned whose face was behind that spectral visage.

I glanced around for my zia and located her easily across the room because we are the only two women in attendance tonight. We locked eyes and she gave me an almost imperceptible nod confirming that my uncle had arrived. She casually made her way over to me and said in sotto voce, "How appropriate that he would choose the attire of a character that has spent his entire life learning everything yet failing to understand anything." She found my hand and squeezed it reassuringly. "Stay close to the actors throughout the evening. It will give the impression that you are a member of their troupe. When I wish to introduce you to someone important, I will do so discreetly. A mask automatically causes the wearer to behave covertly, so no one will give you away." I simply nodded.

Whether they came on foot or by boat, the guests arrived damp and slightly disheveled from the rain. Soon, they all took turns warming themselves by the fire, the wine began flowing, and everyone was in good spirits, in stark contrast to the ominous thunderstorm persisting throughout the evening.

When we were summoned into the dining room for dinner, I sat as far away from my uncle as possible and situated myself between Fabrizio and a writer from Bolzano, where I could keep an eye on Maffio from across the long table. Occasionally, from behind Maffio's mask, I saw his eyes dart in my direction, and I would promptly look down at my plate or turn to the writer next to me and asked him about his latest poem, which instantly caused him to puff up like a peacock. Male writers are often envious men who frequently compete with each other and with the upwardly mobile courtesan, such as my zia, for a patron's support, public attention, and literary acclaim. I could not ascertain whether or not the man next to me actually mistook me for a young boy in female disguise, but I know all too well how often female writers like Zia Veronica have been the victims of the unbridled anger of men, especially those insecure in their own social standing or talents, undoubtedly because she captured the attention of such a prominent literary patron as Domenico Vendramin and profited from his tutelage. Not wishing to ignite his ire, since I would be presenting my own literary work tonight,

I placated the peacock next to me by feigning enraptured interest in his poetry.

It is not only these literary opportunists who unleash unwarranted mistreatment toward my zia. If powerful men such as Domenico Vendramin have helped Zia Veronica survive, powerful men also oppose and abuse her. Zia Veronica's interactions with the prestigious Vendramin Academy, along with her affiliation with other patrician intellectuals, often engender spiteful and injurious attacks on her reputation and character by men who see her status as a threat to their own privilege. I have no doubt that the main reason Maffio showed up tonight was to seek revenge. Despite his privileged status as a patrician son, he wasted his opportunities and became the self-appointed outcast of my family. He owes the difficulties in his own life to no one but himself. Nevertheless, his past inability to support himself or acquire stable employment after he squandered his entire inheritance does not stop him from placing the blame on others. And who better to receive the brunt of his bitterness and frustration than a brilliant, educated, successful woman?

The peacock, having mistaken my casual conversation as an invitation to regale me with his vast intellect, continued his incessant blather without a break and I was greatly relieved when, at last, Fabrizio beckoned the actors into the salone. I excused myself and quickly joined them. If any of the actors found it strange that I was lingering in their company, no one said anything about it. Perhaps they presumed I was merely an anxious new dramatist, wanting to make sure they would perform my work correctly. In any case, they treated me as one of their own and merrily joked while including me in their preparations for the performance.

"I must say," Fabrizio told me, "your commedia raised several eyebrows amongst our troupe while we rehearsed. You are certainly making a very bold statement."

"What is the point of art if not to expand awareness by revealing uncomfortable truths?" I asked.

"Indeed!" he purred melodically, appraising me with newfound interest and, dare I say it, respect?

Having completed their dinner, the partygoers joined us in the salone for the first portion of the entertainment. It is customary for each writer to present their poetry aloud to Signor Vendramin and the other prominent scholars for possible consideration of their financial and public support. These contests turn into a battle of wits to see who best has cultivated both the written and verbal arts. Honest courtesans, such as Zia Veronica, are habitually the favorite ridiculed subject matter of these rivalries, which male writers use as a means of eliminating them from competition and to perpetuate the mistrust of a courtesan's talents by painting her as a dishonest woman.

A skillful conversationalist and gracious hostess, Zia Veronica maintained her composure while deflecting whatever barbs they hurled her way. Her erudite responses defended not only herself but all her fellow courtesans and women in general. She insisted that it was her critics, not she, who contribute to the dissolution of the world.

It was unbearable listening to their insults and just as I was becoming angry with Signor Vendramin for not coming to her defense, he chastised the men and cautioned them not to mistaken Zia Veronica's beauty and charm for frailty. She soon had the opportunity to prove his point.

After all the writers had taken their turn at demonstrating their supposed eloquence, Maffio came forward. He proceeded in presenting a caustic poem, satirizing a caricature of a cortigiana onesta, whose identity was revealed in the final line—Veronica, puttana unica. I felt my blood boil as all the men snickered at calling my zia a unique whore. This affront proved even too much for Signor Vendramin, who stepped forward ready to say something when my zia placed a hand on his arm and stopped him. She calmly and resolutely walked to the center of the salone and stood directly in front of Maffio.

With slow deliberateness, she removed her mask, looked directly into his eyes, and said, "Those who comprehend the true significance of the concept *unique*, express it with praise and admiration. They understand it to describe one who enjoys a shining reputation. One who excels in loveliness or valor and who far surpasses all others in virtue and intellect. Whomever declares otherwise strays from the true definition of the word, patently revealing *his* ignorance."

There was a stillness throughout the room, immediately followed by rapturous applause from all the academics with shouts of, "Brava! Bellissima! Veronica, a veritably unique poet!" The other writers glanced uncomfortably at one another, chastened into silence.

Signor Vendramin walked over to Zia Veronica, held both her hands, and brought them to his lips. This was met with more shouts and another round of applause. He escorted her away from Maffio and they were surrounded, not only by Signor Vendramin's colleagues, but also by the writers who all wanted to avoid any association with Maffio. Zia Veronica's statement having attacked his incompetence as a poet while exposing his incomprehensible hatred of women, Maffio was left standing by himself in the center of the room. I wanted to slap him. We made eye contact through our masks and I willed my eyes to communicate my disgust. I spun away in contempt.

The time had come for the presentation of my commedia and we assembled near the makeshift stage. The musicians played an opening fanfare and Fabrizio made his introduction. "Welcome to our mythological narrative!" he announced. "You are about to enter a pastoral tapestry where you will witness a world of earthly pleasures, aesthetic beauty, virtue, and sensual delights living in perfect harmony. Together they abide in tranquility, camaraderie, and mutual contentment." Applause followed as Fabrizio disappeared behind a backdrop.

The play commenced.

I held my breath as the story reached its climactic scene when the young lovers attempted to reconcile their differences. The maiden, played by a slender, fair, adolescent boy no older than myself, heartbroken by her beau's infidelity, implored him to admit to the immorality of his behavior. "Virtue," she insisted, "resides not in bodily strength but in the vigor of the soul. Although physically weaker than men and lacking the freedom of choice that men enjoy in their amorous relationships, women possess equal intelligence and integrity. Moreover, women tend to be wiser than men because they follow the principles of reason, patience, and humility rather than the insolent acts of violent men. If a woman is unwilling to respond in kind it is not a sign of weakness nor an admission of guilt. It is a conscious decision not to destroy the world by subscribing to physical aggression. Thus, women routinely submit to male power and relinquish their right to rule, not through an inherent inequality or lack of ability, but from an innate desire to preserve the world."

Zia Veronica, who stood behind me, placed her hands on my shoulders, and whispered, "Brava!"

I scanned the masked faces for any trace of shock or condemnation, and noticed several guests shifting uncomfortably and glancing surreptitiously at one another.

The heroine continued admonishing her beau that peace on earth will never be achieved until all traces of male aggression and subjugation are replaced with equanimity and a rejection of the hierarchical differences, which promote divisiveness. Only then will we recuperate a world where nature and reason can coexist, and individuals can live together freely in mutual respect and love.

"Social harmony completely depends on the equal contribution of all men and *women*!" declared the maiden.

Her lover, brought to his senses by her indisputable reasoning, bowed before her and promised to uphold this ideal. They embraced and were joined by a band of fairies and centaurs who danced around them in celebration, accompanied by the musicians.

La fine.

There was a look of uncertainty and apprehension on the faces of all eight actors when they assembled onstage for their bows in the midst of complete silence.

Zia Veronica was the first to applaud and I quickly joined her, followed by Signor Vendramin who looked at his guests expectantly. They began clapping half-heartedly until they noticed Signor Vendramin's expectant look turn to disapproval at their lackluster response, prompting them to applaud more enthusiastically.

Zia Veronica and I approached the actors and thanked them for their brilliant and brave performances.

"Beware of a woman's wanton public tongue!" boomed the voice of Maffio, silencing everyone. I knew not whether his comment was directed at the young actor who portrayed the maiden and was standing in front of me with a look of terror, quaking with fear, or toward me for having written the words that were spoken out loud. "Do you expect us to believe that you attained permission from the Church to present this foul heresy?"

My blood ran cold, matching the sudden chill in the room.

Perhaps because she was so thoroughly aggrieved after having spent the majority of the evening battling misogynistic tirades, my zia whirled around and viciously spat, "If truth is now defined as heresy, and art is no longer allowed to freely express it, then I fear for the future of our Republic with rogues like you who wouldn't recognize the truth if it struck you in the face!"

"Signor," interjected Domenico Vendramin, "this is a private gathering in a private home. None of the work presented this evening is in the open space of the Piazza San Marco nor inside the public forum of the Palazzo Ducale. Therefore, an official sanction is unnecessary."

"I'm not so sure The Ten would see it that way," Maffio sneered and a collective murmur of unease rippled among the writers.

"Signor, I do not appreciate your threats," Domenico responded forcefully. "Nor do I appreciate being lectured in my own house about the regulations that govern the city of my birth.

Need I remind you that I have served as senator and, although retired from civil service, I am well versed in the laws that govern our land."

This retort was supported by several of Signor Vendramin's colleagues adding their opinions in agreement, while Maffio maintained that the rules were absolute. Everyone began speaking at once in an argumentative frenzy. The atmosphere rapidly turned volatile with the simmering hostility felt throughout the evening finally reaching its boiling point.

I gaped at my zia in alarm and asked, "What should we do?"

"Thank you for sharing your talents with us this evening," she calmly addressed the musicians and actors. "It is best that you depart now. No need to dismantle the stage. You may return later after the storm has past, at your earliest convenience to retrieve your equipment."

They all looked deeply relieved and eagerly left the brewing tempest inside for the one outside.

"Come!" Zia Veronica said, grabbing my hand and ushering me out of the salone.

We practically ran all the way to my bedchamber, where she locked the door and began pacing the room. I removed my mask and set it down on my dressing table waiting for her to say something. Finally, she paused and heaving a deep sigh, sat on my bed and motioned for me to sit next to her.

"Francesca," she said, "please forgive me, for I have greatly misjudged the situation. I regret that I sought to urge you toward such a life. It is completely contrary to human reason to subject one's body and labor to such slavery. The servility, the vileness, the inconstancy is a misery I do not wish for you."

"Zia?" I began, but she held up her hand, imploring me to allow her to continue.

"I have been the most fortunate of women to find myself in the companionship of Domenico, who has been the best of allies," she continued. "But men like him are rare, even among his learned, progressive colleagues. And placing you in a position to become prey to the whims of so many men, at the mercy of their support, defiles the memory of your mother, my beloved sister."

"Why do they treat us with such unprovoked disdain?" I asked.

"Honored for Mary's sake, yet despised for Eve's, men have always had an ambivalent attitude toward women. They delight in exalting women to the stature of virginal queen when it serves their agenda, but when faced with social adversities, quickly transform women into devious Jezebels whom they unfairly charge with the social and moral dissolution of civilization."

"But why?"

"Fear. For those accustomed to having all the power, equality feels like defeat. And there is nothing more dangerous than a wounded beast. Francesca, I want you to go ahead and marry Giovanni. Any life with him anywhere will be better than this."

I stared at her amazed, hardly believing what I was hearing.

"Contrary to how women like myself have been described throughout history," she continued, "ours is not the oldest profession, but rather the oldest *oppression*. How can I possibly advocate that for you?"

"Oh, zia!" I threw my arms around her and cried with unimaginable relief.

"Listen carefully," she said through her own tears. "Tomorrow morning, before we send Giovanni back home to Murano, we will discuss plans for your nuptials. The sooner you marry, the sooner you will be safely away from Venezia and that reprobate, Maffio."

"Si," I nodded, wiping my tears. "But that suggests that I will be leaving you much earlier than we had anticipated."

She took my face in both her hands. "Cara ragazza, if it means you will be protected, that is all that matters. Murano is not so far after all. Alfredo and I will visit frequently. And then you must go to Padova and make a new life for yourself!" She placed a gentle kiss on my forehead and hugged me once more. "Now, I want you to remain here in your chamber. If Domenico hasn't already evicted Maffio from the premises, I will see to it that he is promptly removed. Sleep well, my sweet girl. I will see you in the morning."

"Grazie, zia! Grazie mille! Buona notte."

"Buona notte. Lock the door behind me." She blew me a kiss and just before closing the door said, "Your commedia was truly superb!"

As soon as I heard the door click shut I ran over and bolted it. I leaned my back against it and allowed the tears to flow. *Giovanni! We are free!* I couldn't imagine how I would possibly manage to sleep tonight and wait until morning to finally share the good news. My joy eradicated whatever dread I felt earlier and infused me with courage and hope. I *had* to see Giovanni immediately.

I left my chamber and crept through the empty portego, where I could hear the angry voices of the confrontation continuing in the salone. I flew down the stairs and found myself surrounded by the icy acqua alta and darkness.

*   *   *   *   *

Why did I not think to bring my cloak? I scold myself, shivering inside the damp storage room, where a small window allows a meager amount of light to enter. The moon! That must mean the clouds are breaking up and the storm is passing.

I put my shoes back on and feel my way around the walls, locating the shelf where Alfredo keeps his supplies. I touch the coarse woolen blanket he lets me use on those brisk mornings whenever we travel to Murano. Covering myself with it, I feel around some more and discover a lantern. My fingers are stiff from the cold and it takes me several tries with the fire steel before I can finally light it.

I hear something.

"Giovanni? Alfredo?" I hastily pick up the lantern and run out the door into the other room. "Where have you been?" The thick, cumbersome blanket causes me to stumble through the darkness and I plunge headlong into the black cloaked figure of Maffio.

The lantern briefly illuminates the eerie, white mask and my mind has a moment to register who he is before the collision causes me to drop it, sending it crashing down and snuffed out by the water covering the stone floor. Once again, the room is in darkness. I can just make out where the stairs are. I run toward them, but Maffio grabs me by the arm and holds me back.

I struggle to free myself. Holding me with one hand, he grasps my face with the other, twisting me toward him.

"Ah-hah!" he sneers, his face so close to mine I can smell his foul, wine-soaked breath through his mask. He is inebriated. "Of course. Who else, but Francesca? You bear a strong resemblance to your father and I would recognize my brother's face anywhere. Did you and your puttana zia think you could fool me with your elaborate masquerade? I am not at all surprised that she would take you in so that you could follow in her shameless footsteps. All the women in your family are nothing but dirty whores, including your mother!"

I manage to free my arm and, with all my strength, strike him squarely on the long beaked nose of his mask, jamming it into his face before it falls to the floor. Maffio yells in pain and cups his nose, which immediately begins bleeding. I take the opportunity to run for the stairs again, but he is too quick. He seizes me by the hair and pulls me back.

"Aiuto!" I scream. "Someone help!"

Maffio practically picks me up by the hair and places a rough hand over my mouth. I bite him! He lets out a yelp and slaps me across my face. I fall in a large puddle of water, momentarily stunned. He hauls me up by the back of my dress and throws me inside the storage room. Sprawled on the floor, I touch my split-open lip and taste blood.

"So," he says, kicking the rock away so the door will close, and moves toward me, "perhaps I should help instruct you in what makes a good whore."

In the dim light I can feel and hear rather than see him reach inside his cloak and begin undoing his trousers. Rape, although considered a crime of violence, is never severely punished by the Venetian authorities, leaving women of all classes victimized by the aggression of men. Women are rarely, if ever, believed or compensated by society for the physical abuse they endure.

I struggle to stand up, but he pushes me down and begins lowering himself on me. With every ounce of strength that I can muster, I kick him, landing a blow on his shin. He roars with rage and just as he is about to lunge for me, my hand touches the rock that kept the door open earlier. I roll to my side, grabbing hold of it with both hands and hurl the rock toward Maffio's head, hearing his skull crack as it makes contact. He falls on top of me. I scream!

Pushing his body off of me, I scramble to my feet. Blinded by gushing tears and terror, I run to the door and heave it open.

"Francesca!" Giovanni shouts in surprise, standing next to Alfredo, who holds a torch. I collapse hysterically into his arms. "Francesca, what has happened?"

I cannot speak. All I can do is hold on to him as if my life depended on it. After several moments, I motion to the storage room. Both Giovanni and Alfredo glance over at the closed door, then at each other.

"What is it, signorina Francesca?" asks Alfredo.

"In there. He is in there," I manage to say between spasmodic gulps of air.

"Who is?" asks Giovanni.

"Ma . . . Maffio!"

Alfredo and Giovanni exchange alarmed looks. With torch in hand, Alfredo walks over to the storage room. He opens the door and cautiously peers inside before stepping all the way in. After a few moments, he comes back out and utters softly, "He is dead."

I bury my face in Giovanni's chest and cry, "Oh, Dio! Dio!"

"Francesca! Cara mia, what happened?" Giovanni implores.

For the next several minutes I relay all the terrible events of the evening leading up to my unexpected encounter with Maffio. "Where were you?" I ask.

"I am so sorry, Francesca. Alfredo and I were helping the musicians and actors onto their boats. The winds are strong, and we suggested it would be better for them to leave on foot, but they insisted on taking the canals."

"Giovanni! What will happen now? Oh, Dio! What have I done?"

"We must leave," Giovanni replies. "We must leave tonight!"

"Si," agrees Alfredo. "You must go, and I will dispose of the body."

"Alfredo, no!" I gasp. "That would place you in terrible danger."

"No one must connect you nor signora d'Aragona to that villain's death. And you cannot return to Murano," Alfredo tells Giovanni. "That risks bringing trouble to your family."

"Padova," Giovanni says. "We will go to Padova."

Alfredo nods in agreement.

"But how will we survive?" I ask. "Where will we stay?"

"I have the money Signor Vendramin paid me. His generosity is the equivalent of half a year's wage. We can survive on that for a long time and I will find work somewhere. As soon as I can, I will send word to my zio Lorenzo and let him know where we are and that we are safe."

"I have a cousin who owns a small farm along the left bank of the Medoacus Major in the village of Fessio, halfway to Padova. He will take you in and give you shelter. I will inform your family the first opportunity I have and let your zio know to expect your message. I will also tell your zia, signorina Francesca, and we will spread the rumor to explain your departure as two impetuous, impatient young lovers who ran away to elope.

"Oh, Alfredo!" I embrace him. "You have always looked out for me. I owe you so much."

"How will you dispose of the body?" Giovanni asks. "Will it not raise suspicions when he goes missing? Too many people are aware of his attendance here tonight. The Ten may very well send out a search for him."

"From what I know of that delinquent, no one will shed a tear for him, much less bemoan his absence. I will devise it so no one will find his body until the fish have made a fine meal of him and he will be unrecognizable. Even if he is discovered before then, it will look like he perished in the storm."

"This is madness! We will never get away with it!" I cry.

"We must try, signorina Francesca," Alfredo insists. "It is our only choice."

I am filled with both gratitude and incredulity in equal measure at Alfredo's selfless willingness to take on my troubles as his own.

"Giovanni," he says, "bring the blanket. Help me wrap the body in it. We will attach the rock to it, so it will weigh him down."

I watch in utter disbelief as Giovanni and Alfredo carry the heavy bundle from the storage room and out the water entrance to the fondamenta, where it looks like the high tide is starting to recede. When they come back inside I ask, "What did you do with him?"

"We placed him in one of the sandoli," Alfredo says. "Just before dawn I will take him to the marshlands east of Murano. Then I will go pay your zio a visit, Giovanni. By that time, the two of you will be long gone and safely headed to my cousin, Andrea. I promise he will welcome you without question. And now, you must hurry before more guests come down here wishing to depart. I don't think you can afford to wait until morning. Leaving under the cover of night is your best chance to escape undetected."

"Should I not go upstairs and pack some items?" I ask.

"No, signorina!" Alfredo replies. "You must not run the risk of being seen. You must go now!"

"He is right, Francesca," says Giovanni. "We cannot take any chances."

"Wait just one moment," Alfredo says and quickly runs into the storage room. He reappears carrying two blankets, and a leather bag, which he hands us. "It is not much, but it will sustain you until you reach my cousin's farm. Inside is a round of bread, a portion of hard cheese, and a gourd filled with wine."

"Grazie, Alfredo," Giovanni says in a voice choked with emotion.

"May God bless and protect you, Alfredo," I add and embrace him for what I fear may be the last time in my life.

He lets me go and wipes his eyes with his strong callused hands. "Hurry! You must leave right away. Your best route is to head west on il Canal Grande to the Canale Scomenzera, past the mouth of the Canale della Giudecca, into the laguna. Once you are in the laguna, use the Isola San Giorgio in Alga as a marker and stay to the right of it. Continue straight ahead to the town of Fusina, where you will find the entrance to the

Medoacus. From there it is roughly twenty kilometers up the river to my cousin's farm."

Giovanni nods solemnly and says, "My family is forever indebted to you. Come, Francesca, we must make haste."

Giovanni wraps one of the blankets around my shoulders and the three of us exit through the water entrance. The rain has subsided to a drizzle, but the wind continues to whip through the corridor of the canal. The water on the fondamenta has fully retreated and I remain huddled against the building, holding the bag of food and the other blanket while Giovanni and Alfredo use a bucket and rags to bail out the water from the sandolo.

"I will leave this bucket and rags with you in case it rains again," says Alfredo when they finish.

Giovanni holds the sandolo still while Alfredo helps me climb onboard. Once seated inside, Giovanni hands me the second blanket. "Place it over your head," he shouts above the howling wind. "It will protect you from the cold and the rain."

"What about you?" I implore.

"I will need my arms free to row," he replies. "Do not worry. I will be fine. Keep yourself as warm and dry as possible."

Giovanni positions himself at the stern with his oar, Alfredo unties the ropes from the mooring post, and gives the sandolo a shove.

"Addio, Alfredo," I say, barely audible over the wind, and he silently waves back to us. We drift away from the water entrance. The sandolo passes underneath the balconies and large shuttered windows of the place that has been my home for the past seven years. Almost half my life. As Giovanni steers our boat to the right onto the rio di Noale, I take one last look at Alfredo standing at the foot of the Palazzo Vendramin.

I lament that I never had the chance to say goodbye to Zia Veronica and feel an ache in my heart so intense it is like the cold blade of a knife. I wipe my tears with the rough blanket, annoyed by my own sentimentality. *Francesca, you fool! Stop your incessant crying like a child. Giovanni needs you to be strong and level-headed. There is no time for silly tears. It will take all our focus and determination to make it through this long journey.*

We reach the end of rio di Noale, and Giovanni steers us to the right onto the Canal Grande. We instantly feel the wind's force increase once we are no longer protected by the buildings along the narrower rio. He tries to keep the sandolo along the outer edge of this expansive canal where the current is not so powerful. I can see Giovanni straining against the gales, and I feel useless to help him.

I move the blanket off my head so I can watch the palazzi as we pass by and burn their images into my memory. Their facades normally radiating warmth in rose, amber, and gold, now all assume the cold, shuttered look of winter closing in. Where once the soft light of a summer sunset on this resplendent grand waterway created a mother-of-pearl pink, during the early days of autumn it becomes a muted palette of greens and grays. Now it is a monochrome of charcoal and black ink.

After what seems like an eternity, we finally reach the Canale Scomenzera and turn left where we feel the immediate difference in the calmer waters of this slightly narrower canal. We are not on it for very long, but it gives Giovanni a chance to rest before taking on the open waters of the laguna.

Just as our little sandolo arrives at the spot where the Canale della Giudecca meets the Canale di Fusina, it begins to rain again.

No. No! Dio! Please let us cross the laguna without having to bail water.

Giovanni steers us through the tumultuous current where the two canals converge and we join the laguna, which is a menacing, turbulent, rocking sea. I am jostled off of my seat and slammed to the bottom of the boat where the seawater and rain is already collecting.

"Stay down low, Francesca!" Giovanni shouts. "You will be more stable that way. Hold on!"

The waves crash up against our tiny boat. I sputter and cough when I am hit square in the face with salty water, stinging my eyes. I brace myself for another wave.

"Giovanni!" I yell. "We must go back. The water is too rough."

"The wind is behind us now," he replies, and I can barely hear him. "It would be too difficult to turn around. I will try to get us over to Isola San Giorgio. We can take refuge there until the storm passes."

We continue our journey on the roiling sea, and I watch helplessly as Giovanni fights against the truculent, ruthless elements. Over the wind and rain, I hear the roll of thunder. I look at Giovanni to see if he's heard it just as a gash of lightning slices through the dark sky behind him, lighting him up in a silhouette of biblical proportions. The deafening thunder that follows startles me and I scream. The water grows even more threatening as the murky slate-colored waves appear to be breaking from all angles, thoroughly drenching us. We are soaked through.

"There is San Giorgio!" Giovanni shouts. "We are getting close!"

I strain to see the miniature landmass about half a kilometer away. I turn to look back at Giovanni to give him encouragement when another jagged lightning bolt pierces through the thick cloud cover and the sea appears to reach over the stern like the nefarious arm of a giant sea creature, taking Giovanni and his oar with it.

"Giovanni! No!" I scream into the relentless rain.

I drag myself back up to the seat, trying to balance while perching myself high enough to see where Giovanni landed, but I can see nothing.

"Giovanni!" I continue shouting into the dark, wet void. Suddenly I see him six meters off the starboard side, popping up to breathe before getting pounded by another wave. In the absence of an oar, I have no way of steering the boat toward him. Instinct taking hold of me, I lie flat along the bow and anchor myself by hooking my feet underneath the wooden slat that creates the seat across the sandolo. This position allows my arms to dangle in front of the bow where I can just barely reach the water. With a power arising out of sheer desperation and reflex that belies my stature, I use my small hands as paddles to try to turn the boat around to rescue Giovanni. I see him rise to the surface again, hungry for oxygen, just as the sea reaches up and drags me down to an underwater world . . . suspended in time.

* * * * *

I am in a thin place, where the distance between heaven and earth collapses. Where the transcendent, divine, and infinite are made visible. The veil that separates the ordinary physical parts of reality from the extraordinary and metaphysical is now transparent and the mundane is subverted by a sense of awe. All conventional and limited understanding dissolves. Through this window I sense a world of great mystery, delight, inspiration, and profound connection.

I am swathed in bright, warm light. It is fluid, safe, and cushioning, echoing my amniotic origins. I experience voices like a soft, sweet breeze. *Francesca. Francesca.*

Mamma and Papà stand before me, smiling radiantly.

Francesca, they breathe. *Magnificent, courageous girl. Your work is done. Come rest.*

I run into their open arms.

Cradled with infinite love, I reunite with the *ALL.*

E . . .

M

O

I am . . . H

Chapter 17 — FRANKIE

Venice, Italy
Monday, September 2, 2019

"Look!" I proudly announce. "I got five As and one B on my report card!" "Why did you get a B?" My mother asks . . . I don't want to go to school today. I'm so tired from crying all night. But I have to go to school. I have to! I need to get good grades so I can go to college. It's the only way I can escape.

I sense my solitude the moment I open my eyes. The clock on the nightstand shows that it is just a little past 8 a.m. Luciana has long since left for work. I feel an odd, but familiar heaviness. What is going on? Is it just my nervousness about asking Luigi for a job? I force myself out of bed and open the shutters. There is a dull grayness to the morning light, which doesn't help my mood.

After using the bathroom, I walk to the kitchen. Instead of texting me, Luciana has left an old-school note taped to the coffeemaker, which reads:

Cara Frankie,

Buongiorno! I hope you slept well. I have some errands to run this afternoon when I am finished with work, but let's meet up for an aperitivo at Harry's Bar around 17:00. Text me after you've spoken with Luigi. Buona fortuna!

Ciao,

Luciana

Although Harry's Bar has been on my Venice to-do list since the moment I arrived, I have put it off because it's such an overcrowded tourist attraction. Now that the city is returning to the Venetian residents, I can finally look forward to ordering a Bellini from the place where the famous cocktail originated. And if all goes well, it will be the perfect way to celebrate.

I make myself a café latte and take it out to the terrace. As soon as I sit down at the patio table, I change my mind and go back inside to drink my coffee on the sofa. There is a startling chill in the air and the sky is a gray blanket. It is only the second day of September and already autumn is announcing itself. Fall tends to be my least favorite season because I seem to have a more difficult time fending off my blue moods as the daylight hours decrease. But even so, I don't understand why I woke up in such a funk this particular morning, especially after the excitement I felt when I got off the phone with Grandma last night.

What the hell is wrong with me?

I once asked my therapist if she thought I might be bipolar, and she reassured me that I was not. "Then, why do my moods swing so drastically?" I asked her.

"Sometimes the body keeps score," she explained. "Your body may be reacting to a past trauma. Is there something about the fall or that time of year, besides the reduced daylight, that makes you sad?"

Shit.

Yesterday was the seventh anniversary of my parents' fatal car collision. That's why Grandma kept asking if I was okay. She probably thought that was the reason I was calling. She was checking in with me in a roundabout way, undoubtedly trying to avoid triggering me. I never made the connection and of course I didn't ask her how she was feeling. No wonder I fell apart the night before! The looming anniversary and Luciana's story about *Madama Butterfly* could not have hit that wound more directly. It all makes sense now.

I was five years old on 9/11. Despite observing the reaction of all the adults around me, I was too young to have felt the full emotional impact of that day. My grandma once described how bizarre it still feels when the anniversary comes around. "The first year was the strangest," she said. "It was so hard to believe that a full year had already gone by. The entire country was still reeling and the whole world felt different. It completely changed the way we travel, the economy was a mess, and people were very suspicious and fearful. Then before we knew it, ten years had gone by! I couldn't believe it. The shock and horror of those images of the planes going into the World Trade Center remained palpable, but then you blink, and five more years have passed. Each anniversary I display my American flag and I see all the neighbors do the same. There is still an ache in my heart, but it does get less intense each time."

I suppose the fact that, all day yesterday and the week leading up to it, I completely forgot that the anniversary of my parents' accident was approaching is a good sign. Although the memory still feels painfully raw, I guess the sting has diminished somewhat. Or has it? Certainly, my meltdown two nights ago had everything to do with grief and loss, so maybe my body was telling me something.

I glance over at the clock on the wall of the living room. 8:30 a.m., which means it is 11:30 p.m., California time. Too late to call Grandma, and I don't want to risk waking her up by having her phone vibrate with a text since she has taken to leaving her phone on all night next to her bed in case I have an emergency. I'll just have to wait to get in touch with her later, as promised.

I finish my café latte and my stomach is in knots as I head for the shower. I'll treat myself to a nice lunch at Café Florian after I visit the bookstore. My anxiety is making it impossible to eat anything right now, and it will give me something to look forward to regardless of the outcome with Luigi. This is the same trick I often use whenever I have an audition—I plan something fun to do immediately afterwards so the audition is not the main focus of my day. This strategy doesn't always work, but it gives me the illusion of having some level of control.

I finish my shower and take great care in picking the right outfit. I want to appear respectable, responsible and dependable. Why am I so worried? Luigi has already met me. We've interacted on three different occasions and he's always been pleasantly approachable and nice. Besides, isn't my friendship with Luciana and the fact that her parents are allowing me to stay in their home a ringing endorsement?

I return to the kitchen, wash out my coffee cup, lock the door to the terrace, and take one last look around the apartment to be sure all the lights are off. I head out.

The sun is already breaking through the clouds, revealing the promise of piercing blue skies. It's a good omen.

I walk north toward Fondamenta Giurati and catch the almost-empty vaporetto at the Sant'Alvise stop. No problem finding a seat up front this time. I try to relax and enjoy the view of San Michele. I can see Murano, a short distance behind the small cemetery island, as we motor to the Ospedale stop.

After disembarking at Ospedale, I traverse through the hospital complex until I arrive at Calle Tetta, which crosses over two canals and leads me right to the entrance of the Belli Libri dell'Acqua Alta.

Okay, here goes nothin'. If it's meant to be, it's meant to be.

I take a deep breath and step into the courtyard. Everything is just as haphazard as the first day I came here. Does Luigi bring all this stuff inside at the end of the day? I can't imagine where he would find any space inside the store to put it all. Maybe he just covers it with some kind of tarp in case it rains. Well, I guess I'm about to find out.

Just as I enter the front door, I feel that familiar pit in my stomach whenever I have to audition. I'm sure it's my body's reaction to the probability of rejection. I *hate* auditioning.

I walk inside. The store is empty of customers because it's still early. I'm surprised not to see Luigi in his usual spot, seated by the cash register.

"Buongiorno?" I call out. "Luigi?"

"Si?" I hear his muffled voice answer back but can't see where he is.

"Ciao, Luigi. It's me, Frankie."

"Frankie!" he exclaims, popping out from behind a perilously tall stack of hardback books nestled inside a kayak. "What a nice surprise. Come stai?"

"I'm fine. How are you?"

"Bene, bene!" he says coming out from his book maze and walking toward me. "Have you returned for more books about Puccini?"

"No, not today," I laugh lightly. "I actually came to talk to you about something."

"Oh?" he says, eyebrows raised, enhancing his impish expression of delight. "What can I do for you?"

"Luigi, you mentioned that you were looking to hire some help. Were you serious?"

"Si. Certamente. Don't I look like I could use some help?" he asks, gesturing to the piles and heaps.

"Well, I was wondering if I could apply for the job?"

His look of surprise, combined with the fact that he doesn't respond immediately, flusters me, and I continue speaking rapidly before he can refuse.

"If you need a recommendation, I'm sure I can get one from the Hotel Vendramin. And certainly, all my coworkers will vouch for me. I realize a drawback might be that I will need to extend my visa and work permit, but Luciana said that perhaps Sofia could help me with that since she deals with those issues all the time working for La Fenice." He still looks somewhat puzzled and I am starting to lose confidence.

"You would like to work here?" he asks incredulously.

"Yes."

"You are not returning to your home in America?"

"Well, that's just it," I say. "There's really nothing to return to right away. I mean, there's my nonna, of course, but if I can find a way to stay in Venezia, I would love that. And she's totally in support of it. As a matter of fact, she's the one who has been encouraging me to stay as long as possible. I would have to find a job back home, anyway, so why not try to do that here?"

"What about the rest of your family? Your Mamma and Papà won't miss you?"

"My parents are . . . they've passed away. I live with my nonna."

"Oh, Frankie. I am so sorry."

Not trusting my voice, I merely nod in response.

"Well," he says, "this is quite something. You have taken me by surprise. But it is good!" Then, after a pause, "Please let me ask you, Frankie. Why would you like to work here?"

"Oh, Luigi, I've been in love with your bookstore since before I even arrived in Venezia! I saw photos of it on the internet when I was preparing for this trip and I couldn't wait to see it in person. It's even more delightful than I ever imagined!" I want to add that I am absolutely obsessed with this bookstore, but I don't want to scare him off by sounding like a desperate lunatic.

His smile lights up his entire face as he nods appreciatively. "Grazie, grazie."

I wait, trying to appear calm while he contemplates my offer. Then, out of seemingly nowhere he asks, "Frankie, what exactly do you want to do with your life?"

Huh?!

This takes me aback. I thought I was just applying for a job, not entering a philosophical discussion of my life goals.

Normally, whenever I've been asked this question, I would automatically answer with what I've fantasized about ever since I was a little girl singing along to Broadway musical soundtracks—I want to be a performer. But suddenly I am smacked with what I can only describe as . . . divine inspiration? *What the heck.* I've got nothing to lose, so I might as well be honest. "I would love to travel the world and write about my adventures and all the fascinating people I meet . . . and get paid for it."

"Ah, yes. That is very interesting. And why exactly do you wish to write about such things?"

Jeez, this guy doesn't let up. *Dude, how the hell should I know? This idea literally came to me just now.* But after thinking about it for a moment, it hits me. Although this summer has been an amazing life-changing experience, there were many times when I felt extremely isolated and homesick. I was here for over a month before I began feeling that I was finally making friends and gaining some level of confidence with the language. "I think it's so important for everyone to have the experience of feeling foreign," I tell him. "I've come to realize how essential it is in building empathy and compassion for how hard it is to be in a country where you're an outsider, especially where a different language is spoken. And I want to write about that experience, not merely as a tourist, but I want the chance to see what life is like for the citizens of various places. Perhaps that would be a way to educate people, by focusing more on what we have in common rather than our differences."

"Ah-hah," he says and stares very intently at me for what feels like a long time. I try to disguise my discomfort while he continues thinking, but I can sense my armpits getting damp. I feel dizzy. I probably should have eaten breakfast. He smiles knowingly as if he has a great secret and says, "Frankie, you look like a little angel, but I see in you the soul of a *tiger*."

I can't find any words to respond to that. So, I don't.

"You are about to join a very noble lineage. For centuries artists from all over the world have produced some of their most important work while living as expatriates."

"Yes, I know! And many of them right here in Venezia."

"Si. I have a feeling that there is something very important that you are meant to do," he continues. "But you must prepare yourself for the hardest work. Because if you're going to write something that is true, that is real, and something that will actually help people, you are going to have to dig deep. And just when you think you've gone deep enough, you're going to have to go down that extra layer. Perhaps the most surprising moment for a writer is realizing that their story is something richer and even more heartbreaking than the story you've been telling yourself. It takes a great amount of bravery, and it's why I have so much admiration for the writers who do that work. It's a gift to readers and to the world and it takes something extraordinarily courageous in the writer to extract that gift. But make no mistake, it is arduous work, and you must get ready to find yourself in high water. And sometimes the only way to get above the water is to allow yourself to sink, because the act of letting go will give you the energy to come back up."

Completely mesmerized by the profundity of his words, I nod and whisper, "Okay."

After a moment he offers me a warm smile and says, "Also you may want to invest in a good pair of tall, sturdy, rubber boots," he chortles good-naturedly, and this makes me laugh. I don't know what else to say, so I just wait expectantly.

"I won't be able to pay you very much," he says abruptly interrupting my awkwardness, "but I thought what I could offer is food and lodging to make up for it. Sofia and I live upstairs, and we have an extra room. You could stay in Cristina's old bedroom. Would that be something that might interest you?"

I feel like I want to jump out of my skin! "Yes! Oh, my gosh, Luigi! That's perfect. The opportunity to live like a true veneziana would be priceless. I would need to find lodging anyway and that solves my problem."

"Bene! Allora, here's what we should do. Why don't you come over for dinner sometime this week? We can show you where you will be staying, and you can ask Sofia all the questions you have about your visa and permit. And afterward, if you are still interested in the job, we can go from there. Does that sound good?"

"That's fantastic! Yes!"

"Let me have your phone number," he says taking his cell phone out of his hip pocket. "I will give you a call once I've discussed it with Sofia and let you know what day."

"Sure!" I say reciting my number while he adds it to his contacts. "Oh, I must tell you that my job at the Hotel Vendramin will be over at the end of this month and then my nonna and I will be traveling through Italia the entire month of Ottobre, so I won't be able to start until Novembre. Is that okay?"

"Certamente. That is perfect timing because I close the bookstore in Novembre due to the acqua alta, and that will give us plenty of time to get a head start going through this beautiful mess. That is why you will need those boots!" he laughs. "How long did you want to remain in Venezia?"

"I would love to stay a full year if possible."

"I see," he says thoughtfully. "Yes, I think it might take that long to get a handle on all of this."

"When will you and Sofia be returning from Padova?"

"We will only be in Padova the third week in Ottobre because Sofia must return for the final opera of the season, *La Traviata*."

"Oh good! Then I'll be able to bring my nonna to the bookstore before she flies back to the States. I can't wait for her to see this place."

"I look forward to meeting her. Ah! That reminds me," he exclaims. "If you are going to become a member of the Belli Libri dell'Acqua Alta family, there is someone very important you should meet. Gio! Where are you? Vieni qui." I follow Luigi's gaze as he glances over the room. "There you are! Come meet Frankie."

I hear a faint sound but can't tell where it's coming from.

"Gio, this is Frankie," Luigi says, addressing someone I still cannot see. "She is the answer to our prayers. Welcome her to our little family."

On top of a stack of magazines, sitting on the table directly in front of me, jumps a beautiful, sleek, white-pawed, white-tip-tailed, black cat. "*Ciaoooeeew*," he utters, looking directly at me and steals my breath away.

He has the most exquisite eyes I have ever seen.

EPILOGUE

Encino, California
Saturday, November 7, 2020

"But while I may be the first woman in this office, I will not be the last, because every little girl watching tonight sees that this is a country of possibilities!"

On TV Senator Kamala Harris delivers her speech to the American people as the first woman of color to be elected to the office of Vice President of the United States. When she and President-Elect Joe Biden are joined onstage with their families to a cheering crowd, music, and fireworks, I feel like I can finally breathe for the first time in four years.

Grandma, Mayra, and I hug each other and jump up and down like little kids.

"This calls for champagne!" Grandma says and dashes to the kitchen to retrieve the bottle of bubbly she had bought the night before the election. Her faith never wavered.

"Oh, my God!" Mayra shouts. "I'm so relieved. Ha, ha! You're fired!"

"Na-na, na, na, hey, hey, hey, goodbye!!!" we both sing and dissolve into peals of laughter.

My year in Italy was unfortunately cut short when our world was hit with a global pandemic. Italy was one of the first countries to be hit the hardest with large numbers of infections and a high death rate. On February 1st I flew back home and have been quarantining with Grandma since the middle of March. I came home to a country under siege from an invisible, mysterious virus, almost nonexistent leadership from our Federal government, racial unrest and protests, and civil chaos that became even more intense the closer we got to the Presidential election. The past seven months have been filled with anxiety and fear. After several days of uncertainty while the voter ballots continued to be counted, tonight I feel something I haven't experienced since that fateful election night in 2016—hope.

Millions of people around the world have been suffering not only from this deadly contagion, but from the economic hardships brought on by the closure of businesses due to stay-at-home orders and curfews. All live performances came to a complete halt last spring and the future of theatre companies across the nation hangs by a thread. When Mayra was laid off from her job at the Universal Studios Hollywood costume department and could no longer afford the rent on her apartment, Grandma graciously offered her a place to live here with us.

"What is the point of a big house," Grandma said, "if you can't fill it with laughter and the people you love? I enjoy having you girls here. It keeps me young! And I know you're both really worried about the future of the performing arts, but throughout history art has always managed to survive. I'm confident that will never change because people need to feel. We need to know that we're not alone. That's what live theatre does. In the meantime, the three of us can ride this storm out together."

So, when Mayra and I found ourselves unemployed we decided to create a podcast called, *Tiger Soul,* which is an homage to the compliment I received from Luigi. On each episode we discuss pop culture, the arts, feminism, social activism, and mental health all inside our homemade sound studio in one of Grandma's guest bedrooms. We try to exemplify civil, respectful discourse on a wide range of topics, including some very hot-button issues. Mayra and I feel that if we can provide laughter, entertainment, information, a sense of connection, and a brief respite from the mundanity of this "new normal" where people can't physically be with one another, then this crazy year will not have been wasted.

"I propose a toast!" Grandma says, handing us each a glass of champagne. "To the future! Anything is up from the black hole we were just in these past four years."

"Here, here!" I agree.

"Amen!" Mayra adds.

For the next several hours, my phone explodes with text messages.

From Luciana:

> Ciao, Frankie! What an amazing team your new
> President and Vice President are. So happy for all
> of you! Cheers! I miss you!

From Bruno and Giulietta:

> Congratulations! There is reason for hope! We have
> seen the largest global act of cooperation our
> species has ever engaged in. Billions of people
> making small sacrifices for the collective good,
> acting in ways that signal solidarity and connection.
> And now your country has new leadership. Wishing
> you, your nonna, and Mayra continued good health
> and safety.

From Luigi:

> Felicitations! What great news for your country and
> by association, all of us in Italy and throughout
> Europe. Give my love to Gio!

From the moment Luigi first introduced us, Gio followed me everywhere and was my constant companion.

"I have never seen him behave this way," Luigi exclaimed. "It is like you two are soulmates!"

When it became clear that I would need to return to California Luigi said, "You must take Gio with you. If you leave without him, it will break his heart."

As if sensing who has just texted me, right on cue, Gio meows.

"Stand still, Gio," I say, poised to take his picture. "Let's send Luigi a nice photo of your handsome face. Say, formaggi!"

I press 'send' and pocket my phone. Picking Gio up, he immediately purrs as he nuzzles his face against my cheek, his warm breath and whiskers tickling me.

"Oh, Gio! The future looks bright again! We're going to be okay," I say, kissing the top of his head. "We're going to be okay."

. . . ?

AUTHOR'S NOTE

One evening in mid-August of 2016, I sat inside a theatre in Palo Alto, California, listening to a panel discussion at the end of a week-long New Works Festival. A question was posed to American playwright, Rajiv Joseph, in regard to his play, *Archduke*, which he had been working on at the time, as to whether or not he worried about historical accuracy in his plays. He said something which struck me as profoundly brave and, most importantly, liberating: "I am not a historian. If you want accurate history, you should read a history book."

While I am a fan of history, I am also not a historian. I am first and foremost a storyteller. I have taken liberties with dates and characters in order to weave a tale that is, hopefully, both entertaining and informative, while also expressing my love for the city of Venice, the Italian people, their beautiful language, and rich culture. Many of the characters are amalgamations of actual people who were citizens of Venice, Italy during the Renaissance.

ABOUT PATTY FLORES REINHART

Patty Flores Reinhart was born in El Salvador and immigrated to the United States at the age of three. Growing up in Southern California, she launched her acting career and graduated from UCLA with a BA in Theatre Arts. Patty appeared on both English- and Spanish-television in Los Angeles while simultaneously teaching elementary school. Later, she performed with several theatre companies throughout the San Francisco Bay Area, where she lives with her husband and son. Along with her passion for performing and traveling, Patty is committed to raising awareness in order to promote greater representation of BIPOC (Black, Indigenous, People of Color) all across the arts.

Part memoir, part fiction, Reinhart's love of Venice, with its labyrinthine streets, ancient bridges, and crowded waterways, shines through in every chapter of *High Water*. Interwoven throughout the story are parallels of women's past roles and limited choices, presenting a sobering reflection of how much progress has been made—or not—for modern young women of color to control their future and gain acceptance in today's increasingly interconnected global society.

To email Patty directly:
pattyfloresreinhart@gmail.com

To find out more, please visit:
https://www.pattyfloresreinhart.com/